High Stakes

By Danielle Steel

HIGH STAKES · INVISIBLE · FLYING ANGELS · THE BUTLER · COMPLICATIONS
NINE LIVES · FINDING ASHLEY · THE AFFAIR · NEIGHBORS · ALL THAT GLITTERS
ROYAL · DADDY'S GIRLS · THE WEDDING DRESS · THE NUMBERS GAME
MORAL COMPASS · SPY · CHILD'S PLAY · THE DARK SIDE · LOST AND FOUND
BLESSING IN DISGUISE · SILENT NIGHT · TURNING POINT · BEAUCHAMP HALL
IN HIS FATHER'S FOOTSTEPS · THE GOOD FIGHT · THE CAST
ACCIDENTAL HEROES · FALL FROM GRACE · PAST PERFECT · FAIRYTALE
THE RIGHT TIME · THE DUCHESS · AGAINST ALL ODDS · DANGEROUS GAMES
THE MISTRESS · THE AWARD · RUSHING WATERS · MAGIC · THE APARTMENT
PROPERTY OF A NOBLEWOMAN · BLUE · PRECIOUS GIFTS · UNDERCOVER
COUNTRY · PRODIGAL SON · PEGASUS · A PERFECT LIFE · POWER PLAY
WINNERS · FIRST SIGHT · UNTIL THE END OF TIME · THE SINS OF THE MOTHER
FRIENDS FOREVER · BETRAYAL · HOTEL VENDÔME · HAPPY BIRTHDAY
44 CHARLES STREET · LEGACY · FAMILY TIES · BIG GIRL · SOUTHERN LIGHTS
MATTERS OF THE HEART · ONE DAY AT A TIME · A GOOD WOMAN · ROGUE
HONOR THYSELF · AMAZING GRACE · BUNGALOW 2 · SISTERS · H.R.H.
COMING OUT · THE HOUSE · TOXIC BACHELORS · MIRACLE · IMPOSSIBLE
ECHOES · SECOND CHANCE · RANSOM · SAFE HARBOUR · JOHNNY ANGEL
DATING GAME · ANSWERED PRAYERS · SUNSET IN ST. TROPEZ · THE COTTAGE
THE KISS · LEAP OF FAITH · LONE EAGLE · JOURNEY
THE HOUSE ON HOPE STREET · THE WEDDING · IRRESISTIBLE FORCES
GRANNY DAN · BITTERSWEET · MIRROR IMAGE · THE KLONE AND I
THE LONG ROAD HOME · THE GHOST · SPECIAL DELIVERY · THE RANCH
SILENT HONOR · MALICE · FIVE DAYS IN PARIS · LIGHTNING · WINGS · THE GIFT
ACCIDENT · VANISHED · MIXED BLESSINGS · JEWELS · NO GREATER LOVE
HEARTBEAT · MESSAGE FROM NAM · DADDY · STAR · ZOYA
KALEIDOSCOPE · FINE THINGS · WANDERLUST · SECRETS
FAMILY ALBUM · FULL CIRCLE · CHANGES · THURSTON HOUSE
CROSSINGS · ONCE IN A LIFETIME · A PERFECT STRANGER
REMEMBRANCE · PALOMINO · LOVE: *POEMS* · THE RING · LOVING
TO LOVE AGAIN · SUMMER'S END · SEASON OF PASSION · THE PROMISE
NOW AND FOREVER · PASSION'S PROMISE · GOING HOME

Nonfiction

EXPECT A MIRACLE: *Quotations to Live and Love By*
PURE JOY: *The Dogs We Love*
A GIFT OF HOPE: *Helping the Homeless*
HIS BRIGHT LIGHT: *The Story of Nick Traina*

For Children

PRETTY MINNIE IN PARIS
PRETTY MINNIE IN HOLLYWOOD

DANIELLE STEEL

High Stakes

A Novel

Delacorte Press | New York

Published in the United States by Delacorte Press, an imprint of Random House, a division of Penguin Random House LLC, New York.

DELACORTE PRESS and the HOUSE colophon are registered trademarks of Penguin Random House LLC.

LIBRARY OF CONGRESS CATALOGING-IN-PUBLICATION DATA
Names: Steel, Danielle, author.
Title: High stakes : a novel / Danielle Steel.
Description: New York : Delacorte Press, [2022]
Identifiers: LCCN 2021028755 (print) | LCCN 2021028756 (ebook) |
ISBN 9781984821713 (hardback ; acid-free paper) |
ISBN 9781984821720 (ebook)
Subjects: GSAFD: Suspense fiction.
Classification: LCC PS3569.T33828 H54 2022 (print) |
LCC PS3569.T33828 (ebook) | DDC 813/.54—dc23
LC record available at https://lccn.loc.gov/2021028755
LC ebook record available at https://lccn.loc.gov/2021028756

Printed in the United States of America on acid-free paper

randomhousebooks.com

2 4 6 8 9 7 5 3 1

First Edition

To my darling children,
Beatie, Trevor, Todd, Nick,
Samantha, Victoria, Vanessa,
Maxx, and Zara,

May you always cherish the real prizes in life,
truth, honesty, honor, kindness, compassion, love,
May you be loved and well-treated by those around you,
And may you treat them, each other, and yourselves well,
May you be forever safe, loved, and blessed!

I love you with all my heart,
Mom/d.s.

High Stakes

Chapter 1

J ane Addison was rushing around her bright, modern new West Village apartment, getting ready for her first day at a new job. She had gotten her undergraduate degree from UCLA, worked for two years at *San Francisco Magazine,* and then gone back for her MBA at UC Berkeley, in their entrepreneurial program. She was twenty-eight years old, born and raised in San Francisco. Her father was one of the most successful venture capitalists in Silicon Valley. Her older sister, Margaret, was thirty-five, climbing the ladder at a rival venture capital firm. Margaret was married, with two children. Her husband was the CEO of a successful tech start-up, which was about to go public. Jane's life was very different from Margaret's, and so were her goals. For the moment Jane wasn't interested in marriage, and didn't know if she ever would be. Having babies held no particular lure for her. Margaret and her husband had met in business school at Stanford, and they liked their stable, married life and their demanding careers. They seemed comfortable and efficient managing both.

It looked like a hard juggling act to Jane, a lot of responsibility and too much work.

Jane's dream was to own a small magazine one day or, even better, a small publishing house, but she was a long way from achieving her goals. She was just beginning her work life. She had flown to New York to interview for jobs at the major publishing houses, Penguin Random House, Simon & Schuster, Little, Brown, but nothing that interested her and paid decently had turned up. The magazines she had sent her resume to hadn't leapt at the chance to hire her. They told her she was overqualified for the openings they had, and figured she probably wouldn't stay long enough to make hiring her worthwhile.

In the end, the only offer she'd had that excited her came from a friend of her father's, an old classmate of his at Princeton. Bob Benson owned a literary and entertainment agency, Fletcher and Benson, in New York. They represented actors, producers, directors, and screenwriters on the dramatic side, and writers on the literary side. The position she'd been offered was as an assistant to the executive assistant of the number two agent on the literary side, a woman named Hailey West. Jane had met her when she was applying for jobs in New York, and she seemed like an intelligent, pleasant, busy woman, committed to the writers she represented. The agency had some very important clients, and it seemed to Jane like a good interim job until the right opportunity turned up, closer to her goals for the future. She still wanted to work at a major publishing house to learn the ropes, but an entry-level job in publishing didn't appeal to her much, and at least a job in a literary and talent agency sounded like fun. Meeting important writers and movie stars would be exciting. The agency was very successful. She'd interviewed with her father's old friend and the heads of both sides of the agency, Francine Rivers for literary and Allie Moore, head of talent. They were both interesting women, and Bob Benson said that if she did well, she could be a literary agent one day.

Jane's mother came from San Francisco to help her find the apartment in a big, modern, efficient building in the West Village, with a view of the Hudson, in what seemed like a friendly neighborhood. The building had a gym, a pool, and a roof garden for the tenants' use. There was good security and plenty of staff, and her parents liked the fact that she'd be safe there. Her mother had been an interior decorator until Margaret was born, and she still enjoyed decorating their homes and doing whatever she could for her girls.

She helped Jane get her apartment organized and furnished in record time. Jane was thoroughly enjoying it and grateful to her parents for the comforts they provided. She was well aware that she and her sister had enjoyed benefits all their lives that many of their friends hadn't. They were discreet about it, but Jane realized how lucky she was that she could take whatever job she wanted without worrying about whether or not she could pay her rent. Thanks to her mother, she had a comfortable home all set up for her a month after she arrived.

An old boyfriend of hers from UCLA, Benjie Strong, was working for a start-up in New York. He'd been there since grad school. They had reconnected as soon as she got there. They had been dating for a month and had busy, separate lives. He had slept at her apartment the night before, and had his own place with a roommate in SoHo. It had made the transition to New York easier and a lot more agreeable for Jane.

He was making toast in her kitchen when she helped herself to a yogurt from the fridge. She made coffee for both of them with the espresso machine and handed him a cup. He'd been reading *The Wall Street Journal* on his phone and looked up with a smile when she set the coffee down next to him. Benjie Strong was a year older than she was. He was twenty-nine, and looked like he was going to a picnic in cutoff jeans, a T-shirt, and running shoes without socks. He had gotten his MBA at Wharton, and was a bright guy. There was no dress code where he worked. Jane had already seen that the dress code was casual at Fletcher and Benson, but not to that degree. The men wore collared shirts and jeans, loafers or running shoes. The women mainly wore skirts and tops of some kind, and looked put together even if they were wearing jeans, which some did. They wore makeup and their hair was neat. Benjie looked like someone who had the day off. He smiled broadly when he glanced at her.

"Going to a party?" he asked her, and she laughed.

"Compared to you, I look like I'm going to dinner at a fancy restaurant. Going to the beach?" she teased him back.

"I'm a lot more dressed up than most of the guys I work with. Some of them come to work in shorts and flip-flops, if the weather is decent. No one cares what we wear to work." It was the nature of start-ups, they both knew, and most of the employees were younger than Jane and Benjie, fresh out of college, looking like they had just rolled out of bed. No one shaved, or not frequently, and they barely brushed their hair. Games were provided in common areas, vintage pinball machines or video games, a candy bar, and board games to play on their breaks. The whole atmosphere was keyed to the very young. Many of them worked from home several days a week. And in start-ups or companies like Amazon, they often brought their dogs to work. Amazon, Facebook, and others like them had set the trend years before, and made the work environment highly desirable to the "millennials," mostly in their twenties, who worked there. The surroundings at Fletcher and Benson were more polished, since their clients were adults, and the employees were older than those at most start-ups.

The women she had seen there dressed well and she noticed that most of them wore heels to work. She was wearing a short black denim skirt, a striped Chanel T-shirt she had "borrowed" from her mother to bring to New York, and a pair of high-heeled black Manolo Blahnik pumps. Her long blond hair was pulled back in a neat ponytail, and she was going to wear a white Levi's jacket and carry a black-and-white tote. She looked fashionable, but not too much so. She was slim and had a good figure and long legs. There was nothing suggestive about what she was wearing. The skirt wasn't too short, and the heels weren't too high. Her perfume was a light fresh scent one barely noticed. She looked clean and young and pretty, and she was eager to do a good day's work and learn about her new job and coworkers at the agency.

She and Benjie left the apartment together. Benjie was taking the subway to work in Brooklyn, and Jane had called an Uber to take her to Midtown, where the agency was, on Fifty-Seventh Street between Madison and Park Avenue in the heart of the luxury shopping district. It would be hell getting there in bad winter weather, with all the traffic, but it was warm now and a nice area to walk around in during her lunch hour. There were plenty of places to eat or to order food nearby. And there was a kitchen and dining room for employees who brought their own lunch. Many of the employees ate at their desks while they continued to work. The working conditions were extremely pleasant at Fletcher and Benson, even if they didn't provide all the games and snacks offered by start-ups. None of that mattered to Jane.

"Have a good day," Benjie called out to her as she got into her Uber and he headed for the subway. She wasn't madly in love with him, but they had a good time together and shared some of the same interests. They didn't want to live together but saw each other a few times a week on an exclusive basis, which meant that neither of them was dating anyone else. It suited both of them. They had dated briefly in college at UCLA and were enjoying a replay of it now. It made being in New York more enjoyable, having someone to share it with. Benjie had had a serious relationship in business school, but they broke up when he graduated and moved to New York. Jane had never been seriously in love, and she didn't regret it. She wanted to get her career off the ground first and stay focused on that. Her work was important to her, more so than romance at the moment.

It took her half an hour to get uptown in morning traffic, while she read *The New York Times* online in the back seat of the Uber. They arrived right on time, and she followed a mass of people into the building where Fletcher and Benson occupied two floors. She went straight to the executive floor, gave her name to the receptionist, as she'd been told to do, and was about to head for a seating area, when a tall, heavyset man with white hair nearly collided with her, and then looked her over appreciatively. She didn't know who he was but felt instantly uncomfortable at the way he stared at her. His eyes went straight to her chest, and then took in the moderately short skirt, and glanced past her legs and then back to her face again. He stood in her path like a boulder in a stream, and she had to walk around him to get away from him. He didn't step aside and continued staring at her.

"Are you here for an interview?" he asked her in a deep, gravelly voice. "You can come and work for me if you like." As he said it, the receptionist met Jane's eyes with a knowing look and shook her head almost imperceptibly.

"I'm starting a job today," Jane said in a subdued voice. She didn't want to be rude, not knowing who he was, although she thought his behavior was crass and unacceptable.

"Receptionist?" he asked, making a very broad assumption that if she was a woman, she must have a low-level job. He was out of step with the times.

"In Ms. West's office," she said quietly.

"That's good news," he said. "Well, welcome aboard." And with that, he headed down a long hallway, and Jane took a seat to wait for Hailey West's executive assistant, who appeared a moment later. Julia Benning smiled at her warmly in welcome. She was a pleasant-looking woman in her late forties or early fifties. She took Jane first to the office of Francine Rivers, the head of the literary department. She explained on the way that the heads of both the literary and dramatic departments wanted to see Jane again to welcome her. Julia said that it was customary for them to see the new hires who were going to be working in the executive offices. She left Jane outside Francine's door, and told her she'd come and get her after Jane met with Francine and Allie Moore, the head of talent. Jane had met both women previously during her interview.

Standing there alone a minute later, Jane felt a rising wave of panic seize her as she knocked on Francine Rivers's door. Jane could see her through a wide glass panel: a stern-faced woman in black slacks, a black blazer, and running shoes, with her dark hair pulled back in a messy bun. She was frowning as she concentrated on her computer. She turned when she heard Jane knock and signaled for her to come in, then waved her to a chair. Jane realized then that Francine was speaking to someone on speakerphone and looking at a book cover on her screen.

"It looks all right to me, Elliott. If they make your name any bigger, there won't be room for the title on the cover. And I think the red foil makes your name really pop. I like it."

"The whole thing looks off-balance to me," a disembodied voice came from the speakerphone. "The British cover was much better."

Francine Rivers looked irritated but tried not to sound it when she responded. "Do you want them to make the title smaller?" she asked, only half in jest, and the male voice at the other end answered immediately.

"Yes, I do. Tell them to try that."

"I'll take care of it right away," she assured him, and ended the call and then turned her full attention to Jane.

"I'm sorry. One of my badly behaved 'children.'" She smiled a wintry smile at her. "Hell hath no ego like a narcissistic author. He won't be happy till his name fills the whole cover." She looked closely at Jane then, as Jane noticed that Francine had dark, serious eyes and a slightly sour, jaded expression when she wasn't smiling. "I get all the problem ones. Some of our big authors are challenging. They can be very insecure, like children, and jealous of their competitors. Don't worry. Hailey gets all the nice ones. But she's friendlier than I am, and has more patience," she said, almost smiling. "So welcome to the mother ship. We're delighted to have you join us."

She had seen Jane's grades from business school and was duly impressed. Bob Benson had already told her that Jane was the daughter of an old friend of his from Princeton. And he had told Francine who Jane's father was. She recognized the name, of course. Jane was obviously bright and had a good education, so there was justification for hiring her, and not just because of a college friendship between her father and the head of the agency. She had gotten the job on her own merits. Her contacts had merely gotten the door open, not landed her the job. "What made you want to work for a literary agency? Do you write?" Francine asked her. That was frequently the reason bright young people applied for jobs at the agency. They somehow thought that if they worked for an agent, their own work would be discovered, which wasn't how it worked. And most aspiring writers never made a career of it anyway. They didn't have the persistence or the talent. Even after all these years as an agent, it still amazed Francine how hard it was to find a good new writer, especially one who had more than one book in them.

"No, I don't write," Jane answered her. "I want to learn more about publishing," she said naïvely, still feeling nervous and sensing the tension around her. Francine was her big boss and seemed very serious to her, as the head of the literary department at the agency. "And being an agent is part of it," Jane said as an afterthought.

"We're problem solvers," Francine explained. "Most writers want a mother or a nanny, and need one. That's basically what we do—we nurture them, in addition to getting them book contracts and negotiating for them. We're their advocates and translators and liaisons between the writers and their publishers. Some of the problems are ridiculously small, and others are enormous and harder to solve. You'll see it all firsthand in Hailey's office. She's gentler with her writers than I am. Occasionally I lose my temper and scare the hell out of them. It whips them into shape, though." She smiled a tired smile. "I do that with the publishers too. Being an agent is like being a referee at times. At other times, you need a gentle touch to close a deal, or so I'm told. I prefer threats, leverage, and force, myself. It always works for me," she said, and laughed. She looked as strict as she said she was, and as dedicated to her job. Jane readily believed her. "This is not a playground. It's hard work," Francine added for emphasis. She seemed like a take-no-prisoners kind of person. Jane wouldn't have called her bitter, but there was something cold and unhappy about her.

As they were talking, the heavyset white-haired man whom she had seen earlier in the reception area appeared in the doorway. He opened the door without knocking, ignored Jane this time, and looked straight at Francine.

"Seven? The usual?" he asked, and Francine nodded, looking irritated. Jane noticed that her new boss's eyes went dead after he spoke. Francine nodded assent again and he left her office, leaving the door half open. He didn't bother to close it, although it had been closed when he arrived.

"That's Dan Fletcher, one of the two heads of the agency," she explained to Jane without further comment.

Jane nodded. "I saw him this morning when I arrived." She didn't comment either.

"I hope he behaved. He doesn't always when attractive young women are involved. No one has explained the Me Too movement to him. I hope he didn't say anything inappropriate," she said, still looking annoyed.

"No, not really. He just looked me over and assumed I was here to interview for a receptionist's job."

"He thinks that's what I do too." Francine smiled. And then she told Jane how to find Alabama Moore's office, the head of the talent side of the agency. Francine said she had work to do. Jane stood up and thanked her for her time.

They shook hands and Jane left Francine's office and made her way down the long hallway, with countless offices on each side, and people busy at desks inside them, looking at computer screens or talking on the phone.

Jane's only worry was that Dan Fletcher would appear again and harass her, or invite her into his office, an invitation she had no intention of accepting.

She found Alabama Moore's office after a few wrong turns. She had to double back once, but she finally found the office with her name on the door. As the head of the dramatic department, she had a huge office. Allie Moore was on an exercise bike when Jane knocked and walked in. She was wearing a white Chanel jogging suit and listening to something on headphones. She smiled and stopped pedaling as soon as Jane entered the room feeling awkward.

Alabama Moore had a dazzling smile, and Jane thought she was very beautiful. She had met Allie in her initial interview and was impressed by her then. She had a mane of blond hair and big blue eyes. She was wearing no makeup and her face looked young and smooth. Jane wasn't experienced enough to recognize the work of a great dermatologist combined with an expert plastic surgeon or to realize that Allie Moore had had "work" done, along with Botox shots and fillers. She looked as if she were around Jane's age. Jane would have guessed her to be about thirty, when in fact she was forty-three. Her figure was slim and lithe in the white velour jogging suit that molded her flawless body. She got up at four on weekdays so she could be at the gym religiously at five A.M. She owned a loft apartment in Tribeca. She hopped off the bike and invited Jane to join her in the seating area in her office, which consisted of a comfortable couch, two big easy chairs, and an oval coffee table. There was expensive contemporary art on the walls, and her smile was warm as Jane observed her and the effect she created in the outfit she was wearing. It had been a good choice.

"It's great to have you here," Allie said enthusiastically. "You'll like Hailey a lot. She works incredibly hard and is the consummate professional. I'm the official renegade, the rebellious child of the Fletcher and Benson family. I have to be, to deal with the actors, writers, and producers I represent. Some of them are barely more than kids, and they act it. Others should have grown up years ago and never will. They all get spoiled working on movies where people cater to their every whim. But some of them really deserve praise and attention because they have such huge talent. The badly behaved ones get away with it, and will never realize how spoiled they are, until it's all over for them.

"I grew up with Hollywood parents, so I'm used to it. My mother is a well-known actress, you'd know the movies she's been in, and my father produces hit TV shows. My parents' lives were enough to convince me that I never wanted to be on stage myself. I went to USC film school, but I decided I wanted to be an agent.

"My mother trained me to deal with divas from the time I was two. I worked for CAA, Creative Artists, in L.A. for a few years after I graduated, and then I came to New York to work at William Morris Endeavor. Then I met Bob Benson and he made me an offer I couldn't refuse, so now here I am, thirteen years later, and we represent some wonderful talent.

"I'm proud to be here, and I love what I do." She beamed at Jane and was all innocence. "Are you interested in the dramatic side? Maybe you can do some projects for me sometime before they lock you away forever in the literary world. The talent side is much more fun," she said mischievously as Jane thought about it for an instant. She had never considered being an actor's agent or even a writer's agent. This was kind of a sidetrack for her, to learn more about the business, and had been her father's idea when she didn't find a job in publishing at first. She was in love with books, much more than film. But Allie made the dramatic side sound appealing too.

Jane also suspected that there was a lot more to Alabama Moore than she was admitting. She was obviously very bright, her face was smooth and guileless, but her eyes said something different. She was a keen observer and noticed everything, and her welcome was much warmer than Francine Rivers's. Francine seemed tougher. There was something bitter about Francine that came through her pores. Allie seemed to love her job and Jane had the feeling that she lived and breathed for her career and would have killed anyone who inter-

15

fered with it in any way. They were both highly successful professional women, who seemed competitive while trying to appear as though they weren't. She had a sense that either woman would attack if she felt threatened. This was the big leagues, and they were playing for high stakes, for their clients and themselves. The women who worked at the agency were pros in every way. They had fought hard to get where they were, and it showed in an intensity about their jobs.

Julia Benning, Hailey West's executive assistant, appeared while they were still in the seating area in Allie's office, and a moment later, she whisked Jane away to Hailey's office, which immediately felt like a safe haven to Jane when she got there. The atmosphere was different in Hailey's office than in Allie's or Francine's, and Julia was a gentle guide. There was a desk for Jane near Julia's, which she could consider home base, and an office just messy enough to feel human but not chaotic. Julia showed Jane the closet where she could leave her things, and then the espresso machine. They had their own. Julia felt like a fellow student and upperclassman, showing Jane around her new school.

Hailey was in a meeting in the conference room with a major author when Jane got there, and she returned to her office an hour later. She was smooth and professional and slightly younger than the two department heads Jane had seen that morning.

Hailey was thirty-eight years old, and had an extremely responsible position as the number two agent in the literary department. She was wearing a white blouse, a well-cut, straight navy blue skirt, and high-heeled sandals. She had dark hair and wore it loosely pinned up on top of her head. It gave her a softer, more feminine look than the other two. Jane had noticed photographs of three young children on her desk, but Hailey made no mention of them when they spoke. She was entirely professional and all about business. It was obvious that Julia liked her and respected her, and when Hailey went into her own office and closed the door, Julia filled Jane in on the rest.

"She has three kids," Julia said as they each had a cup of coffee during a brief break.

"Divorced?" Jane asked her, curious, and Julia shook her head.

"Widowed. And her kids are young, a girl, eleven, and two boys, six and nine. The little one was just a baby when her husband died five years ago, at forty-three. He had an aneurysm and died while he was jogging. He was a publisher. She was an editor and used to work for him, and she quit when she had her kids. I think she stopped working for about six or seven years after she got married, and then he died, with no money and no insurance, so she had to go back to work. She couldn't get a job that paid enough as an editor, so she came to work here. Bob Benson knew her husband, so he gave her a job, and now she's number two on the literary side. She needs the job to support her kids. She's totally professional and never misses a day, even when they get sick. A lot of people who work here don't have kids. Employers are always afraid that people with young children won't be reliable, but she is totally committed to her work. She never talks about her kids. It's all about the writers she represents. Francine Rivers has two teenagers and works hard anyway. Allie Moore doesn't have kids. You have to be dedicated to your job here, and willing to work long hours and drop everything when one of our clients has a problem or a crisis. People with kids can't do that, especially single mothers. Hailey is as dedicated to her writers as she is to her kids. She's all about business when she's here. She doesn't stay home with sitter problems. I don't know how she manages, but she shows up no matter what goes on at home. She's good to work for, you'll see. She's very fair." Julia showed Jane around the rest of the office then, and pointed to a project she was working on, and a slew of foreign book covers she had to send to Phillip White to approve. He was Hailey's biggest author, a huge bestselling success. "He hits one out of the park every time," Julia said, describing him. Jane knew who he was and liked his books.

By the time Hailey came back from her next meeting in the conference room, which Julia had set up for her the way she liked it, Jane had been shown where everything was in the office. Julia was neat, efficient, and organized, and anticipated Hailey's every need, after having worked for her for several years.

"I have to be a mind reader sometimes, although not often, and hope I guess right. I try to anticipate what she'll want so she never has to ask for anything. If she does, I've failed."

"She's lucky to have you," Jane said with genuine admiration for her. "I don't know how you keep it all straight."

"You'll get used to it. I've been doing this for a long time, it seems like a lot at first, but you'll get into a routine once you know her. She's very clear and straightforward in her requests. She'll tell you what she needs. Just do what she says. Don't put a spin on it or try to improve it. Listen, and follow her directions. That's what matters most. Don't decide you know a better way or a better system. You'll guess wrong and screw it up that way. And if you don't hear or don't remember something, ask her. That's what she wants. Don't be afraid to ask her questions. Better that than to guess wrong, especially if you don't know her well. Your asking her questions just saves time in the end." It made sense. Hailey sounded like a practical person from everything Julia said. "You're the first assistant I've had," Julia said with a smile. Bob Benson had created a job for Jane after Hailey had told him that her assistant could use some help. She was swamped.

"What about you?" Jane asked her. "Are you married? Do you have kids?"

Julia laughed in answer.

"Hell, no. Being an assistant is like being married. I'm married to her life and my job. I love it. I don't have time for a husband and kids. That boat sailed without me years ago. I'm fifty-one. I used to want to be an agent, but decided I'd rather be an assistant. Fewer headaches. And Hailey deals with the really crazy writers herself, so I don't have to. It's a perfect job, and there's a lot of satisfaction in it, if you do it right." Jane knew she wanted more than that in the long run. She didn't want to be an assistant forever. She either wanted to be an important agent one day, like Francine and Allie, or Hailey, or own a magazine or a small publishing house. That was still her dream. She wanted to run her own business and be her own boss, not work for someone else. "No guts, no glory," her favorite business school professor had said, and she liked the concept. She saw this job as a stepping-stone to bigger things, and she intended to learn all she could while she was here. She had big dreams. This was just the beginning to her. If she was going to make sacrifices in a job, like long hours, hard work, and a lot of stress, she wanted to do it for herself. She didn't want to still be an assistant at fifty-one. With her father's help to get her started, once they agreed that she was ready, Jane was sure she could go far. That was why she had gone to business school. She wanted to be Bob Benson or Dan Fletcher, not just a member of someone's staff. But this was fine for now, and it sounded like fun, even if stressful at times. They were all busy, and the nature of the business included pressure.

Hailey kept Julia occupied until lunchtime, and Julia gave Jane several projects she could handle on her own. At lunchtime, Jane ordered a salad from one of the restaurants they used to have lunches sent in. She went to the kitchen to get a fork and a soda out of the fridge, and was about to go back to her office to eat while she worked, when Dan Fletcher appeared. He caught her when she had the refrigerator door open, and scraped past her so he could rub up against her. She wanted to turn around and slap him but resisted the urge. Instead she turned around and looked him in the eye. For a second, he looked like he was going to grab her. There was no one else around.

"Is there a problem?" she asked him, momentarily oblivious to the fact that he was her boss and one of the two owners of the agency.

"Not for me. I understand Bob and your father were classmates at Princeton. We'll have lunch and you can tell me about it sometime." He pretended not to see the look of fury in her eyes, and his hand brushed her bottom as she walked past him. He was bold to a shocking degree, and apparently got away with it. No one dared call him on his behavior because of who he was. She went back to her office, shaking with rage. Julia saw the look on her face and was worried.

"Something wrong?"

"How the hell does that lech get away with it? First he squeezed by me, so he could rub up against me, and then he put his hand on my ass."

"Oh. Dan. He does it to everyone. Just ignore him," Julia said with a shrug.

"I'm not going to ignore him," Jane warned her. "I'm going to call him on it if he does it again."

"He's harmless. He's married with kids," Julia said, as though that made a difference.

"I don't care. That's sexual harassment," Jane reminded her.

"He's the boss." She said it as though that absolved him of everything.

"That's my point," Jane said, and dug into her salad. "I'll call a lawyer about it if I have to." She was still seething, remembering his rubbing past her in the kitchen, his body pressed against hers. He was disgusting.

"You'll never get another job if you call a lawyer," Julia said practically.

"I'm not going to put up with it," Jane said, and ate her salad in silence after that. She wondered how many women in the office he'd done that to, who kept their mouths shut to keep their jobs. She couldn't imagine him doing something like that to Francine Rivers. She was tougher than that, and looked like she wouldn't tolerate it for a minute. There was an undercurrent of anger in Francine, which Jane suspected would cause her to erupt with very little provocation. Jane couldn't guess if Francine's anger came from her job or her personal life, but she didn't seem like a happy woman. She had a fabulous career and was highly respected, but Jane could sense that something was amiss somewhere in her life.

Jane had no way of knowing that Francine's husband had walked out on her with the nanny, divorced Francine, and married the nanny as soon as their divorce was final. Fortunately, she had never given up her job as an editor at a major publisher. But she could no longer afford to keep it after the divorce. She had taken the job at the agency and was promoted with astounding speed. She was a very talented editor and had a real ability to discover promising young writers who blossomed with her direction and guidance. Several of them were writing bestsellers now. The pay as an agent was better, but the child support her ex-husband gave her was meager. He'd had two more children, so she got nothing from him anymore. She made a very healthy salary, but supporting two children on her own ate up what she made very quickly. At forty-five now, she had dealt with ten years of financial struggles, trying to provide the best she could for her kids and save for college, without taking loans. It took a heavy toll on her. She hadn't cared about her looks for years. Her daughter, Thalia, was seventeen, and next year Francine would have college to pay for. She wanted her to go to an Ivy League college if she could get in, which cost a fortune. Her son, Tommy, was thirteen, and would be entering high school the same year that his sister started college, and they were applying to the best private prep schools. Francine lay awake every night, trying to figure out how to pay for everything. She always found a way, but she had nightmares about what would happen if she ever lost her job. And even with it, and a highly respected position, she spent everything on her kids. There was never anything left for her.

She had moved out of the city to a respectable area of Queens after the divorce, to save money. She missed living in the city, but sent both her kids to private schools, and wished she could do more for them and put aside money for their future. She made too much to qualify for a scholarship for Thalia in college. Bitterness over not having anyone to help her and having a deadbeat ex-husband had been a way of life for Francine for so long that she no longer remembered what it was like to live without it. Constant struggles and financial problems after the divorce had toughened her, and she set the bar high for anyone who worked for her. She tried to be gentle with her authors at the agency, but she found it hard to be sympathetic at times.

Her children complained that she was never home, stayed at the office too late, and never got back early enough to make a decent dinner. She rushed home as soon as she could, put a frozen pizza in the oven, and helped with homework, but most of the time she was too tired to spend much quality time with them. She wanted to be outstanding at her job so she would never lose it. It was her greatest fear, that she'd get fired and wouldn't be able to support her kids in their fancy schools. She made a healthy salary, but her ex-husband had proven to her how uncertain the future could be. Her work was draining, and her life a constant vicious circle of too much work, a lot of stress and pressure, and supporting her kids. It tainted the way she saw the world around her. She knew only too well how competitive the agency was. If you slipped for a minute, someone else would have your job. And she was willing to fight anyone to the death to make sure that didn't happen to her. Worrying about it didn't make her pleasant to be around, and she hadn't had a man in her life in years.

* * *

Later that afternoon, Jane met Merriwether Jones, the CFO at the agency. Her life, as Julia described it, was a perfect example of total success. She was beautiful, a Harvard MBA, nice to everyone, friendly and charming. She was married to a writer, who stayed home to take care of their five-year-old daughter, Annabelle, while Merriwether made a huge salary at the agency. According to Julia, her husband Jeff was a handsome hunk, and they were crazy about each other. She was warm and encouraging to Jane when Bob Benson introduced them. She was one of those women who proved that you could have it all, a family, a happy marriage, and a great career. She reminded Jane of her sister, who was a high achiever who had it all too. Merriwether lived in a townhouse she had bought in the East Eighties. She had grown up in Boston, and her family expected her to get a great education and use it to become successful and make a lot of money, and she had.

Jane's father's old friend, Bob Benson, seemed to have it all too. He was married to a famous entertainment lawyer, had three sons, two in college and one still in high school. They lived in Greenwich, Connecticut, in a beautiful house, and he and his wife both had successful careers. He seemed like an all-around nice person, and everyone said he was a pleasure to work for.

By the time Jane got home that night, after a long Uber ride back to the West Village, her head was swimming with all the people she had met and the information Julia and Hailey had shared with her. Every one of the women who had important jobs, including Julia, was fully focused on her career. And Jane had the feeling that all of them would have been willing to kill to protect their jobs, if anyone tried to interfere with them. Their work ethic appeared to be excellent, and they set the bar high for themselves and everyone around them. The one who appeared to be having the most fun was Alabama, with all the actors she represented. Francine was the toughest and hardest. Hailey seemed to be on an even keel, and Merriwether appeared to be the happiest, with the most well-rounded life. Meeting their expectations was going to be a lot to live up to, and Jane just hoped she didn't disappoint them.

"So how was it?" Benjie asked when he showed up with dinner for them that night. She was grateful to see him. She was too tired to cook and would have gone to bed without dinner.

"Interesting. Action-packed. And my head is exploding with all the information," she told him over couscous and fragrant Moroccan chicken ordered from a favorite restaurant of theirs. He was thoughtful that way, and he had brought a half bottle of champagne so they could celebrate. He was on a tight budget, but always generous with her. "I've never met so many smart, interesting, successful women all in one place. They're all focused on their careers, and are a lot to live up to."

"You don't know them that well yet, who they really are. All you saw today is what they wanted to show you."

"They're divorced, widowed, single, and one is happily married. They're juggling kids, their jobs, and their clients. I don't know how anyone can do all that and get it right, but they seem to. All I want to focus on is my job. The head of the literary department is very tough and seems angry. I guess they're all tough in one way or another, or they wouldn't have their jobs."

"Just make sure you don't end up like that. There's more to life than work," he reminded her, then kissed her and cleared the remains of dinner away, while she went to take a shower.

It didn't sound like fun to him, but he also knew that Jane was more ambitious than he was, and her family expected a lot from her. It was a vast difference between them. Her father had driven both of his daughters hard to become high achievers, and her sister Margaret's success in finance was a lot to compete with. He didn't envy Jane, despite everything her parents had provided for her. They expected a lot in exchange, and she didn't want to disappoint them. His parents just said they wanted him to be happy, whatever route he followed. He wasn't sure the Addisons ever thought that was important. Neither did Jane. All she thought about was what she was going to accomplish in the coming years.

It was a race she was going to run every single day. And the race had started in earnest now with her first serious job. He didn't envy her at all. In fact, when he thought about it, he felt sorry for her. She was going to miss out on a lot in life if she continued on the path she was on. She was driven by a force he didn't really understand. It was a white-hot fire within her. She had to meet her parents' high expectations and her own. It was a tall order for anyone. And dating her wasn't easy either.

Chapter 2

H ailey left her office half an hour later than usual, which was
always a problem when she did. She never made a point of it,
and stayed until her work for the day was done. But a late call from
an author, a crisis Francine or Bob wanted help with, or a delay of
any kind caused her problems with her babysitter, who never wanted
to stay overtime. She had several other sitters she could call, and
often did, if one of the kids was sick. She never mentioned it being a
problem to Francine, who had kids of her own. Hers were teenagers
and had been latchkey kids for years. They were three and seven
when she got divorced, and she taught them early to be independent. She had her daughter watch her little brother at an early age
until Francine got home, and managed without full-time babysitters
even when they were very young. They went to a neighbor if they
had a problem, which they seldom did. They had learned to be self-
reliant. She tried to save on childcare as soon as she could and didn't

want to waste money on help. Her kids learned to fend for themselves and were unusually responsible now as teenagers. She was proud of them. They had managed for years without child support from her ex-husband, and they all lived on her salary. Her ex spent the little he made on his new family and ignored his old one. She was bitter about that too.

In Hailey's case, it was different. Her husband had died so suddenly that she wasn't prepared in any way. Her children were young and there were three of them. Arianna was six, Bentley four, and Will eight months old when Jim died. She had no choice but to rely on sitters when she went to work at the agency where she was lucky enough to find a job. She couldn't support them and herself on what she would have made as an editor, pay for childcare, and still live in the city. They had been spending all of Jim's salary to live in a spacious apartment in Gramercy Park downtown and lead a pleasant life with three children, with her not working. Everything changed the moment he died, with no insurance and almost no savings, and no salary of her own. She had no family to help her. Jim's father had died when Jim was young, and his mother had died of early Alzheimer's. Hailey had no one to turn to and had to rely on herself and the people she hired in order to go back to work. At least all her children were now in school full-time. The sitters picked them up after school and brought them home. Hailey took them to school in the morning before she went to work. She tried to be home no later than seven every night, no matter how busy she was, and she never used sitters on weekends. She had had no social life to speak of for the past five years. She couldn't afford one. She was more of an anxious mother than Francine, and didn't want to leave her kids alone.

Francine had taught hers to be independent early on. It was a difference of philosophy they had discussed several times if they saw each other socially.

Hailey had been lucky to find an inexpensive two-bedroom walk-up apartment on the West Side. She and Arianna slept in one room, and Bentley and Will slept in the other. The building was safe and in a modest, mixed neighborhood.

She never talked about her kids casually at work, or that it was occasionally a struggle to get help with them. If they got sick at school, she did everything she could to find someone who could pick them up and keep them for her so she didn't have to leave work to do it. She never reminded anyone at the office that she had children to deal with. She made work her priority during office hours, and her children the rest of the time, and she never complained about it. It was a constant juggling act. It might get better when they were older, but she was still in the thick of it with young kids.

It was seven-thirty when the cab dropped her off, and she hurried up the steps of her building. When she had time, she took the subway home, but she had been in a hurry, so she hailed a cab as she walked out of her office building. She let herself into the apartment, and she could hear them talking in the kitchen. The kindly Jamaican woman, Felicity, who babysat for them on most days, had made dinner for them, as she often did.

Hailey threw her coat over the couch in the living room and hurried into the kitchen. Only Arianna and Bentley were at the table, and Felicity was putting their dishes in the dishwasher. Dinner was over. She had missed it, again. It was a struggle to get home early enough to eat with them.

"Where's Will?" she asked them. Her six-year-old son was noticeably absent.

"He threw up all day, Mom," Arianna, her eleven-year-old daughter, said with reproach in her voice. "And I need help with my math homework." It was Hailey's worst subject too, and always led to arguments and tears when Arianna didn't understand the problems, and neither did her mother. "And I have a science paper due." They gave her a mountain of homework, and Hailey could hardly keep up with it in the little time they had together at night.

"We'll deal with it when the boys go to bed," she said, trying to sound calmer than she felt, and turned to Felicity, who was eager to leave now that Hailey was home. She had children of her own, teenagers who got into mischief if she stayed too late. "Does Will have a fever?" Hailey asked her. It was the second time in three weeks that he'd been sick.

"No," Felicity said, shaking her head. "But he threw up three times after I picked him up at school. He's sleeping now. He didn't want dinner."

"He threw up all over the little rug in our room," nine-year-old Bentley informed her with a look of disgust.

"I put it in the washing machine. It's drying now," Felicity reassured her. It was one less thing to deal with as Hailey sat down at the table with them, and tried to focus on them and clear her mind of everything she'd done at the office since that morning. This was their time now. She led a double life, a literary agent to some very high-powered writers by day, and a mother to three children who needed her full attention at night. She felt constantly guilty about them because of the time she couldn't give them.

She had loved being a full-time mother when Jim was alive. Her life had been a relay race ever since he'd died, trying to cover all the bases, and being mother and father to them. They all resented how hard she worked, and the fact that she couldn't speak to them openly when she was at the office. She told them they had to wait until she came home at night to deal with their problems. But sometimes they forgot and called her anyway. She got off the phone as quickly as she could when they did that. She wanted no crossover or overlap between her two lives. She had to be two people now: a mother and an executive. She managed it as efficiently as possible, although sometimes it got out of hand. She was very organized, which averted crises whenever she could manage it. A surprise illness or an accident turned everything upside down, as it had today. Arianna and Bentley still remembered their father, although dimly. Will had been a baby when he died, and never knew him. Arianna often said that "if Dad were alive things would be different." Bentley said it to mimic her, and in both cases what they said went straight to Hailey's heart and convinced her that she was failing, but she couldn't do anything differently. They had every spare moment of her time when she wasn't working.

"Can I watch TV tonight?" Bentley asked her, fully aware that it was against the rules on a school night, but hoping she'd forget or let him do it. He was a handsome blond boy who looked like his father. He was all arms and legs and tall for his age, as was Arianna, who was tall and blond too. Will looked more like her with dark hair. He still seemed like a baby at six and loved to cuddle with her. He was always hungry for affection, and loved curling up with her to read a book or watch TV. She tried not to think about the manuscript she had brought home to read. One of her authors wanted her comments on it. She put it out of her mind as she got to work with Arianna on her homework, and as always, within half an hour, Arianna was in tears, and Hailey was close to it. The problems made no sense to her either, and the explanation in the workbook wasn't clear to either of them. They eventually got them done. Bentley was asleep on the couch by then, since he couldn't hang out in his room with Will feeling so sick. She had checked on Will after Felicity left, before starting on the homework, and contrary to Felicity's report, Will did have a fever. Not an unusually high one, but enough to make him feel rotten. She gave him children's Tylenol and he went back to sleep.

They got started on Arianna's science report, but halfway through, Arianna couldn't concentrate anymore. She was too tired. Hailey promised they'd finish it the next day.

"If you don't come home late again," Arianna growled at her. She was more critical of her mother than the boys were, but she needed her more for homework, and resented having babysitters instead of her mother. She was extremely adept at making her mother feel guilty.

"I come home as fast as I can," Hailey said defensively.

"Except when some stupid writer calls you about his dumb book, and you'd rather talk to him than be at home with us."

"That's not true and you know it. I'd much rather be here with you, but I have to work" because your father didn't bother to think about us and get life insurance in case something happened to him. But she never said those words or criticized him to her children.

She got Arianna to take a bath and let Bentley go to bed without one. He was deeply asleep by then, and she carried him to his bed, got him into his pajamas, and checked on Will again. He felt cooler, and she hoped it would be a short flu and not a long one, and that they wouldn't all get it. Felicity had agreed to come in for the whole day the next day, but said she couldn't the day after, so if Will wasn't well by then, Hailey would have to find another sitter from her long list to be with him. If absolutely necessary, an elderly neighbor downstairs was willing to stay with them, but she couldn't keep up with them, and Hailey only used her when she ran out of other options. It was a daily juggling act.

It was nearly ten o'clock when she finally sat down to read the manuscript. It was well written, as his work always was, but by then she was so tired that in half an hour she was sound asleep on the couch. She hadn't had time to eat dinner and she fell asleep with the lights on and her clothes on, which was a common occurrence. Arianna's words were still echoing in her head when she fell asleep . . . *you're never home with us . . . you come home late every night . . . you care more about your stupid writers than you do about us.* Every one of those words was a dagger to her heart, and none of them were true. She hoped that Arianna didn't really believe that, but she feared she did.

The next morning, she would have to get them all ready for school, feed them breakfast, decide if Will was still sick and if he needed a doctor. Then she had to get to the office on time, well dressed and looking civilized, and explain to the writer why she hadn't finished reading his manuscript yet. For eight hours or more in her office, she had to pretend to herself and everyone around her that her mind was clear, her heart was light, her job was all-important to her and the only thing that mattered, and that she didn't have three kids at home,

one throwing up with a fever, and the others waiting to do homework with her. She was leading a double life and had for the past five
years. There was no end in sight until her kids grew up, which was
light-years away. Some days, most days, she wondered how she
would survive it.

Allie Moore's life was at the opposite extreme of Hailey's. Allie couldn't
even have imagined a life like Hailey's, with three children she was
responsible for, and not a spare moment for herself to read a magazine
or get a massage. Hailey ricocheted between the office and home every
day, meeting other people's needs and never her own.

Allie only had herself to think of, and rarely wasted time thinking
of anyone else. She spent most of her time considering her looks and
how much fun she could have. She loved working with young actors,
celebrating their victories with them or consoling them in their losses
when they didn't get a part. She loved helping them build their careers, and doing all she could to give them a boost up to the top.

She made their careers fun, and she loved sharing the excitement
with them. Because what was life if you didn't have a good time?
And she had constant ongoing affairs with the flavor of the month. If
you added sex to the mix, then what could be more perfect? Most of
the young actors she represented didn't need to be convinced, and
they fell easily for her charms. Who wouldn't? She was young, exciting, powerful, had a flawless body, and looked years younger than
she was. It was fun for her.

Sometimes she'd just sit back and look at the photographs of the
young actors she represented and pick one she hadn't tried yet. It

was like shopping online, not even online dating, because most of the time, the men were so in awe of her and what she could do for them that she got to make all the decisions.

She never made promises she couldn't keep. In fact, she made none at all. She wasn't trading sex for jobs. They got the parts or they didn't. All she did was invite them out to play, and if they wound up in her bed in the end, what harm was there in that? They were consenting adults.

She had come across a photo of Eric Clay that afternoon while going through their files. He was waiting to hear about a lead part in a new TV series, and expected word from the producers any minute. He had auditioned for it and had a good shot at getting the part. He'd been waiting to hear back from them for a month, and was seriously worried about it. She called him that afternoon between meetings, to ask how he was.

"No news yet," he said glumly. "I think it means I didn't get the part. You know how they are. You audition, they tell you that you were fantastic, and then you never hear from them again."

"Not at your stage, Eric," she said in a soothing tone. "I know the producers. We've done a lot of work with them before. They're great guys, and have an eye for talent, but they're flakes. They can never make up their minds, and then suddenly the project gets green-lighted, and it takes off at jet speed. Not hearing from them for a month doesn't mean a thing. And I saw your audition tape, it was fabulous." Eric was twenty-six years old, a well-trained, very talented young actor. He could play anything from comedy to Shakespeare, and was one of the best-looking men she'd ever seen. He got a lot of work and had been in a series before for a short time. Women fawned over him, and on top of it he was bright and a nice guy. They'd have to be crazy to turn him down for the part, and they weren't. "What are you doing tonight? Can I take you out and cheer you up?"

"What did you have in mind?" He was hesitant. He didn't do drugs or lead a wild, crazy life. She didn't do drugs either, but she liked going out with handsome young guys.

"Whatever you want, dinner at a deli, something simple. If you don't feel like going out, we can order in at my place." She knew he lived a few blocks from her in Tribeca.

"That sounds just right. I didn't want to have to get all cleaned up and dressed. I'm wearing sweats. I was going to go to the gym, but I already went this morning. I'm taking boxing classes to keep busy and in shape. But I'd rather hang out at your place than the gym tonight. Can we order sushi?" He sounded like a kid when he asked, and she smiled.

"Of course. Whatever you want." She was the agent for all purposes: food, friendship, hand-holding, sex, whatever the situation warranted and the client wanted. Her employers knew that she dabbled with the clients occasionally, or they suspected it. She was seen with handsome young actors on their roster at events from time to time, but they saw no harm in it. What she did after hours was her business. Things could get pretty loose with actors sometimes, and she was old enough to know how to handle it. As long as she was discreet, they didn't care what she did. It was different and somewhat more serious on the literary side of the agency. Alabama Moore was the best actors' agent the agency had ever had, and everyone loved her.

Allie got home half an hour before Eric was due to arrive. She showered and put on jeans and a thin pink V-neck sweater without a bra. Her implants held her breasts up nicely. They hadn't been as perky at twenty as they were now, and had been a lot smaller before the surgery. Her body was amazing, with lean, smooth flesh, and not an ounce of fat anywhere. She was in fantastic shape from her daily workout at the gym and yoga classes. She put the time in to keep her body toned, lean, lithe, and trim, and it paid off. She made good use of it regularly. She wasn't indiscriminate or sloppy about it. She chose her partners carefully and had affairs that usually lasted about a month. Then she moved on. They always ended on good terms, and she and a number of her young male clients shared a secret from then on. It added a little spice to her work. She enjoyed that and so did they.

She turned down the lights in her loft and lit some candles. She pulled out the menu for the sushi restaurant she preferred for Eric to look at when he arrived, and she put some music on. She set the stage just enough to make her apartment appealing and the mood right if he was so inclined. If not, the atmosphere was cozy and re-laxed, and they would share a soothing evening. There was no harm in that. She couldn't imagine trading the life she had now for a hus-band and children. She loved her freedom and the variety of part-ners that had been her way of life for years. She had no desire to be tied to one man, or for an intimate relationship, and the thought of children terrified her. She would much rather spend the night with someone like Eric than some boring guy her own age, or a child. She had no maternal instincts at all, and never had. She loved her career and where it had taken her. She had grown up among actors, and she was familiar with their quirks and fears. Their narcissism didn't bother her, since she was similarly focused on herself, so they didn't shock her with how self-centered they were.

Eric arrived five minutes late and brought a bottle of good French wine. He opened it so it could breathe for a few minutes and glanced at her appreciatively.

"You look hot, Allie," he said with a slowly spreading smile. "It cheers me up just looking at you."

"That was the whole idea of your coming over tonight," that and some other things she had in mind. The invitation was obvious. He kissed her then and slid a hand under her sweater. Her implants were recent and felt more real than the last ones, with new technical improvements. In any case, he didn't complain. He seemed to like them. He took her sweater off gently, pulled her down on one of the couches, and slid a hand into her jeans as she unzipped his and released him. They didn't waste any time and were making love within minutes. He was an adept lover, and made it last as long as they could both stand. Her yoga positions served her well, and they were both breathless when it was over. He glanced at her cautiously, afraid she might have regrets.

"Are you mad at me?" he asked her, fondling her breasts again, and then kissed her nipples. "I couldn't keep my hands off you once I saw you in that little pink sweater. You're so damn hot, Allie." She grinned and laughed. She was a fun companion and great in bed.

"What part of that do you think I'd be mad at?" she said in a husky voice. It was the best sex she'd had in years. She hadn't guessed he'd be quite that good. He had surprised her, which was rare for her.

"Well, if you're not mad," he said, smiling too, "let's do it again." And they did. They made love three times before they ordered sushi at midnight, and twice afterwards. He spent the night, and he strolled around her apartment naked the next morning when she got up, and joined her in the shower. He was a gorgeous sight to behold.

"That was an incredible night last night," he said with a look of wonder once they were dressed. They had surprised each other. "Can I see you tonight after work?"

"You're not bored yet?" she asked, and kissed him. He slipped his hand into her jeans again.

"Do I look bored to you? I may have to show up at your office. I'm going to be having withdrawals by lunchtime."

They made love again in her kitchen before she left for work and he went to his boxing classes, after promising to be back that night. She could sense easily that they were going to have a fabulous time for the next few weeks, maybe a month, and she had taken his mind off the part he wanted so badly. Now he wanted her even more. She was glad she'd called him. It was good for both of them. It was one of the many perks of her job that she loved, having easy access to men like him. Although after the acrobatics of the night before, and his ability to make love again and again, she was beginning to think he was unique. He was definitely her favorite client for now.

Merriwether's evening started out peacefully when she got back to the townhouse on East Eighty-Fourth Street, where Jeff had been trying to write for several hours. Their daughter, Annabelle, was already asleep, as she always was when Merriwether got home. Their part-time nanny, who came in the afternoons so Jeff could write, had put Annabelle to bed before she left.

Jeff looked irritable when she got home, and she poured them both a glass of wine.

"How's the book going?" she asked him. She'd had a good day at work. She loved the balance in her life: her home life with him and her hard-driving career as the CFO of the agency. She loved having a grown-up life. It wouldn't have been enough for her, staying home with a child and no longer working. She'd grown up in New York and came from a family where excelling and material success were all-important. Jeff was from an L.A. family of "creative people" who had accomplished nothing and didn't care.

"It's not," he answered about his book, and took a long sip of wine. "Annabelle was a pain in the ass this morning. She said she had a stomachache so I let her stay home from school, in case she was getting sick. She was fine. She interrupted me every five minutes until lunchtime when Amalia finally came in and took her off my hands, and by then I was too distracted to write. I just wasn't in the mood. It's hard shifting gears from childcare to writing." Annabelle was usually in school until Amalia, their part-time nanny, came in, and most of the time he enjoyed being with their daughter. He said that having a job would interfere with his writing. And now their daughter did.

Merriwether was thirty-seven years old and had supported them since they'd married seven years before. She didn't mind Jeff not working. She made more than enough money to support them both, and their daughter. And one of these days, Jeff would make big money with his writing. He was forty-two and had a lot of creative years ahead of him. Merriwether thought that he had talent. He just needed encouragement and more drive. Hailey agreed. She was his agent, and she encouraged him and gave him editorial advice when she read his manuscripts. He had sold one book, a thriller, three years before, and nothing since. He said it was a dry spell, and Merriwether was sure he'd find his voice eventually. Some days his writing went better than others. And he never pushed himself too hard. He said the writing had to "flow." Merriwether was driven and had been an overachiever since she was a child. It was the only thing that got her parents' attention and approval. She had gone to Harvard because both her parents had. Her father was the head of a corporation and her mother was a corporate lawyer. She was an only child.

"You seem to be getting home later and later these days," he complained as they drank their wine. There was cold chicken in the fridge, but neither of them was hungry yet. Merriwether liked to unwind at night after long, stressful days.

"It's been busy at the agency," she said.

"If you came home earlier, you could see Annabelle before she goes to bed," he commented, which made her feel guilty.

"I see her at breakfast," Merriwether said defensively. He didn't usually complain about the amount of time she spent with their daughter. "And I see her on weekends. That's what fathers do, who work all day and don't see their kids at night. I spend more time with her on the weekends than most fathers who're out playing golf."

"So you see yourself as the man of the family now?" he said, looking annoyed.

"It's the role I have as the breadwinner. That doesn't make me a man, but I have long days at work," and a big salary to show for it, which she didn't say. Dan Fletcher and Bob Benson had been good to her. "This is what we agreed to when I got pregnant, and you wanted to quit your job and write full-time. I agreed to earn the money so you could spend time at home writing and be with our child." Merriwether hadn't felt ready for a baby yet at thirty-two, but the arrangement they'd made suited her. She was free to have a career, and he could stay home to pursue his. It seemed fair to both of them at the time. And suddenly he was complaining. She was surprised. "Do you want to go back to work?" she asked him. He'd never had a serious job, but had dabbled in PR and special event planning, which he hated. He hated schedules, responsibility, and authority, but he was handsome, charming, and sexy, and she loved him, so she overlooked his faults.

"No, I don't," he said. He liked things as they were. He just hadn't expected Merriwether to be so deeply committed to her job. "If I did get a job, would you stop working?" he asked her.

"No." She was honest with him. "I love my job. And even if you go back to work, we can't afford to have me quit." With her Harvard MBA, she could command a salary he couldn't. Her taking on the breadwinning so energetically had been a godsend for him. It had seemed the perfect arrangement. "What are you really complaining about?" she asked, puzzled by the underlying message, which wasn't clear. "Are you mad because I make more money than you do? That's pretty normal. It takes a long time to earn big money as a writer. You probably won't make a lot of money for the next five years. That's fine with me." She gave him all the space he said he needed to be creative.

"Or never, if I never sell another book."

"You will. You're still young for a writer."

"But not young if I try to get a job and go back to work. I've turned into this gigolo that you support, and people consider my writing a hobby. I'm kind of the nanny around here," he said, and sounded bitter for the first time. She hadn't realized he felt that way. He'd never put it that way before, in an acid tone.

"You're not a gigolo, Jeff," she said gently, and came to sit next to him on the couch. She kissed him, and he put his glass down and put his arms around her.

"I need to sell a book," he said in a choked voice, and she could tell he was near tears.

"You will. Lots of writers have long dry spells, and then they have a big hit and it all takes off. You just have to keep plugging. Hailey thought your last book was fabulous. Everybody loved it, even the critics, and thrillers are hard to write." He looked pleased when she praised the book.

"We had seventeen rejections, some from publishers I've never even heard of."

"Every writer has that experience, except a few really lucky ones," she said, trying to encourage him.

"I read about a woman the other day whose first book was published when she was ninety-two," he said. "That'll be me with my second one."

"No, it won't be, silly. You stalled for a little bit, it will pick up again soon. You just have to keep at it."

"Sometimes I think I'm just kidding myself about being a writer. Maybe I'll never sell another book, and the first one was a fluke. I feel like a fraud, sitting here while you go to work every day and support us. It's hard to feel like a man when your wife pays all the bills."

"We knew it would be this way. I never expected you to make a fortune overnight." She didn't say that his salary had been negligible before that. She was destined to be the real earner in their marriage, unless he sold a huge bestseller one day. Short of that, she would be supporting them, and she didn't mind.

"Will you try to come home from work a little earlier?" he asked her with a plaintive look in his eyes. "Annabelle and I miss you. It's boring and lonely here without you." He sounded pathetic but she didn't want to promise him something she knew she couldn't do.

"We get so busy at the office, and they need me there, Jeff. I can't just get up and leave at five o'clock. I'm the CFO, not an agent. And the agents don't leave that early either." He nodded, and neither of them said anything for a while. They finished their wine and had dinner in the kitchen, and it pained her to see how unhappy he looked. She didn't know what the answer was, except that he just had to keep writing and hope he sold another book. She couldn't solve the problem for him. And she wasn't going to jeopardize her career for him. She couldn't. But knowing he was unhappy and resentful wasn't going to do anything for their marriage. She could hear warning bells going off in her head when she thought about it. She hoped it was just a phase he was going through as part of the creative process. If not, and he was serious, they had some rough times ahead. She hoped that their marriage was strong enough to survive it. But for the first time in the seven years she had been married to him, she wasn't sure they would. It was a frightening feeling, and when they went to bed that night, he turned his back to her and went to sleep. The fire had gone out of their relationship, like the air seeping out of their tires slowly, as he lost confidence in his work. And more and more, he was taking it out on her.

Francine took a cab to the familiar address when she left the office. As usual, on those nights, she left the office late. It was nearly seven o'clock by then, and she left in the clothes she'd worn to work that day, a pair of black jeans, a gray sweater, and her running shoes. She hadn't brought anything fancier with her. She couldn't see the point of dressing up. She ran a brush through her hair, and left it down because she knew he liked it that way, and he would complain if she didn't. She didn't bother to put on makeup, and just brushed her teeth and washed her face in the office bathroom. She looked plain and unadorned when she put on her black trench coat. She had stopped dyeing her hair and let it go gray, which aged her. And she didn't care about that either. He had never mentioned it to her. She looked like a plain, serious woman leaving work. She used to dress up for these occasions, but now she realized it was what it was, and there was no reason to pretend it was something different. She couldn't lie to herself.

She gave the cab driver the address on Central Park West. She had been going to the same address for ten years. The apartment belonged to people she had never met. It was a pied à terre, which no one used anymore, but they kept it. The owners lived in Montana now, a well-known actor and his wife. The actor was very old and in poor health. He hadn't been to New York in years but kept the apartment as an investment. Dan Fletcher took care of it for him, and used it for his own purposes, with the owners' permission. They didn't mind, and were happy to have him go there and check on it.

He hadn't bothered to turn on all the lights when she arrived. The apartment looked gloomy and unoccupied, as it always did. It had the feeling and the smell of a place that was seldom used. A cleaning service came to clean it once a week, but there were none of the small personal touches of a home that someone loved and lived in. It felt airless and forgotten. They used to have dinner afterwards but hadn't bothered to in years. And she needed to get home to her kids. Dan was usually drunk and passed out by the time she left. He spent the night there twice a week and told his wife he had meetings in town. It gave her a chance to have dinner with her women friends, which she liked. And he went to the office from the apartment the next day.

Francine rang the bell and Dan Fletcher, her boss, the owner of the agency, opened the door for her. There were a few lights on behind him, and she knew her way around the apartment after ten years of meeting him there twice a week.

"You're late," he said as his only greeting. He had a glass in his hand with scotch and ice cubes in it. She could tell he had already had more than one drink. She knew him well. He handed her one too, after she took her coat off, and she sipped the drink. She hated scotch, but it made her visits there easier, and the effect was quick.

He didn't bother to stop in the living room with her, and walked straight into the bedroom as she followed him, carrying her drink. She set it down on a round table. The apartment had probably been pretty once, or interesting. They had some good paintings, some Remington sculptures of cowboys with horses, and there was a view of Central Park from the bedroom windows. She stood and looked at it for a minute as Dan Fletcher watched her, wondering what she was thinking. Then he took a long pull of his drink and set his down too. He took his jacket off and threw it on a chair, unbuttoned his shirt, and when she turned around, he was standing in his boxer shorts, bare-chested, with his socks on, and lay down on the bed. She knew what she had to do. She had been doing it twice a week for ten years.

She took her clothes off quickly and left them in a heap on the chair. Her body was still in good shape. She looked her age at forty-five, and she was an attractive woman even if she no longer cared how she looked. She glanced at him once. He was lying on the bed, with his eyes closed, waiting for her to get started. He took off his boxers and threw them on the floor, but left his socks on. She did what she had promised to do so long ago, for reasons she justified to herself in the beginning, but she no longer could. He had taken her out to dinner the first time, and she was flattered, and didn't think she should refuse. She'd had too much to drink, and later she had wondered if he put something in it. She was almost sure of it afterwards. The next thing she knew, she was at the borrowed apartment. She couldn't remember getting there. She was thirty-five then and better-looking. Her husband had just left her with two young children and too little money to live on and support them and herself. She had taken the job at Fletcher and Benson for the salary they offered her to become an agent. She could just barely manage to live on what she made before that as an editor and support her children, living in a small cheap apartment she'd rented in Queens. The salary she'd been offered as an agent made a big difference to help pay for her children's schools. She needed the job desperately with her ex barely able to make his child support payments then. Everything rested on her.

The next thing she knew that first time, Dan Fletcher was making love to her. She felt dizzy and sick, but she didn't have the strength to stop him. She was too drunk or too drugged. The next morning, she felt sick at what had happened. She had left her children with the sitter all night. And he spelled it out to her. If she agreed to meet him twice a week for sex, she would get regular salary increases and promotions and her job would be secure. And she would be promoted in a short time to head up their literary department. If she wouldn't agree, or stopped meeting him, she would be out of a job and he'd find a reason to fire her, and he'd see to it that she never worked again.

She couldn't believe the position she was in or what he was proposing to her. But she needed the money and the job security for her kids. If he fired her and blackballed her, she'd have no way to support her children. She had no one to turn to, and no boyfriend or husband. So what difference did it make to anyone if she did what he wanted? He told her he'd see to it that her reputation would be destroyed if she didn't agree, and who would believe her if the head of the agency lied about her? He said he'd be sure that everyone knew she was a whore if she left or he fired her. From the look on his face, she believed him. He had all the power, and she had none, and two children to support. She told herself that she was doing it for her children, and there was nothing she wouldn't do for them. How bad could it be? Terrified to lose her job and be disgraced, she had made her pact with the devil, and met him faithfully twice a week. She thought maybe she could get out of it eventually, but once she knew him better, she knew she couldn't. He would destroy her if she tried to escape or reneged on their agreement. He reminded her regularly of what would happen if she stopped meeting him, she'd be out of a job, accused of some kind of malfeasance. She no longer cared by then. Something had gone dead inside her. She believed all his threats to ruin her and expose her as a whore. Having sex with him was the only real job security she had if he would blackball her, and she was sure he would. In exchange, he lived up to his end of the bargain and made her head of the literary department in less than a year. All she had to do was keep having sex with him. As long as she did, no one ever knew. Only she did. And she could keep her job, her salary and reputation. He controlled her by fear, threats, and black-mail. And every time he told her what would happen if she stopped coming or left, another part of her froze inside. She felt numb and half dead and did what he wanted. She couldn't afford not to. He ruled by terror.

In lucid moments, she told herself that this was what prostitutes did, and she was no better than they were. The rest of the time, she didn't think about it. She just did it, and let him do whatever he wanted to her, just to keep her job and security for her kids. For the past five years, he had taken Viagra when he met her, which made it easier to satisfy him. It really was a wonder drug.

He liked coming inside her once she had aroused him, and some-times he came all over her, depending on the mood he was in. De-grading her was part of how he controlled her, until she felt like nothing. She was a hollow shell by then. He never bothered to talk to her, and she wondered why he didn't hire a hooker instead. It might have been more fun for him. He told her once, on a rare occasion when he talked to her afterwards, that he and his wife hadn't had sex in twenty years. He said she was a frigid bitch, and he would have divorced her, but she would have taken all his money. So he had sex with Francine twice a week instead. It seemed to be enough for him, although he was known to be a lech in the office and grabbed a random feel of the female employees whenever he could get away with it. He felt he had a right to. No one was going to challenge the boss and risk their job. They just avoided him as best they could. But Francine couldn't, she had too much at stake. Because of her job, she and her children could live in an apartment in a decent neighborhood in Queens. They went to good schools, and she tried to put money aside for their education, and college one day, so she could stop meeting him. But that time never came. If he destroyed her professional reputation, where would she go and what would she do? It was easier to just keep having sex with him, no matter what it did to her.

Ten years earlier, he had made her stay longer, have sex with him a second time, or give him a blow job before she left. Now he was satisfied with once. He was too drunk to have sex again after that. There was no conversation, nothing personal when they met. It was strictly physical for him, and mechanical for her. She couldn't imagine why he did it. It meant nothing to him either. It was just physical release. He didn't need to make any effort with her, she was a sure thing. She needed the job as head of the department and the money she made. He gave her a "bonus" in cash on Christmas, which paid for the extras her kids needed, things that came up more and more often as they got older. Lessons, tutoring, trips, vacations. She tried to save as much as she could. School tuitions were high and even more than the money, she needed to protect her reputation so she could get another job one day. She doubted he would ever let her leave him without destroying her. She believed his threats.

For years she had been ashamed of what she had let him blackmail her into, but now she no longer cared. It was a disembodied act she performed twice a week with a man she loathed. If he had died, she wouldn't care. And if she lost her job and reputation, she would have been short of money for Thalia and Tommy, particularly with high school and college looming. She had told herself in the beginning that if she met a man she cared about, she would stop seeing him, try to find a way out somehow, and look for a new job, even in another field, but she hadn't met anyone, and no longer wanted to. Her emotional life was over. She had no emotions left. She was empty. He had destroyed her by humiliating her and with his threats to destroy her. She wasn't a woman to him, she was a thing, an object he used for his convenience, like a prostitute he picked up on the street but didn't have to pay. She was free, she was clean, he knew she'd show up every time. She was too afraid not to. She even went when she was sick so he didn't get angry. He had an ugly temper. She had been a decent woman with a heart and soul until she met him. Her husband had crushed her when he left with a twenty-three-year-old nanny, and Dan Fletcher had finished her off. She did what he wanted willingly to keep her job and reputation. She thought of giving it up when Tommy finished college, but that was still eight years away.

Afterwards, she went to the bathroom and cleaned herself up. She didn't want to stay long enough to shower there, and she had to get home to her kids. She stayed less than an hour now. By the time she dressed, he was snoring loudly, lying flat on his back, in the same position he'd fallen into when he rolled off her. He was rough and crude, but she was used to that now. She couldn't imagine making love with a man again. The thought of it disgusted her, almost as much as he did. But this wasn't love, it was just sex.

She let herself out of the apartment and walked to the subway nearby. The doorman tipped his hat as she left. He was used to seeing her, and could guess why she showed up twice a week. He no longer bothered to announce her when she arrived. He knew her.

She changed trains and got home at eight-thirty as she always did. Thalia was out with friends. It was senior year for her, and hard to keep her home now during the week. She had already flown the coop in her own mind. Freedom was just around the corner.

Tommy was sitting glued to the TV, eating a frozen pizza he had heated up himself. He didn't look up when his mother came in. She sat down on the couch next to him for a minute, feeling filthy as she always did after her meetings with Dan.

"How was school today?" she asked him, and he shrugged.

"It sucked, like it always does. I hate my teachers. We had basketball practice today. The coach kept me on the bench for the whole game."

"Why?" she asked gently. He was an unhappy child and had been for years. He had minor reading issues and had had remedial classes for that.

"The coach hates me," he said in a flat voice. It made her realize that he mirrored a lot of her own emotions. So Dan had broken him as well, without ever meeting him. And Thalia couldn't wait to leave. Francine had never succeeded in making their plain, poorly furnished apartment a happy home for them. There was no joy in it, just as there was none in Francine. The apartment reflected how dead she felt. She spent all her energy at work, determined to do a good job, and was too tired and drained to do anything that required emotional input from her when she got home from work. And twice a week, she returned broken again. He broke her over and over and over again, with his threats and degrading comments, until she couldn't heal the broken parts anymore, and didn't try.

She went to take a bath then, and came back in a pink terrycloth bathrobe to tell Tommy to go to bed. He lumbered off to his room without hugging her. He had decided he was too old for that a year ago, when he turned twelve. She was going to her own room when Thalia walked in. She was wearing a pink hoodie and jeans and a pair of pink running shoes that Francine had given her. She spent what she made on her children, and rarely bought anything for herself. And she saved the rest for their college fund and better days.

"Hi, where were you?" Francine asked, as she always did.

"Out. With friends," Thalia said in a surly tone.

"What friends?"

"What difference does it make? You don't know them. You're never here."

"I'm always here," Francine corrected her. "I'm here every night."

"Yeah, after dinner, so you don't have to cook for us."

"I get here as soon as I can. You're old enough now. You could wait."

"For what? I can put my own frozen pizza in the oven. So can Tommy. We don't need you for that."

"I know that. We should make an effort to eat together," she said, as though it was a novel idea. She wanted to give them a normal, happy life, which no longer seemed possible. Francine had been dead inside for too long.

"What, and pretend you care about us, or you're interested? You don't even talk to us when you come home, you're so fried from the office. And as soon as you eat, you pull out a manuscript you have to read."

"It's my homework." She tried to smile at her daughter, but it didn't work. Thalia had ruled her out as a mother around the time she had turned thirteen. It had been a hard road with her ever since.

She'd had a hard time with both her kids for the last few years. Sometimes she felt as though they hated her as much as she hated herself for what Dan had blackmailed her into doing for ten years. She had kept her job but lost her self-respect and damaged her relationship with her children.

Thalia went to her room after that, and Francine turned off the lights, then went to her own room. She lay on her bed, thinking about them, wondering where she had gone wrong. They no longer saw their father and hadn't for years. He wasn't interested. He had a new family, a wife and two little girls, still the same woman he had left with ten years earlier. He lived in Detroit, was an ACLU lawyer, and had stopped sending child support years before. And she didn't bother to fight him for it.

Francine had brought home a manuscript to read, but she couldn't concentrate on the nights she met Dan on Central Park West. She used to cry on those nights, but she no longer did. She had no tears left. For herself, or anyone else. Somewhere deep within her there was rage for what she let Dan do to her. But she couldn't connect with that either. She really was dead. And her kids knew it too. That was the worst part. She had died when she met Dan Fletcher, the first time they'd had sex. She could fake it at work and pretend she was still a human being. But she and her children knew it wasn't true.

Jane and Benjie watched a movie on TV. She had so much new information floating around in her head, she didn't want to go out. She kept thinking of all the people she had met at the agency, particularly Allie, Francine, and Hailey. She wondered what their home lives were like, if they had boyfriends, and she knew from Julia that Merriwether, the CFO, was happily married. She wondered if the other three were happy. She thought Allie was, but Francine seemed profoundly depressed, and so negative about life. She didn't say it, but it came through her pores. Julia said it was the result of her bad divorce. And Hailey seemed energetic and positive, although Jane thought she couldn't have an easy time, widowed with three young kids.

All three women were clearly dedicated to their careers, but Jane couldn't help wondering what the rest of their lives were like. Who were they, other than busy agents in a highly successful agency? She questioned if she'd ever get to know them beyond their professional facades. What sacrifices had they made to be where they were?

Francine seemed as though she had paid a high price for what she'd achieved. She looked as though she had the weight of the world on her shoulders, and Allie presented as though she was entirely carefree. Hailey was the consummate professional, business-like, focused, and cool, despite the pressures of her job. So far all Jane could see was what they wanted to show her. She had a feeling that there was much more to each of them, and she wondered what secrets lurked behind their well-polished masks. She was curious about them.

"You didn't hear a word of the movie, did you?" Benjie asked when it was over. He was visibly annoyed.

"I did," she insisted, but he was right. "I was thinking about the women at the agency. My head is full of everything I've seen and heard so far. I'm trying to figure it all out."

"Let me know when you're in the mood for a real date," he said petulantly.

"I just started a new job. I need to figure out the players, and I want to get it right," she said as he stood up.

"You're already changing," he said, watching her closely, and not liking what he saw. She seemed distracted and distant and less interested in him. She had too much on her mind.

"I'm not changing. I need to focus on my job."

"Yeah, whatever. You want to be one of them so badly, you can taste it."

"I want to do it right, Benjie," she said, tired of his complaints. It had been a long and very full day. He picked up his jacket and looked at her. He had the feeling that he'd already lost her, and he was right. She was a million miles away, and the movie hadn't held her interest.

She was much more interested in the agency than in Benjie or the movie she had paid no attention to at all.

He left a minute later to go back to his apartment, and Jane realized again that he was right. She was changing. And tonight, she had other things on her mind, and she wasn't sorry to see him go. He suddenly seemed like a child.

Chapter 3

The morning after Will's fever from the stomach flu, Felicity came to stay with him, but she arrived late, so Hailey was already rushing before she got to the office. She hated being late because of childcare issues. It always seemed unprofessional to her, and set a bad example to the other agents, and even her assistants, now that she had Jane working with Julia. Hailey believed that personal issues should never interfere in the workplace.

She took a cab to work and had just sat down at her desk when Phillip White called her. Being asked to represent him was a major coup and a feather in her cap after he had met several of her colleagues, including Francine. As the head of the literary department, Francine always got first crack at all the bestselling authors. She must have been having a bad day, because Phillip told Bob Benson he found her lifeless and disengaged, and he preferred Hailey. He liked her energy and enthusiasm, particularly about his work. She had done her homework and read his last three novels, and an earlier one to get a sense of his work and the recent direction he had taken, and she made intelligent comments about them.

Since Hailey had worked as an editor previously, although Phillip had a longtime in-house editor, he thought Hailey would make additional helpful suggestions when she read his manuscripts. His instincts about her had been right. She had been working with him for two years. He felt she was a good negotiator, and her editorial comments were superb as she came to know his work better. He was very happy with the arrangement and was quick to call her with any problem he had with his publisher.

She could hear immediately that he was upset when she answered.

His latest book was on the *New York Times* bestseller list, in third position, and he had done two recent interviews with *The Washington Post* and *The Wall Street Journal,* hoping to push the book further up the list. Instead, it had plummeted to eleventh on the list, which was not the result he'd wanted. He felt that the publisher's publicity department had handled it badly, and he wanted Hailey to complain. The competition was still on the list the second week. And she didn't disagree with him entirely. She thought they had managed the book poorly. They had outdated information in their bio of him, which he felt had contributed to two lackluster interviews, and he blamed the publisher for the book slipping down the list. She reminded him that the book might go back up the list. Usually his sales were solid, but she was planning to call the publisher anyway with some complaints herself about how the interviews had been handled. This was her job, to call the publisher to order and keep a close eye on what they were doing.

"Thanks for taking care of it, Hailey," he said warmly. He'd had a long career as a successful novelist, achieved huge sales every time, and was worthy of the publisher's close attention.

"I think book sales generally have been slipping for everyone lately. It could be the time of year, or bad weather. It's not just you, Phillip. We've seen it across the board with all our authors."

"That's because the publisher is doing a lousy job," he grumbled.

"I don't disagree with you," she said calmly. She had a soothing way of speaking to him, which always made him feel better. She was intelligent and sensible. She listened to him, was honest with him when she didn't agree with him, and championed his cause fiercely when she did. She was respectful of his enormous talent and was proud to represent him.

"They should have held the book back by a week or two, instead of dropping me into such a tough list. I'd have made number one a week or two later. That wasn't smart of them." She agreed with him about that too.

"It's already on my list of complaints. I'm going to call them this morning. And I'm not thrilled with the cover for your next book that they just sent us. What did you think of it?"

"I hate it," he said bluntly. "I already sent them an email about it. It's dark and depressing, and it'll get lost in the bookstores. It's supposed to be our book for the holidays. No one is going to give it as a gift with a cover like that." He sounded deeply concerned and she had been too, when she saw it. "I got an email from the publisher this morning. She said they'll get back to work on it and send me something else when they have it."

"Good. I'm relieved to hear it." Hailey spent half an hour on the phone with him, and, as always, he was reassured by the time they hung up.

She called the editor-in-chief at his publisher after she spoke to him, and registered all of his complaints as well as her own. The editor agreed that they were valid. Hailey liked dealing with Phillip's work. He was a terrific writer and a reasonable person, and a pleasure to work with. He never wasted her time.

She had another call from an author as soon as she hung up. Marianne Thornton was furious that her publisher had placed more ads for a rival author than they had for her latest book. The other woman's book was higher on the list than hers, and she blamed the publisher. She was an author who was always unhappy about something. She complained so often that Hailey could sense that the publisher was exasperated with her, as Hailey often was herself. She had an endless list of gripes, and if her current book didn't do well, it was always the publisher's fault and never her own. She wrote mysteries and some were better than others. Her most recent one had been a dud in Hailey's opinion, and it wasn't selling well. Hailey tried to pacify her, and spent half an hour on the phone, which would have been better spent doing something else.

She had a call from a young author after that. She had run her most recent check from the agency through the washing machine by mistake and needed a replacement. Hailey told Julia about it and asked her to handle it with accounting. She was about to call another author who was late delivering a book that they had already gotten one extension for, and the publisher was going to be furious this time, when Felicity called her. She didn't like getting calls from home at the office unless it was an emergency, and she sounded curt when she answered. Felicity told her that Bentley's school had called. He had just thrown up, and they wanted him picked up and taken home, which was a problem. Will was still sick and running a slight fever again, and Felicity didn't want to take him out, and she couldn't leave him at home alone to pick up Bentley.

"I can't pick him up," she said in her lilting Jamaican voice as Hailey glanced at her watch. It was almost noon, she had been on the phone all morning and had a mountain of work on her desk she hadn't gotten to yet, new submissions and a dozen emails to answer from both writers and publishers. She'd been planning to work through lunch, but she had no one else to pick up Bentley, and it would take her longer to find someone who could than to do it herself.

"I'll pick him up," she told Felicity. She grabbed her bag after she hung up and told Julia she'd be back in forty-five minutes to an hour, then rushed downstairs and hailed a cab. She was at Bentley's school in twenty minutes and had the driver wait outside. Bentley looked miserable when she got to him, and she had him in the cab with her in five minutes. They got to their apartment fifteen minutes later. She took him upstairs to Felicity, and then rushed back down the stairs, headed for the subway, and was back at her desk in under an hour. She grabbed an apple and a yogurt from the office fridge and took them back to her desk so she could answer her emails. They had doubled in number while she was out, and she spent the next hour answering them, and the rest of the afternoon going through the submissions on her desk. Two of them were from unpublished writers who wanted the agency to represent them. She handed their manuscripts to Julia and asked her to have a look at them and give her coverage on them, summarizing the stories and offering her opinion as to whether they were worthwhile or not.

She spent the entire afternoon dealing with minor but time-consuming problems. Most of her days were like that.

Francine had had a busy morning too. One of her biggest authors wanted to cancel a TV appearance on the *Today* show, two days before the scheduled date. Francine knew it would not only hurt her book, but would make the producers of the show furious and loath to have her on the show next time.

"I really think you should do it, Anne. The repercussions just won't be worth it. The publisher is going to be pissed, and so will *Today*." She spent an hour trying to convince her to go on, and finally did. She was an important author and a difficult woman, and Francine had to handle her with kid gloves.

She got two calls from writers who said they were going to be late with their books, which meant a call to two different publishers to try and get extensions for them. One publisher agreed and the other didn't, so she had to send an email to the writer, telling her that the publisher had refused to grant an extension. As soon as she finished the email, she got a call from Tommy's school. The assistant principal told her in an outraged voice that Tommy had hit a boy in school and gotten into a fight with him during recess. It turned into a schoolyard brawl, and they were sending Tommy home for a day since it wasn't the first time, and they wanted him to go home and think about it. Francine knew he would be delighted to stay home and watch TV, but she didn't think that was good for him.

"This is the third fight he's been in, in just over a month. Is there something happening at home?" The assistant principal sounded concerned about him, and Francine was too.

"He says he's not happy at school," Francine said. "I'm not sure why."

"He's exhibiting very aggressive behavior, Mrs. Rivers," the assistant principal said disapprovingly. "I was going to write to you and suggest therapy, some form of counseling. He's clearly having issues. He kicked the water fountain after the fight today and left a dent in it. Destroying school property isn't acceptable behavior either. We had to talk to him about it." She hesitated for a moment, and Francine could tell that the woman had something more to say but was being guarded about it. "He says you're never home. You come home after dinner and he and his sister have to fend for themselves. I do think counseling would be a good idea, for both of you. I can give you some names if you like." Francine hated hearing what she had to say, that Tommy was so disturbed at the moment that he was getting into fights. And the school clearly blamed his mother for it because she worked late. Maybe therapy really was needed. It sounded like it to Francine, and she looked dejected when she got off the phone.

Her assistant buzzed her again less than a minute later to tell her that another one of their big authors was on the phone. This one was a major diva. She was scheduled for a book tour and she didn't like a single one of the hotels where they had booked her. She said she would only stay in five-star hotels. If she was going to have to get up at five every morning for hair and makeup to do TV, then the publisher would have to get her better accommodations. She wanted a suite, which Francine was almost positive the publisher wouldn't pay for. The author in question was successful, but her publisher was not known for their generosity.

Francine tried to tell her as simply as she could that she doubted the publisher would pay for more luxurious hotels for a book tour, and she knew the reaction she was going to get. It came within seconds. The author informed her that if they didn't put her up at the best hotels in each city, she wouldn't go on tour. This meant that radio and TV appearances would have to be canceled, as would the book signings, photo ops in each city, and interviews with major newspapers. A book tour had a million components and moving parts. It was up to the publisher to arrange, and the PR person if there was one.

"They're going to be very upset if you cancel, Barbara. That's not a small threat." It was up to her to manage her client, and she couldn't.

"Precisely. So tell them to get me better accommodations. And I want a car and driver in each city. I'm not going on the road like some gypsy or taking cabs to a TV show at six in the morning." She had done tours before and knew how grisly it could get if badly arranged. "I want to go first class, in every way, or I'm not going. You should have told them that before." So now Francine was to blame too.

Francine got up from her desk and made herself a cup of coffee after the call, to give her some energy before she called the publisher and delivered her client's message. She knew already that it would be a heated exchange. The client in question was notoriously stubborn, and never backed down once she took a position. The author was absolutely capable of canceling the tour if she didn't get her way, which Francine felt was a big mistake.

Francine wandered into Allie Moore's office with her cup of coffee, just to get a break. She'd been going full speed all day. Allie had had her hands full too. They all did on a daily basis. It was the nature of the business, and the downside of being an agent. You wound up spending your whole day arguing for or against something with the client or the publisher, or a nasty journalist, or someone who had done something they shouldn't. Half the time, she felt like a kindergarten teacher or the police. She had long since discovered that stars in any field could be surprisingly childish, either because they were spoiled, which was the case with most film stars, or they didn't live in the real world and had no notion of how ordinary people lived or what they put up with.

Allie glanced up at Francine when she walked in with her coffee, and smiled when she saw her.

"You look like you've had a hard day," she said, wearing jeans and a sexy red blouse with her blond hair cascading over her shoulders. She was in exceptionally good spirits after a very active night with Eric Clay. They were having a ball together, which Allie considered one of the best perks of her job. A never-ending supply of young male bodies to play with, which was all she wanted. Long-term relationships were not her M.O. and not what she had in mind. She liked short, hot, and fiery with no strings attached on either side. The only thing she wanted in her life long-term was her career. But the brief affairs she embarked on with great regularity were a lot of fun while they lasted. When they stopped being fun, she cut the cord and disappeared, almost always before her partners could. She liked being in control of when they started and when they ended. And she never got in over her head. She didn't like complications in her life. And in her opinion sex was a lot less complicated than love.

"When don't we have a hard day?" Francine said, and sat down in a chair across from Allie's desk, which was so big, it dwarfed her, and she looked like a beautiful child at a desk, like Alice in Wonderland.

"My days aren't usually so bad," Allie commented, thinking of Eric the night before. "It must be in the stars. Some days are crazy. Maybe it's a full moon or something. At least your writers are saner than my actors and actresses. I have a young star on a series who just got pregnant for the second time in two years, by a different guy each time, and they'll have to shoot around her. The producers are pissed, and she's begging me not to let them fire her. I had a young client this morning who got arrested for assaulting a cop. He was drunk and on drugs at the time, and he's scared to death he'll lose his part on a soap. And this isn't the first time for him either. He wanted me to find him an attorney, and I did. Then we've got a really nasty one coming up. A big Hollywood star whose name you'd recognize immediately. He slept with a fourteen-year-old girl, who he claims he thought was twenty. They got drunk together, and now she says he raped her. He's ruined. They're kicking him off the movie he's making, and in the current atmosphere, he'll go to prison if they convict him, as he should. It'll all be in the headlines by tomorrow. He has a famous wife, four kids, and he just flushed his career down the toilet.

His wife is going to divorce him, and I think it's a safe bet that his career is toast. That's the worst I dealt with all day. Then there's this crazy old actress I love who's on a sitcom. She wants to bring her six Chihuahuas on set with her, and the director says they bark constantly and he's allergic to them. She says she won't go to work without them. Sometimes I think we deal with crazy people all day. I don't know how you go home to kids at night. If I didn't get to play at night, I'd probably go nuts."

"I already am nuts," Francine said with a grin.

She went back to her office then to call the publisher about the book tour, and Allie took a call from a producer. It was the call that Eric had been waiting for, for weeks. She listened to what the producer had to say with a serious expression, and her face broke into a broad smile. He got the part he had been so desperate for. She couldn't wait to tell him, but decided to save the news until that night. He could stand a few more hours of suspense and then they could celebrate together. The producer was as excited as Allie knew Eric would be. It was going to make his career even bigger. She was happy for him, and she loved being the bearer of good tidings.

Hailey was still at her desk, trying to make order from chaos at the end of the day, and she had made progress. She had given Jane her first big project. She'd given her a manuscript from an unknown writer who wanted the agency to represent him, and asked her to read it and report back to Hailey with her thoughts. Hailey was going to have someone else in the office read it after Jane, but it was a good project for her, to get her feet wet. And it would give Hailey a sense of what Jane was capable of and how well she could analyze a manuscript's potential.

Hailey was finishing the last of her emails before she left for the day when Bob Benson walked into her office. He was always calm, always smooth, always pleasant, and Hailey got along well with him. He slipped into a chair across from her, and she stopped writing her emails and smiled at him. He was married to Martha Wick, the biggest entertainment lawyer in the business. They both had massive careers, and Hailey wondered how they managed it. They had two sons in college, and the youngest was a senior in high school. That seemed centuries away to Hailey, who was still in the thick of things, with three very young children. Bob admired the fact that she never made it a problem at the agency. She never even talked about them, and she worked as hard as was needed in the office, and stayed as late as she had to, sometimes later than everyone else.

"I just talked to Phillip White," he said casually, and she nodded.

"I talked to him this morning," Hailey told him. "He was upset about his on-sale date and his position on the list, and some problems with the publicity department. I called them after I talked to him. They apologized for bringing the book out a week or two too soon, but there's nothing they can do about it now. It's too late to change."

"He mentioned that to me." Bob nodded. "Actually, this is about something else. I got a call from James Stewart, the head of sales. They want Phillip to do a book tour. I know he hates them and tries to avoid them, but they really think it would give his sales a huge boost. Seven cities in two weeks, the usual dog and pony show. TV, radio, interviews, not out in the sticks. Washington, Boston, Chicago,

Denver, L.A., Dallas, Atlanta. It's a big push, but two weeks isn't too bad," Bob said. Hailey looked worried.

"He'll never do it," she said. She knew Phillip and his boundaries well. They'd discussed it before, and he always refused to do book tours.

"They're promising to do it in a really first-rate way, first class all the way. I just talked to him, and he said he'd do it." Hailey looked stunned as she stared at her boss. "On one condition," Bob continued.

"And what's that?"

"That you go with him. He said you're the only one who could make it tolerable. He knows you'd organize everything for him and protect him. And I think he's right. The tour could be really important for him, and it will be stressful and exhausting. I know you can handle it. As a personal favor to me, would you do it, Hailey?" He looked at her so earnestly that she couldn't refuse, but she had no idea what to do with her kids for two weeks. That was a lot of babysitters to corral and schedule, not to mention a fortune to pay them, but this was her job, and she couldn't turn down her boss or their most important client. She wanted to cry, thinking about it, but he had really put her on the spot. Her future promotions were on the line here. And the book tour depended on whether or not she'd do it.

"When is it?" she asked without committing.

"You'd leave in a week. They want to put it together pretty quickly, to give a final boost to his new book that just came out. It's either that or wait a year for the next one, and they don't want to do that. They think they can kick him into the number one slot, even at this late date. Since he never does them, the book tour would have a big impact. It would start a week from today." She nodded, thinking, and decided to do it to keep her boss happy. She'd figure it out somehow.

"I'll do it," she said quietly. "But only because it's Phillip. I really can't start doing tours on a regular basis. It would be a hardship for me to organize."

"I understand. I won't ask you again. It means a lot to me that you agreed this time." He stood up then, smiled at her, and left her office a minute later. Mission accomplished, for him and Phillip. For Hailey, it was just the beginning of utter panic and chaos, trying to find people to stay with her kids, and she knew they would be upset about all the things she'd be missing while she was gone. But her career was important to her too, and it was what kept them eating, paid their rent, and provided what they needed. But how did you explain that to a six-year-old who wanted his mother at home? He'd have to make the sacrifice this time, they all would.

When Allie left the office that afternoon a little earlier than usual, no one questioned it. She came and went as she needed to. All the agents did. They had meetings offsite all day long, went to visit their clients on the sets of movies being made or series being taped. The literary agents were more stationary, and spent their days on the phone, then read manuscripts at night. They usually only left at lunchtime, for fancy lunches with publishers or clients.

Allie bought a bottle of Cristal and a big bouquet of red roses, and arranged them in a vase when she got home. She had sent Eric a text and confirmed that she'd be waiting for him after he went to the gym. She ordered caviar and had it delivered to her apartment, took a bath, and dressed carefully in a filmy white dress you could see through. She wore a white lace thong under it and nothing else, you could see her breasts clearly and she didn't mind, she knew he'd like that.

She put the stereo on and lit candles a few minutes before he was due to arrive. The champagne and caviar were in the fridge so he didn't see them as soon as he walked in.

All he did see was Allie, glowing when she opened the door, her long blond hair cascading past her shoulders. The moment Eric saw her, he grinned, stepped into the apartment, swept her off her feet, and spun her around and then kissed her.

"Good God, you look gorgeous! Sweet Home Alabama!" He still couldn't believe how lucky he was that she was having a relationship with him. She was the head of dramatic at the agency and a big deal, and a magnificent-looking woman. "What's the occasion? What are we celebrating? It's not my birthday. Is it yours?" he suddenly wondered but couldn't guess. He wanted to take her gauzy dress off but loved the effect in the meantime.

Allie smiled up at him for a minute and kissed him. He was wearing gym clothes, but had showered before he came over. She could see every inch of his gorgeous body.

"I got a call today. . . . I have good news for you." She was beaming and he was puzzled. "You got the part, Eric. You got the series. The leading role. This is going to make you a big, big star. You could win an Emmy or a Golden Globe, and I know you can do it. You're in! Congratulations!" He pulled her into his arms and kissed her hard. She could feel him shaking with excitement and she was happy for him. His legs felt so wobbly, he had to sit down on the couch, and he pulled her down next to him and kissed her again.

"I can't believe it. I was sure they'd forgotten about me."

She laughed.

"No one could forget you, baby. I'm so proud of you!"

"I'm proud of me too," he admitted, laughing. "This is thanks to you, Allie. You made me audition for it when I didn't want to. And you pushed them. Oh my God, I can't believe it."

"I can." She went to get the champagne and the caviar then, and brought it out to him as he lay on the couch, grinning, thinking of the good times that were ahead. He opened the bottle of champagne, poured them each a glass, and toasted her. Then he set his glass down, kissed her, and gently took off her dress, and she lay next to him on the couch, her perfect body exposed, with the lace thong.

"I have to be the luckiest man alive," he said, and pulled off his gym clothes. They were two exquisite people with perfect bodies, and it looked like ballet in slow motion as they began making love. Life had never been sweeter, and all he wanted to do now was share it with her. It never dawned on him for a minute that she was seventeen years older than he was, and he wouldn't have cared. He figured she was maybe three or four years older, but that was the last thing on his mind as he entered her with a gasp and a hard thrust as she arched her back, and the dance began in earnest. It was a victory dance for both of them. For Allie and Eric it was a perfect night, and it didn't get better than this.

Chapter 4

J ane had begun to feel comfortable and at ease at the agency. She liked working for Julia as her immediate supervisor, with Hailey as her boss. She loved the fact that they were giving her projects with substance, and a chance to read manuscripts and write synopses and evaluations of them. She had passed with flying colors on the first one, and Hailey gave her several more. She gave insightful, intelligent feedback. She had to read the manuscripts at night, so she was less available to Benjie. He was complaining, but she needed to focus on her career now. She loved working for the agency, and could see it as a long-term job until she was able to set up a business of her own one day. She admired all the women she worked with. Each one seemed to have carved out the right niche for herself, and she hoped to do the same.

She went to the office kitchen one day at noon for the salad she had put in the fridge that morning and was annoyed to see Dan Fletcher there again. He seemed to hang out in the kitchen at lunchtime, hoping to cop a feel when the assistants came to get their lunches. The narrow kitchen gave him ample opportunity to rub up against their bodies, and he didn't hesitate to do so. They never called him on it. They were young and afraid to.

Jane paid no attention to him and was scowling as she walked straight to the fridge for her salad, avoiding contact with him. Someone had moved the salad to a lower shelf, and as she bent over to get it, she could feel a hand slide between her legs from behind. She was wearing thin linen slacks, and she could feel his hand stroke her through the fabric. She wheeled around and stood up so fast that it threw Dan off-balance and she grabbed his wrist hard and stunned him.

"If you touch me again," she said in a normal voice that anyone could hear, "I'm calling a lawyer, or the police. Is that clear?"

"Whoa . . . 'though she be but little, she is fierce,'" he said, quoting Shakespeare. He looked unfazed by her reaction as she dropped his wrist. Bob Benson walked into the kitchen in time to see and hear the exchange. Jane walked past both of them with her salad and headed back to her office, where Julia looked at her strangely. Jane looked angry, with a determined expression.

"Something wrong?" Julia thought maybe someone had taken part of Jane's salad and she was annoyed. That happened. Some people just took what they wanted, regardless of who it belonged to.

"That asshole stroked my crotch," Jane said, fuming.

"What asshole?" Julia looked stunned.

"Fletcher. The guy is a total pig. I told him if he did it again I'd call a lawyer or the police."

"He does that shit all the time," Julia said sympathetically. "Sorry, Jane."

"Why do people put up with it?"

"Because he's the boss. He's got the winning hand."

"Not anymore. Does anyone read the papers? Guys like him lose their jobs and wind up in jail now. People a lot bigger than him."

"I know. But it takes a lot of guts to go after someone like him."

"If he does it again, I will," Jane said, and dug in to her salad. Julia went back to what she was doing on her computer.

Bob Benson was in Dan Fletcher's office by then. He walked in quietly and sat down. Dan smiled at him as though nothing had happened.

"I walked in at the tail end of that exchange between you and the new girl working for Hailey," Bob said with a serious expression.

"Great tits," Dan said without hesitation, "and they're real, none of that new fake crap. They must fill them with rocks. Hers are the real deal."

"How do you know?"

"I copped a feel when she first got here. I was checking her out."

"You can't do that," Bob reminded him, panicked over what Dan said and his remorseless attitude about it.

"Who says?"

"The world. Women. The law. Times have changed, Dan. We could lose the agency over something like that. You may think it's funny, but no one else does. People take that kind of sexual harassment very seriously these days. If she ever did call a lawyer, or the police, you'd be in big trouble. We both would. Martha is handling nothing but cases like that right now. It's a very big deal."

"Oh for chrissake, a little feel here and there won't kill them. They're not virgins, for God's sake. Girls give blow jobs in school at thirteen these days. By the time they come to work here they're old hands. They can't play innocent."

"They don't have to play at all. They have a right not to be touched or manhandled or stroked or fondled. You have to keep your hands to yourself, and you can't make lewd, suggestive comments. Dan, I'm counting on you to behave." Bob was very serious.

"What a fucking bore," Dan said, looking annoyed.

"Never mind if it's a bore, just rein it in, right now," Bob said, and went back to his office with a rock of terror in his gut.

Dan Fletcher was a loose cannon, and he also drank too much. Bob was well aware that he drank when he went out to lunch, not just wine but hard liquor even before lunch, which loosened his behavior even further. He was a walking menace, and Bob was beginning to wish he'd retire. A sexual harassment suit from an employee was something he did not need. And a younger employee was liable to blow the whistle on him faster than an older woman of another generation, who might hesitate. As far as he knew, no one else in the office was a problem, but Dan Fletcher was. That made the agency vulnerable since he was co-owner with Bob. But Dan was loyal and they'd started the agency together, which meant a lot to Bob. He put up with some of Dan's behavior because of it. But not if he went too far. As far as Bob knew up to this point, Dan was all talk and no action, like some men his age. He never thought Dan was dangerous, but what he'd just seen was seriously out of line.

Hailey never heard about the exchange and was too busy to notice that Jane was upset. She was desperately trying to line up sitters to spend the night for two weeks, when she went on tour with Phillip White. It was a mammoth effort figuring out how to cover every waking hour for three kids for two weeks. But she had to do it or she couldn't go. Felicity had agreed to give her a week, but she couldn't do more. She had her own kids to keep track of, even though they were older. Her sister had agreed to come up from Jamaica for that week. For the second week, Felicity could pick them up at school and stay until bedtime, but that was all. Hailey used three other sitters to fill in on various days, and the schedule she was blocking out in timeslots looked like she was running a hotel or an airline. She spent every evening making calls and her children were desperately unhappy she was going to be away. She was going to miss the school fair, Bentley's first big science project, and Arianna had the starring role in *Annie,* which Hailey was going to miss. It was a disaster, but not going would be too. She didn't have a choice, she had to do it.

She never mentioned to Bob Benson what an agony it was for her to cover the two weeks for her kids, and all that she'd be missing. The children each cried about it at various times. It ripped Hailey's heart out and she had tried to explain to them how important the trip was and that she couldn't get out of it. She suggested a trip to Disneyland at a later time to console them, but no one wanted to go. They wanted her at home for everyday life, and the events that mattered to them. She felt like a monster leaving them, and she still had two weekends and several days to cover. She had an idea and called her yoga teacher in desperation. She hadn't been there lately, but the teacher was a nice woman, liked kids, and had offered to babysit before. She needed the money. She could barely pay her rent from the money she made teaching yoga. Hailey called her and explained the situation to her.

"I'd love it! It really comes at a good time for me. They're renovating the studio, and we haven't had classes for four weeks. Could I bring my dog?" Hailey had visions of a Great Dane moving in, or a pit bull that would attack them. "She's a teacup Chihuahua. She's fourteen years old and she sleeps most of the time. I can't afford to put her in a kennel so I can babysit, and I would hate to do that to her."

"Perfect. No problem." She was willing and able to cover all the days and nights Hailey had left to fill, and by the end of the week, she knew the kids would be all set. It was a patchwork of people, and the kids were unhappy about it, although they loved the idea of a dog staying with them, since Hailey refused to get one. It would be one more thing to take care of and pay for, and she had enough with three kids.

"Can we keep the dog?" Will asked, wide-eyed.

"No," Hailey said firmly, "but you can have fun with it while it's here. It's really little, so you have to be gentle, Will. And it's old."

But at least she was covered. She hoped Phillip White never asked her to do a tour again. She just couldn't do that to her kids, and it was going to cost her a fortune to pay all the sitters. She felt sick every time she thought of missing Arianna in *Annie* and Bentley's science project about the importance of water. He had promised to save it for her, and she was going to ask one of the mothers to video the performance. It was the first time she had let them down that badly in her five years of single motherhood. It was a terrible feeling and by far outweighed any pleasure she might have had joining an important author on tour. She was sorry she'd said yes, but Phillip White was thrilled and Bob Benson was grateful to her. Hailey felt that breaking her kids' hearts and disappointing them was just too high a price to pay. She wondered for the first time if she should mention more often that she had children, instead of being discreet about them. They were her life, although she kept that a secret at the office in order to seem professional. But she loved them, and even though her career was important to her, this time she had sacrificed her children for her job, and she had the terrible feeling that she had betrayed them. In this instance, she could either be a good mother or an efficient employee. It was a choice. She couldn't be both.

Francine was trying to set up an appearance for one of her authors on *Good Morning America* on the pub date of his new book. She knew that the show wouldn't book him during sweeps week, when ratings were all-important to them, since the author was a quiet man who wrote political thrillers. His books did well, but he wasn't exciting enough for them to put on during the week that ratings counted most. She needed the calendar to tell her when sweeps week was, and wandered into Allie's office to see if she had it. She was out, and Francine walked around her desk to see if it was on her bookcase, desk, or somewhere obvious where she didn't have to dig around for it. As she stood behind Allie's desk chair, she suddenly saw the photos on the computer screen. At first she thought they were young actors. They were a beautiful pair, naked and entwined. The photos weren't pornographic, but they were very close to it, and extremely sensual, and in one you could guess that they were making love.

She didn't mean to stare at them, but she couldn't help it. And then suddenly, with a jolt, she realized that they weren't of a young actor and actress. The photos were of Allie and Eric Clay, the actor who had just landed the starring role in next season's biggest series. Francine knew he was Allie's client, and that she went out with her clients occasionally, but she'd had no idea that Allie and Clay were involved. She was staring at them as Allie walked back into her office.

"Seen enough yet, or do you want me to show you some more?" Allie said as she crossed the room, and Francine jumped.

"I was looking for the sweeps schedule for ABC," she said, embarrassed to have been caught looking at the photos, but Allie had openly left them on her computer screen. "Sorry, I wasn't looking for those," she said, indicating the screen. "I didn't know you were dating him."

"What I do in my off hours is my business. I don't need permission from the agency."

"No, but it'll be a big deal in the tabloids if they get wind of it."

"Why?"

"Because he's going to be a big star now, and you're his agent."

"And older than he is, right? So fucking what?"

"Are you out in public with this?" Francine asked, curious.

"Not really, we spend most of our time in bed," she said boldly, angry at Francine for snooping at her desk and commenting on it. She'd been looking at the pictures herself, admiring him, and forgot to turn her computer off when she went to the restroom.

"I don't blame you. I just think it could be dicey. Be careful that someone doesn't find out and make a big deal of it. It could go viral and that would look very bad for the agency."

"Who I date or sleep with is no one's business, and certainly not the agency's."

"It is if you sleep with your clients. He's young enough to be your son. That might not look so great in the press either. They could say it's a Me Too issue, if you promised him a part."

"He's not complaining," Allie said angrily.

"I can see that," Francine said. He had a huge erection in one of the pictures. "You should be careful with those, Allie."

"At least I'm not sleeping with our bosses, just the clients," she said pointedly, and Francine looked horrified. It was her worst fear that people at work would find out that she was Dan Fletcher's whore and had been for years. There had been whispers about it, but no one had ever come right out and said anything before. She liked to believe that no one knew. But maybe Dan had been bragging. It was possible. He was neither discreet nor honorable, and he talked when he drank too much.

"What's that supposed to mean?" Francine pressed her.

"That's up to you, Francine. I don't give a damn who you sleep with. And who I fool around with is no one's business." It looked like a lot more than fooling around, and the truth was that Eric said he was falling in love with her, and she cared about him too, more than she expected to. She didn't want it to get too serious with him, but it was heading there. They spent every night together in his apartment or her loft, and they went out openly when they felt like it. They weren't hiding, and felt they had no reason to. Anyone could have spotted them at any time. They got along better than she had with anyone in years. Their age difference wasn't an issue to them, and Allie wasn't going to stop seeing him because Francine said it could go viral. If it did, they'd deal with it. They weren't ashamed of being together, and he said frequently that he was proud to be with her.

"Just watch your ass, Allie. I'd hate to see you or the agency get in a mess over this. I'm sure he's a nice guy, but you've got a lot at stake here. If someone puts the wrong spin on it, it could look nasty. You got him a big part, a starring role, and now you're sleeping with him. It could sound like shit in the press."

"We'll deal with it if that happens. It's not your concern."

Francine left Allie's office quietly, but they were both shaken up by the exchange. Francine wondered if Bob knew about it. She guessed that he didn't. These days you had to be damn careful about who you slept with and how it looked. And Allie wasn't careful. She never had been. She did whatever she wanted. On the other hand, Francine knew that what she was doing, and had been for years, wasn't pretty either, and would look bad too. She was mortified at the idea that anyone knew about it, as Allie had hinted. Dan was such a disgusting old pig, and a despicable human being. He wasn't young and beautiful and a sweet kid like Eric. But Allie was at risk there too, whether she admitted it or not.

When Francine got home that night, she had an email from Tommy's school. He was in trouble at school again, and got in another fight. Francine was exhausted from her workday, but she loved her kids. She sat down with Tommy and tried to talk to him about it.

"What happened? Why are you getting into all these fights?"

"The other boys keep calling me names. They say I don't have a dad, and call me a bastard. They said you were probably never married to my dad. I know I have a dad, but no one has ever seen him." Neither had Tommy. Tim Rivers hadn't seen his son since he left New York with the nanny years before. He lived in Detroit now, with the nanny he married and the two children he had with her. Tommy was three the last time he saw his dad, and Thalia was seven. Tim had traded one family for another. He had a noble job, helping the indigent. And he had been a decent person when they met. He had never made a good living even when they were married, and they'd lived on her meager salary as an editor, at nearly subsistence level, which was why she had taken the agency job when he left. It gave her a huge salary increase, but still wasn't enough now, with two kids to support and college less than a year away for Thalia. And Thalia deserved to go to a good college, and had the grades. Even a state university would cost money for books, dorms, and all the rest. Francine had been putting aside whatever she could for years, but it was never enough. And her ex couldn't help her, and didn't want to.

But the more pressing problem was that Tommy was being bullied. He was a slight kid, short for his age, with some learning disabilities. He was in a remedial reading class. She wondered now if the school was right and she needed to get counseling for him. She was going to look into it before things got worse.

"I'll talk to your teacher," she promised. "You'll be going to high school in the fall if you can hang on till then." It was late to find him a new school for the rest of eighth grade. It seemed like a long wait till the fall to him and even to her. "I'll think of something. I promise."

She had one idea. It wasn't ideal, but it was a possibility, she was going to tell the school that he was being bullied. He looked a little more cheerful when he went to his room. Thalia came home a few minutes later. Francine smiled at her, and Thalia looked sullen, which was her standard attitude these days. "How was your day?" her mother asked her.

"What do you care?" Thalia spat at her with venom, and Francine sighed.

"I do care, or I wouldn't ask you. What are you so pissed off about all the time?"

"What do I have to look forward to, Mom? A shit college? You went to a decent school. I never will. We can't afford it, according to you. I'm going to have to take student loans, and I'll be paying them off forever. So I'll be poor forever. What part of that sounds happy to you? And wherever I get accepted, we won't be able to afford it. It's not just tuition, we'll have to pay for the dorm, and all the extras that add up."

"I've got some money put aside. Not for four years for the two of you, but enough to help. You can get a job while you go to school, and I'll help with the student loans." She made good money at the agency, but private college for two kids cost a fortune and so did life these days. Francine was constantly worried about money. And whenever she paid off one big bill, she got four more. New York was an expensive city. And tuitions were astronomical.

"Why doesn't my dick of a father pay something? He's a lawyer, for God's sake. He owes you years of back child support, and you never even went after him. He got off scot-free from us."

"There was no point going after him, Thallie, he makes no money. He's an ACLU lawyer. He and his new family must be living pretty close to the poverty level."

"So are we," she said angrily.

"No, we're not. We don't have everything you want, fancy trips and clothes like some of your friends." Francine tried to keep expenses down. "But we have a decent apartment, we live in a safe neighborhood. We have food on the table. You both go to good private schools."

"I've been invited to the senior prom, and I can't go because I don't have a dress. You made me wear one of yours last time and I looked ridiculous. I looked like I borrowed it from my grandmother." Francine hadn't bought herself a new dress in years. She bought clothes for work and that was it. Thalia's classmates had designer dresses, which Francine refused to buy for a seventeen-year-old and couldn't afford.

"Then let's buy you a really nice dress this time," Francine said, wanting to improve something for her. She could see how bleak life looked to her daughter. When Thalia looked down the road ahead of her, she saw no hope, no joy, no future, except a mountain of debt and nothing to balance it. "We'll go shopping on Saturday." There was a flicker of hope in her daughter's eyes, and she wanted to fan the flames of that.

"Yeah, maybe, we'll see," she said, grabbed a bag of chips from the kitchen, and went to her room. But she didn't slam the door this time, which was something.

Francine called Tommy's school the next morning and reported to the assistant principal that he was being bullied. She requested some form of security and protective supervision for him. She asked for recommendations for therapists in the area, and the assistant principal promised to email her some names. It wasn't much, but it made Francine feel like she was doing something for her children. She couldn't just let them drift and take care of themselves. She needed to do more than just buy groceries and school supplies for them. She felt so hopeless herself most of the time that she had forgotten to give them hope, and something to look forward to. The school had promised to watch over Tommy and make sure the bullying didn't happen again.

When she got to the office, she made a cup of coffee and waited for Dan Fletcher to arrive. He came in late as usual, and as soon as he walked into his office, she followed him in and closed the door behind her. He looked surprised. They never talked at the office. He gave a start when he saw her facing him, with a hard look in her eyes.

"I need a raise," she said, with iron determination.

"Talk to HR," he said coldly. She had the glory of being the head of the literary department, but she hadn't had a raise in a long time and she needed it now more than ever for Thalia and Tommy. "You're not worth it," he said harshly, and took refuge behind his desk. She looked dangerous. "You're lucky you still have a job," he added.

"You're lucky I don't go to the press or the police," she snapped back at him. He looked angry, but she wouldn't back down.

"My son needs a therapist, he's being bullied at school, and I'm never home because I work here till all hours. And my daughter is going to college."

"You're not worth what I pay you now," he said brutally to fob her off.

"Maybe not. But I show up twice a week to have sex with you, and I have for ten years. That's worth something." There wasn't even a shred of friendship between them. Just sex and money. But she needed the money now for her kids, just as she did when she accepted his rotten deal and allowed him to blackmail her into sex with him.

"If you make trouble for me, I told you what would happen. I can turn the whole publishing industry against you if I wanted to, and you'll never get another job." He had used that threat to control her for ten years.

"And who's going to show up for you twice a week? I've lived up to my end of the deal," she reminded him. "I need the money for my kids." She realized then that they never even called each other by name. He had never called her Francine, and she had never called him Dan. "I could go to Bob Benson," she said, and he looked frightened, "and tell him you've blackmailed me into having sex with you for a decade." But she was too ashamed to do that and too afraid to risk her job if she stopped meeting him, and he knew it. He had her by the throat, but at least he could pay for it now. She deserved a raise and he knew that too.

"You're a bitch," he snarled at her. "I'll take care of it. Now get out of my office." She turned on her heel and walked out. She was shaking when she went back to her office and HR notified her that afternoon that there would be a raise in her next paycheck. It wasn't huge, but it would help, for Tommy's therapy and whatever Thalia needed, in addition to a prom dress and college. She wished she had the guts not to meet him on Central Park West anymore, but she didn't. His threats were too believable. She was convinced he was capable of telling some lie about her, firing her, and casting enough doubt about her character that she wouldn't get another job. And she couldn't afford to lose the one she had, even if it included sex with Dan Fletcher. She had done it for so long, what difference did it make now?

She had passed Allie in the hall on her way back to her office.

They didn't speak to each other after their altercation the day before over the naked pictures of her with Clay. *We're all whores in our own way,* Francine thought, *and we make the compromises we have to.* At least hers were for her kids. She had no idea what Allie's excuse was, other than having fun and sleeping with younger guys.

Merriwether had had an argument with her husband that morning too. Jeff wanted her to go to a party with him at the Whitney Museum. It sounded like a nice evening, but she had promised to spend some time after hours with Bob Benson, discussing how they were managing the agency's money, and how Goldman Sachs was handling their investments. She'd been promising to spend time on it with him for months, and she'd never gotten to it.

"Why is the agency always your priority and never me or Annabelle?" Jeff had said angrily, and she felt guilty as soon as he said it. He was right. Her job was her priority and always had been. It was the truth she always tried to hide.

"I love you," she said. "I want to be here for both of you, but if you expect me to carry everything financially, then we both have to make sacrifices. I have a big job, Jeff. I have responsibilities. I can't be here to play the little woman every night." He had slammed out of the kitchen and gone upstairs to the office where he wrote every day. She had taken Annabelle to school, and her daughter looked at her with big sad eyes. Merriwether didn't know how to explain it to her.

She used to think she had the perfect life, and a perfect marriage, and she no longer did. She no longer believed there was such a thing. There had to be balance in a relationship, and equality—they both had to put something in. She was supporting them and using everything she earned to give them a good life, while Jeff contributed nothing and pursued his writing career. And he claimed he spent more time with their daughter, to make her feel guilty. In fact, their nanny spent more time with her. Merriwether couldn't do it during the week when she was working. She spent her weekends with Annabelle, and Jeff played tennis with his friends and did what he wanted. He considered weekends his "days off."

He didn't spend time with Merriwether and their daughter on the weekends because he claimed that he did that all week long, but he didn't. He wrote all week, or said he did, and played all weekend. Merriwether realized that she was lonely with him. They used to have a real relationship, but they no longer did. They had an arrangement in which she did all the work and contributed all the money, and he contributed nothing, and complained about her working to make her feel guilty. She could no longer figure out what he brought to their marriage.

She came home late every night because she was tired of hearing him complain about her. All he did was make her feel guilty for providing them with a good life, which he never appreciated. It was a lopsided arrangement. She was getting tired of his making her feel bad about it. She was the "bad girl" who supported the family. She was tired of being scolded all the time. She was a good girl. A very good girl. The only person who didn't think so was her husband.

Benjie sent Jane a text that afternoon. He wanted to go out to dinner and a movie, and then spend the night at her place. It sounded like fun, but she was excited about the manuscript Hailey had given her to read that night. It was a big deal for Jane to be evaluating unknown writers who wanted to be represented by the agency. Their fate was in her hands, and it was a vote of confidence on Hailey's part, and Jane didn't want to blow it. She had promised to have the latest one done by the end of the week, and she didn't want to let Hailey down.

Jane texted him back. "Can't. Have to work tonight. How about this weekend?"

He answered. "Do you sleep there? Third time you've turned me down. Still room for a guy in your life? Or have you traded real life in for your career?"

"Really sorry. Just got a big project. Hope to be free by Friday."

His final response was "Never mind. I get the message loud and clear." She hated texts for things like this. He was obviously pissed at her. He had warned her when she took the job not to give up her personal life for her career. Wasn't it possible to have both, she wondered, a relationship and a job? Why did it have to be one or the other?

She wondered if she'd hear from Benjie again, or if he was done. He never had to work late. But he wasn't on a career path either. All he had to do was show up for work, hang out with the other kids in shorts and flip-flops, play Catch Phrase at lunchtime, hang out at the candy bar, have a beer at the keg on Friday afternoons, and bring his dog to work if he had one. Jane had a grown-up job that was putting demands on her, and she wanted a promotion eventually and a real career one day. It was what her parents expected of her and what she wanted for herself. Benjie didn't want his job to interfere with his fun. She wondered if he'd want to be Peter Pan forever. He wasn't an adult. She was trying to be one.

Allie and Eric had dinner at a neighborhood deli that night. A few people recognized him from the show he'd already been on, but most people didn't.

"It's all going to be very different a year from now, you know," Allie warned him as he ate a hot pastrami sandwich and she had chicken salad.

"How so?" He looked surprised.

"People are going to recognize you everywhere you go. They'll want your autograph and to have their picture taken with you. The paparazzi will stalk you and start rumors about you. People will be watching you all the time. It's different. Right now you can do whatever you want." He hadn't thought about it yet, but he realized that she was right. He wasn't sure if he'd like it or not.

"I don't care what people do, as long as I can be with you when I'm not working," he said adoringly.

"What if the press hounds us?" she asked him, watching to see how he'd react.

"So what? We have nothing to hide. And if they drive us crazy, we'll find a nice comfortable cave and hide there. I love you, Allie, I don't care what the press says about us."

"I'm older than you are," she said, as though revealing a dark secret to him. He smiled.

"I know. I don't care. I looked you up on Google the first time I went out with you. Big fucking deal. You look younger than I do."

She grinned. "So you think we're okay?"

"Better than okay. We're great and I love you." She looked happy and relieved. Francine had made her nervous when they'd gotten in an argument over their pictures and the fact that Allie was dating a client seventeen years younger than she was. It was happening very fast, but she liked it. "Now let's go home to bed before I tear your jeans off right here at the deli." She laughed. He paid the bill, and they raced home to her apartment. They were breathless from running when she unlocked the door to her loft and he slammed the door behind them, then pulled her to one of the comfortable living room couches. He had her clothes and his own off in seconds, and made love to her as passionately as he had every night since they had started dating. She felt as though she was flying and could do anything as long as he was with her. It was an incredible feeling. And when he made love to her again, nothing else in the world mattered to either of them but the two of them together. It was all new for her. For the first time in her life, Allie thought she was actually in love.

Chapter 5

Hailey's extraordinary organizational skills came into play from the moment she picked Phillip up in a chauffeur-driven SUV, and they were driven to the airport. She had snacks in her tote bag for him, Tylenol in case he had a headache, eye drops if his eyes got tired before he went on TV. She had her laptop, an iPad, her phone. She had a spare printout of their schedule in case he had forgotten his. She had booked a VIP service to get them on the plane. They flew first class to Boston, which seemed silly but was fun. Phillip had a glass of champagne, since he was a nervous flyer. She handed him a magazine and *The New York Times,* and he looked perfectly relaxed by the time they took off.

Before they arrived, she had made sure that he had a suite at the Four Seasons, and she had a plain double room down the hall from him. She was close enough if he needed her. He had an interview with *The Boston Globe* that afternoon. It went smoothly, and he was booked for a morning show the next day, so they would have to get up early. He had gone to Harvard, so after the interview, they took an Uber to Cambridge and walked around the campus. He showed her all his old haunts. They had dinner that night at his favorite restaurant from his student days. He said they had the best steaks and burgers in Boston. He enjoyed her company thoroughly. She was a great audience for his stories. Most of them were funny, and she was comfortable with him. They got an Uber back to the hotel after dinner. She had ordered all his favorite snacks for his room, and a bottle of a good French Bordeaux. She had made everything easy and effortless for him. Her function, she realized, was to be half wife and half mother, making sure that he felt comfortable and at home on the trip.

Book tours were grueling and stressful, and wore thin after the first city or two, and this was only the beginning. She wanted to give him enough space that he didn't feel intruded on, but also support when appropriate. It was an art sensing what he needed when and being an almost invisible presence, there to assist him but not crowd him. She chatted with him when he wanted to, and was at ease being silent. And she left him alone to go to her own room to make phone calls and answer emails, to keep up with some of her other clients.

When she knew they'd all be at home, she called her children, and they were happy to hear from her. Will cried the first time she called and said he missed her. But by the second day, he was getting adjusted. She FaceTimed with them, and Arianna tried on her *Annie* costume for her. Felicity was with them, and Hailey told them all about Boston and visiting Harvard. It was the first time she had ever left them, and as much as she missed them, she was surprised to realize that it felt good to be on a grown-up trip where she could actually watch a TV show or read a magazine, or just relax, without worrying about who had had a bath, who had done their homework, who had a stomachache, or hadn't eaten enough dinner. For the first time in the five years since Jim died, she didn't have to worry about them every moment and be on duty. She had two full-time jobs now, as a mother and as a literary agent, and she was on vacation from one of them, although she was still working at the other. But for once, she wasn't doing both.

Phillip was easy company, he was polite and considerate, and she enjoyed making the trip easy and comfortable for him.

"I feel like I don't have to worry about anything or handle anything. You take care of it all. It's almost like being a child for two weeks, with an incredibly thoughtful, efficient mother. You're awfully good at this, Hailey," he complimented her on the way to the studio the next morning at six-thirty. They wanted him there before seven for makeup if he needed it, and then to wait in the private dressing room they provided him. He had worn a good-looking gray suit, a light blue shirt, and a navy tie. He looked very handsome and respectable, conservative but not boring. He had asked her advice about the tie, and she told him which one she preferred.

He'd had his pre-interview the night before over the phone, so the questions they asked weren't a surprise. The interviewer was a very attractive woman who had actually read the book, and the questions were intelligent. He had written a clever political thriller with a twist at the end, which had even surprised Hailey. Phillip was charming on TV and told some funny stories about when he'd been an under-

graduate at Harvard. It was a perfect interview. He was calm, relaxed, and appealing. It was over by eight-thirty, and they were back
at the hotel by nine. She ordered breakfast for him while he changed
out of his suit and walked into the living room of his suite in jeans
and the blue shirt he'd worn on TV. His breakfast arrived a few minutes later. She left him alone to enjoy it and went back to her room
to get organized for the next engagement. He was doing an important local radio show, and after that, they were flying to Chicago that
afternoon. It was a city she had always liked, although she didn't
know it well.

The radio show he did at lunchtime was fun, with an engaging
host, and Hailey was impressed by how smoothly Phillip handled it.
He was a pro. And although he said he didn't like book tours, he did
them well. She continued to smooth the way for him and tried to
foresee any problems, so they could avoid them.

She sat next to him on the plane, and they were about to take off
in a few minutes when Felicity had the children call her. They Face-
Timed her again, and she got a minute or two with each of them
before she had to hang up when the plane was about to take off.
Phillip looked at her after she ended the call.

"I just realized something about you. You never talk about your
personal life."

"I try to be professional," she said quietly.

"How many children do you have?"

"Three," she said proudly, and he smiled.

"That's a lot of kids. I knew you had children, but I never thought
about it. I thought maybe one or two."

"They're good kids, and pretty easy most of the time."

97

"Boys? Girls?" He was curious about her now.

"The oldest is a girl, Arianna. She's eleven. Bentley is nine, and Will is six."

"He looked cute on the phone." Phillip knew she was widowed, but he didn't know much else. "How do you manage all that, and a job too?"

She laughed. "I run my ass off all day, and then I run my ass off at night. Then everybody goes to bed, I do some work, and it's over until the next day. I do homework with them before they go to bed." Listening to her made him feel guilty.

"Leaving them must be complicated," he said. "I never thought about all the organizing it must take for you to be away for two weeks. Do you have a nanny?" She shook her head.

"I'm their nanny. I have several babysitters I call on. It's a little patchy, but I managed to get people to be there every day. I even hired a yoga teacher with a Chihuahua for next week. The kids are excited about the dog. They want one desperately, but I figure I've got all I can manage as it is."

He was impressed by how she had masterminded it all, and still took care of him too. "This is actually the first time I've left them. I think they're okay with it now. It'll be good for them. They'll be happy when I get back." She hoped it was true and hated thinking about the performance of *Annie* that she was missing. "You don't have kids, do you, Phillip?"

He shook his head as the plane took to the skies. She didn't think he did, but he might have older ones she didn't know about. He was forty-eight, ten years older than she was.

"No kids. That actually was what ended my marriage. Originally we were in complete agreement. No children. And then over time, she realized that she did want them, and I didn't. I have nothing against children. I just didn't want any of my own. I had a very painful childhood, with an alcoholic mother and a cold, hard, somewhat cruel father. My mother died in her fifties of cirrhosis. My dad wasn't very old when he died. He was a glacial, mean person. I still remember some awful scenes from my childhood, of my mother drunk and my father verbally abusing her. I'm an only child, so I didn't have anyone to share it with, or to comfort me. I've been writing about my father all my life, trying to figure him out. I'm beginning to think I never will. But I learned to live with it. I just didn't want to take a chance that I'd turn out to be a father like him. I don't think I would have, but I didn't want to risk it. So eventually my wife and I got a friendly divorce, so she could have kids with someone else. It came down to that in the end, and I think our marriage had run out of gas by then.

"We were married for nine years, which is a fairly long time these days. She remarried very quickly afterwards and she has a boy and a girl now, and I think she's happy. We had our time. It was finite, not forever, and we were pretty young when we married. I was twenty-six and Sandy was twenty-three. We've been divorced for thirteen years now. I think I wanted to be alone anyway. It allows me to write as much as I want, during any crazy hours. My writing's been better since she left. I think she interfered with the airwaves somehow. She's a writer too. She writes young adult books, they're very good. We still talk from time to time. She's an important piece of my history. I don't want to lose that, even though we're no longer married."

"That makes sense," Hailey responded. "I feel that way too for my children's sake. I try to keep the memory of their father alive for them. It's been five years now, and the memories start to fade, both good and bad. I'm not sure if that's a good thing or not. My husband died very suddenly at forty-three. He didn't have life insurance or any savings to speak of. We had a nice life. We lived off his salary and spent it. So I went back to work after he died, and now here I am. He was a publisher and I was an editor. I loved it, but I couldn't support the kids on that, so I became an agent, and they pay me decently. I try to keep the two worlds as separate as I can, so my family doesn't interfere with my job. I need the job. And I enjoy it immensely."

"Now that I know more, I'm touched that you left your children to be here with me. If I'd known all the responsibilities you have, I wouldn't have asked." She could tell he was a kind man. He had always been kind to her. "I'd like to meet them sometime," he said as they headed toward Chicago.

"Who?" She looked distracted, thinking of the next leg of the trip.

"Your kids," he said, and she smiled. Maybe he would one day, but for now, they had work to do. She had always liked Chicago. It was a small, cosmopolitan, lively city. They were going to be staying at the Four Seasons, and he would be doing another morning show the next day.

He read for the rest of the trip, and she dozed off for a while. They had gotten an early start and had been busy all day. He woke her gently when they were about to land. She smiled, and he carried her tote bag for her when they left the plane. She had a car and driver waiting for them, and they were both excited as they drove into the city at dusk. It was a beautiful night in a pretty city. The view was fabulous from his suite on the forty-fifth floor. They decided to have room service that night, and he invited her to join him. He told her all about his next book over dinner. It sounded fascinating, and she couldn't wait to read the first draft, since he always wanted her to read them and make suggestions.

Francine managed to get an appointment with one of the therapists, a few days after she had been given the list of names. There had been a cancellation and she grabbed it. She came home earlier from work to take Tommy, and they were in the room together for the first session. The therapist was a woman and she was very warm and friendly. Tommy seemed to like her, and so did Francine.

He told her all about being bullied at school, and how scary and upsetting it had been. He complained about his mother coming home late from work and never being there in time to have dinner with them. Francine said it was true, and that she frequently had to stay past business hours, and the commute to and from Queens added close to another hour. There was just no way she could get home any sooner. She had a very demanding job. Tommy said he understood but didn't like it. He wished she'd get a job where she could come home earlier. She said that wasn't in the cards for the moment.

On the whole, nothing dramatic happened, no terrible revelations. Tommy seemed comfortable and at ease when he left, and when asked, he said he'd like to go back again. He said he felt safe there.

Francine had met Dan on Central Park West the night before. She had thanked him for the raise and he didn't comment. There was no pretense of warmth between them. And she knew that the raise had also been to ensure that she didn't blow the whistle on him, and tell Bob Benson about their arrangement for the past decade. He held threats over her head of what he could do to her, but she had the goods on him too.

Merriwether stayed after hours to work with Bob Benson, as she had promised, the night of the Whitney Museum party. It was a cocktail party for their big benefactors, with a dinner afterwards. Jeff had left the house looking very elegant and handsome in a tuxedo.

Merriwether and Bob meticulously went through their accounts and discussed what kind of bonds they should buy and how their investments were doing. Bob liked their financial discussions. She always had an intelligent, well-informed viewpoint, and a great head for finance.

He asked if she wanted to have dinner afterwards. Jeff was out anyway, and Annabelle had been put to bed hours before, so they went to a small French restaurant a few blocks from the agency. The food was excellent, and they both relaxed sharing a bottle of wine and dinner.

They talked about various problems at the agency, and Bob opened up to her about his concerns about Dan Fletcher.

"He just doesn't get that he can't behave that way. One of these days, one of the young women in the office is going to bring a suit against us. My wife tells me all the time about similar situations, and it can get very ugly. I'm not sure he ever follows through, but he lays hands on whoever he wants to. I'm scared to death we're going to wind up with a Me Too situation. Martha seems to handle nothing but those cases these days."

"She must have a very interesting practice," Merriwether said. "Entertainment law must really be fun."

"She enjoys it," he commented. "And it was good for us to be in the same industry. We had a lot to talk about for a long time, until her practice grew and she never came home at night. I think she enjoyed her work a lot more than she did raising our children." Merriwether felt guilty as soon as he said it, because sometimes she felt that way too.

"You've been married for a long time," she said, intrigued by him.

"Twenty-eight years. We're more friends than anything else now. I have great respect for her and what she's accomplished," but it didn't sound like he was in love with her. He could have been talking about a close friend or a sister. "It's hard having two big careers under one roof," he admitted as they ate dinner and each had a second glass of wine. "You get pulled away from each other eventually. You both get busy, then one day you look up and you're miles apart, and you have nothing in common anymore, except history."

"I'm not sure it's any easier having one career under one roof. We agreed early on that I would be the breadwinner. I was better equipped to do that with a Harvard MBA, and Jeff wanted to stay home and write. It seemed like the perfect arrangement, especially when our daughter was born. He didn't have a job he loved, and I had started at the agency, which was exciting for me. And it still is." She smiled at him.

"And now?" he asked her.

"He resents the hell out of me. He thinks I've become a heartless machine and only care about my job, which isn't true. But it's hard to go home at night, knowing you'll be berated and criticized. I seem to stay later and later all the time. I hate going home," she admitted, "but I have a great time with my daughter on weekends. And during the week, I love my job. I think he resents that I enjoy it so much and that I've done well at it."

"Martha and I had those issues too. We both loved our jobs. She used to complain that I came home late every night, and it was even harder with the commute to Greenwich. She made a point of getting home earlier, for the boys. I never saw her or the boys during the week. Everyone was asleep when I got home. But I loved what I was doing, and so did she. But then somehow we headed in opposite directions and lost each other along the way. We've stayed together and I respect her enormously. She's the best entertainment lawyer in the business. But it hasn't been a marriage in the real sense in years."

"I think Jeff and I might be heading there," Merriwether said. "I have no idea how it happened or when, but all of a sudden he's angry all the time, and he resents everything I do. He thinks I'm a terrible wife, and maybe he's right." It felt good to confide in Bob, and he clearly understood.

"I'm sure you're not a terrible wife," he said kindly, "but you may be a terrible wife for him. You got too big and too successful, and it makes him feel inadequate. In our case, with my wife and me, after a while we were like two guys living together, talking about business all the time. Her cases, my clients, the only thing we had in common were our sons. Everything else disappeared. And in my opinion, kids aren't enough to make a marriage. You may stay together for their sake, or claim that you are, but to make a marriage work, you need more than kids, you need a little bit of magic, and a lot of love. Martha and I lost the magic years ago. I don't know where it went, but we woke up one day and it was gone." Merriwether looked sad as he said it.

"I think that's what happened to me and Jeff. The crazy thing is I can't even tell you when or why, but all of a sudden, there's no buffer, there's no forgiveness, there's no compassion. He's angry all the time, and I'm tiptoeing around feeling guilty, and I'm not even sure for what. Making too much money? Working too hard? Being successful, or a woman with a big job? I don't know what my crime is, but I'm tired of being the bad guy, while I pay for everything and work my ass off to give us a good life."

"I think you're heading down a slippery slope here. If a man becomes successful and makes a lot of money, he's a hero. If a woman does, it's a very different thing. You have to be married to someone very solid and confident about himself to be able to tolerate that, otherwise he'll punish you for what you are and he isn't, and what you've accomplished and he hasn't. Even some successful men can't tolerate it, but a man who isn't successful is liable to end up resenting you and punishing you for what you've achieved."

"I think that's where we are," Merriwether said. In a way it felt better to say it out loud and hear the explanation for it. In another way, it just felt sad. Jeff was so angry at her now, all the time. She felt like a failure in her marriage. "I used to think we were happy. I no longer do."

After they left the restaurant, Bob put her in a cab to go home. He had to catch the last train to Greenwich and didn't want to miss it. He didn't have an apartment in the city, and didn't want to stay at a hotel. Merriwether thanked him for dinner. She'd had a lovely evening. He was smart and wise and funny and wonderful to talk to, and it sounded as though he had lived what she was going through. She wondered if it was possible for a woman to be successful and have a solid marriage. She had always believed it was, but now she wasn't sure. Maybe one did have to choose between marriage or a career, but that seemed pathetic to her. She still believed you could have it all, with the right man.

From Chicago, which turned out to be as delightful a city as Hailey and Phillip both remembered, they went to Denver, which had its own natural beauty with the mountains around them. They spent two days there, and from Denver they flew to L.A. and spent four days there. Phillip did a morning show and a late night one. He did a book signing at Book Soup, and two radio shows. It was a whirlwind tour, and Hailey kept everything moving swiftly and smoothly, with a minimum of stress and inconvenience for Phillip. With each city, he was more impressed by her and how capable she was. She made everything easy for him, and even fun at times. She was perfectly prepared in each city. She knew where to go and who they were meeting. She averted a minor crisis at one of the TV shows when the publisher hadn't sent the book. She sent their driver out to buy one in time for them to have it on the show. And she was good company. He loved talking to her.

Phillip handled each appearance graciously, and was surprisingly relaxed on TV, and even enjoyed it. They both liked Dallas. Hailey had never been there before. Atlanta had less charm. It was a big, businesslike city, but the interviews he had there were some of the best, and they only spent a day there. By the time they got to Washington, D.C., they were almost sorry the tour was ending. Phillip had worked hard and done his part. He never complained and Hailey saw to it that he had nothing to complain about. On their last night in Washington, he took her to a splendid elegant dinner at The Lafayette, across from the White House, and spotted two well-known senators and a congresswoman dining there. They both enjoyed the evening and talked about the tour and the cities they'd visited. His publisher was thrilled with the number of appearances he'd done, and how well it had all gone. They couldn't have hoped for a better result, and he looked at Hailey with a grateful smile.

"You made this a terrific experience, Hailey. I used to have nightmares about going on tour. You made it a first-class event every step of the way."

"Thank you." She smiled back at him. "I enjoyed it too, and I didn't think I would." Her children had survived it with the patchwork of babysitters she had provided. The yoga teacher with the Chihuahua was the biggest hit. Will had squealed and said she let them eat ice cream for breakfast, watch TV on school nights, and stay up late, but Hailey didn't mind. She was just relieved that they were happy. Arianna's performance in *Annie* had gone well, and Hailey couldn't wait to see the video when she got home. She was bringing back a few souvenirs from each city for each of them, and an autograph for Arianna of a teenage rock star she'd met on one of the TV shows. She was a particular favorite of Arianna's, and Hailey knew she would be thrilled.

Phillip looked at her as their plane landed in New York.

"I'm not going to know what to do with myself tomorrow when you're not there to tell me where to go. I'm going to miss you, Hailey. Let's have dinner next week sometime."

"I'd love that." She was tired from the trip. Paying close attention to every detail had required concentration every moment of every day, but the results had been rewarding, and she hoped it would help his book. It was a wonderful book and deserved to be a huge success. She was happy to have contributed to that, and that he was happy with the tour.

The last car and driver were waiting for them at the airport. She said she could take a cab into the city. He didn't need to worry about her.

"Don't be silly. I'll give you a ride. Where do you live?" She told him and he smiled. "You live a few blocks from me. I'll take you home." He had an apartment at The Dakota on Central Park West. He'd had it for years, since his books first became successful. Many famous actors, directors, artists, and writers lived in the building.

It took them forty-five minutes to get to the city, and another fifteen to cross to the West Side, through Central Park. He was surprised by how small and shabby her building was. She was always so well dressed and impeccably put together that he had somehow assumed she would live in a fancier building. It had never occurred to him that she might be struggling financially. The street was all right, but her building wasn't pretty. He got out to help her with her suitcase, and when he saw that there was no doorman, he offered to take it upstairs for her.

"Don't worry, I can manage," she said, slightly embarrassed to have him see her unattractive address, but her bag was heavy and he wouldn't let her take it.

"I'd love to meet your kids," he said with a shy smile, which surprised her, knowing that he wasn't very interested in children. She hesitated but then invited him to come up, and he carried her bag up the two flights of stairs and waited while she fished the key out of her handbag. The moment she stepped inside, there were squeals of delight and excitement. Will threw himself into her arms and almost knocked her down. She picked him up and carried him as Phillip stood behind her and watched them. He realized now what she had left behind to do the tour with him. Seeing them made it real to him, and he understood the sacrifice she'd made leaving them and was deeply touched. Arianna was looking at him shyly, and Bentley politely stuck out his hand to shake Phillip's, when he put the suitcase down.

The living room was small but everything was neat and clean, and the apartment was cozy and inviting. The yoga teacher was standing in the kitchen doorway. She had helped the children make a cake for their mother with pink icing and sprinkles that spelled out "Welcome Home Mom." A tiny white long-haired Chihuahua was barking frantically. It was loving chaos, and Hailey hugged and kissed each of them and held them close to her as Phillip smiled at the scene. He didn't want to intrude, but he was enjoying it, and it told him more about who she was than anything else could have. This was who she was too, not just the woman who had escorted him so efficiently through seven cities in two weeks.

"I think I'm leaving you in good hands," he said before he left her to celebrate her triumphant return with her children. He walked out quietly after saying goodbye to her, and as soon as the door closed behind him, Arianna looked at her intensely.

"Is he your boyfriend, Mom?"

Hailey was shocked at the question.

"Of course not. He's my client. He's an author, which is why we went on the book tour, so he could go on TV and give interviews, so more people would know about his new book." She knelt down and opened her suitcase then, and started handing out the small souvenirs she'd brought them from every city, sweatshirts and pencils and tiny teddy bears, a Dodgers cap for Bentley, and the autograph from her favorite rock star to Arianna. She squealed when she saw it.

"You *met* her?"

"Phillip was on the same TV show with her, so I asked her for her autograph when we were in the green room together."

"What's the green room? Is it green?" Will wanted to know.

"No, it's not green. It's a waiting room, kind of like a living room, where people wait to go on TV. They have lots of things to eat, and I watched the show from there." It had been fun for her too.

Xena, the yoga teacher, gathered up her things and got ready to leave a little while later, and the children were sad to see the dog go. Her name was Pamela and they loved her. They all said they wanted a Chihuahua, except Will, who wanted a Great Dane. He had seen one in the park, and said it was big enough to ride, like a pony.

Hailey thanked Xena before she left. "You really saved me. I couldn't have done the tour without you." She wouldn't have had enough babysitters to cover the full two weeks.

"You have terrific kids. I'm going to miss them. Call me anytime to babysit. We're best friends now."

It took a while for everyone to settle down. And while they were going through the gifts she'd brought them, she went and changed into her nightgown and bathrobe. It felt good to be home in her fuzzy slippers and robe, with her children around her. Will looked to her as though he'd grown. Bentley was the same sturdy boy, and Arianna suddenly looked more grown up. Maybe it had been good for them to manage for two weeks without her. No one was complaining. Will said he wanted chocolate ice cream for breakfast, with chocolate sauce and marshmallows, like Xena gave them.

"I think we'll give the ice cream breakfasts a rest for a while," Hailey said, laughing. "Cornflakes tomorrow."

"Yerghk," Will said, and made a face.

"Maybe pancakes. I'll get up in time to do them."

"Yum. Xena didn't know how to do pancakes, so we had ice cream."

"That makes perfect sense," she said, happy to be home with her children. The book tour had been interesting and rewarding, and hopefully good for Phillip's book, but there was nothing as sweet as being back with them. She had missed them more than she realized or wanted to admit while she was gone. She'd been busy doing what she had to do. She had enjoyed working with Phillip. He had been a gentleman and good company for the entire trip.

He thought about her in his silent, orderly apartment in the Dakota. He had enjoyed her company too, but seeing her with her children had added another dimension to her. She was a warm, loving woman. Leaving them for two weeks to help make his book a success had been an incredible gift. He didn't know how to thank her.

Will and Arianna crowded into her bed with her that night and she let them. Bentley wanted to sleep in his own bed. He was too old to sleep with his mother. Arianna and Will snuggled up next to her like warm puppies, happy to have her home. The last two weeks had been an adventure for them, and for Hailey too.

Chapter 6

Hailey got a warm welcome when she got to the office the next day. Julia and Jane were thrilled to see her. Jane had read and done coverage on all four books Hailey had given her before she left. They were sitting on Hailey's desk, with Jane's reports clipped to each of them. She had enjoyed reading them, and thought that at least two of the writers, and possibly three, would be good candidates as clients for the agency. She was thoroughly enjoying her increasing responsibilities, admired Hailey, and loved working with Julia.

Julia had everything organized for Hailey's return, and brought her a cup of coffee. Francine dropped by to check in with her, and she was smiling.

"How was it? How did it go?"

"It went great." Hailey beamed at her. "He's a total pro. And incredibly easy to work with."

"Did you sleep with him?" Allie asked as she slipped into Hailey's office unnoticed.

"Of course not." Hailey made a face.

"Too bad. He's hot."

"Yeah, and he's my client," Hailey reminded her.

"We don't all sleep with our clients." Francine gave Allie a disapproving look.

"No, just our bosses," Allie said under her breath, and slipped out again, while Francine gave her a murderous look. Hailey ignored the comment and pretended not to hear it, although she had heard the rumors about Francine too, and didn't believe them.

By lunchtime, it was as though she'd never left. Clients were calling to complain. One of her favorites called to say he was late with his deadline, and Hailey laughed. He was late with every book, but he was a talented young writer so his publisher put up with it. When Hailey went to the kitchen to get a yogurt, she saw Allie walk into Bob Benson's office and shut the door behind her. Half an hour later, Hailey could see them still engrossed in earnest conversation through the glass wall of Bob's office. She wondered what that was about. They all heard about it later, on the news.

Rod Talbott, one of their biggest stars, had been arrested on criminal charges, for raping a seventeen-year-old actress. He had allegedly drugged and raped her. Two other young women had already come forward and said that he had raped them too. He had been kicked off the movie he was making. He was one of the agency's biggest clients on the dramatic side, and everyone at the agency was upset about it. He always seemed like such a nice guy and was kind to everyone when he came to the office.

Allie said it to Hailey and Francine, before anyone else did. "His career is over. You won't be seeing him here again. I spoke to Bob about it. We're taking him off our roster. He won't work again anyway. And the way things are now, he'll go to prison. Guys like that don't get away with it anymore. This is a big deal, and the girl is a minor." It was all over the news that night. He had called Allie and asked for her help to find a criminal attorney, and Bob wouldn't let her do it. He wanted no part of it. They had other clients who had been in trouble with the law before, but nothing as shocking as this.

When Hailey got home that night, there was the biggest bouquet of roses she'd ever seen in a vase on the coffee table. Three dozen pale pink long-stemmed roses, and the card read, "I can't thank you enough. Phillip." He was amazingly gracious and generous. Arianna stared at the roses and then at her mother when she came home.

"He *is* your boyfriend, Mom. Is that why you went on the tour with him?"

"He is *not* my boyfriend. And I went because my boss asked me to." Arianna didn't look convinced.

Hailey watched the video of Arianna in *Annie* that night and she was terrific. She told Arianna how proud of her she was. Arianna really had been wonderful, and she had a lovely voice. Hailey would have loved to get her singing lessons, but they couldn't afford it.

Felicity had left chicken curry for them that night, which was one of their favorites. Hailey was putting the dishes in the dishwasher when Phillip called her. She was pleased and surprised to hear his voice. She smiled as soon as she heard him.

"You sent me the most outrageously beautiful roses I've ever seen," she said gratefully. "I was going to email you tomorrow."

"You deserve a whole garden for what you did for me. I missed talking to you today. Are you free for dinner on Friday?"

"If I can find a sitter. I may have worn them all out while we were away. If I can find one, I'd love it." She had missed talking to him too. They chatted for a while, and she promised to let him know as soon as she could about Friday.

And in the morning she had even better news for him. They had just gotten word that the tour had worked its magic. His book was going to be number one on the *New York Times* list next Sunday. She called to tell him, and he let out a whoop.

"And I owe it all to you," he said in a choked voice. He'd been number one on the list many times before, but it always felt like the first time, and he had worked hard for it on the tour. Coming up from number three, after it dropped to number eleven, was nearly impossible to achieve, and Hailey had helped him do it.

"I didn't do all those interviews and charm them, you did," she reminded him, and refused to take the credit for it.

"Now you have to find a sitter so we can celebrate," he said.

"I'll work on it today," she promised.

Bob Benson heard the news and came in to congratulate her.

"Good job, Hailey. Well done. That really is some tour you did with Phillip. The publisher is thrilled. They set up some great interviews for him but you got him through it."

"He really deserves this," she said kindly. He was working on a new book and told her he'd have a first draft to show her soon. He really appreciated her comments. He liked the independent editor he used, but lately he'd had more faith in Hailey's suggestions.

After Bob left her office, she asked Jane to make a copy of three of the manuscripts she'd done coverage on. She wanted to give them to Francine to read, after seeing Jane's rave reviews on them. Jane had said that the fourth one wasn't worth pursuing.

"Do you mind making copies for me?" Hailey asked her, and Jane beamed.

"Of course not." She was pleased that Hailey had faith in her comments and was going to show Francine the three manuscripts to decide if they should invite the unknown authors to become clients of the agency. They were always looking for new talent. Jane headed to the copy room with the manuscripts, and had just fed one of them into the machine, when Dan Fletcher followed her in. She hadn't noticed. She had her back to the door and the machines were noisy, so she hadn't heard him, or the door close behind him. She was standing in front of the copy machine, when suddenly she felt his full weight behind her as he crushed her against the machine, reached around her, and fondled her breasts. He was a tall, heavyset man, and for a moment, she was so startled and frightened, she couldn't scream or fight back. She squirmed around to face him to push him away, and he continued to lean his full weight against her to pin her against the machine, and ran a hand up under her skirt and into the thong she had worn to avoid panty lines in her skirt. He pulled the thong down easily with a firm grip and forced his fingers into her. She struggled and slapped him as hard as she could, and he had the mark of her hand on his face as she fought free of him and the copy machine kept churning.

"You pig!" she shouted at him, but no one could hear them in the small soundproof room with the big copy machine working. And no one could see them with the door closed.

"I can get you fired anytime I want to, you little bitch. You think you're such a smart-ass. Come to my office at lunchtime and blow me or you're out of a job," he said in a voice filled with venom and anger as he rubbed his cheek where she had slapped him, but it had gotten his hand out of her at least.

"You sick old fuck. I warned you," she said, shaking with rage. She pulled the door open and walked out of the copy room and ran back to her office without the manuscripts. He emerged a few minutes later and hurried down the hall to his corner office.

Julia had seen Jane rush into her office. "Problems with the copy machine?" she asked her. "We need new ones. The damn thing nearly ate a manuscript of mine yesterday." Jane sat down then and Julia could see that she was shaking. "Are you okay?" Jane nodded and didn't answer her, and a few minutes later, she went back to the copy room and got the manuscripts and the copies. She looked calmer when she came back to the office and put them on Hailey's desk for Francine.

It was almost lunchtime, and as soon as Julia left for lunch and Jane was alone, she made a phone call. She knew exactly who to call, and when she said who she was and where she worked, she got an appointment for six o'clock that night.

Hailey hung up the phone in her office, looking pleased. She had found a sitter for Friday night. Xena said she'd do it, and she'd bring

Pamela, her dog, with her. The kids would be thrilled. She called Phillip then to tell him, and he was happy too.

"I'll pick you up at eight," he said, "or is that too early or too late? I don't know how that works with the kids."

"It's perfect," she said. He knew exactly where he wanted to take her to celebrate his number one book. "I might have the first draft of the new one to give you by then." He sounded pleased. He'd been working nonstop since he'd gotten home, energized by the success of the trip.

The news was still full of stories about Rod Talbott, and additional victims coming forward to accuse him. Everyone at the agency was talking about it. His fall from grace into disgrace had been rapid.

"That's going to be Dan Fletcher one of these days," Merriwether said, looking worried when Bob stopped by her office to see how she was.

"He's a seducer, not a rapist," Bob commented. "And as far as I know, he plays with consenting adults." But he worried about Dan too. Especially when he drank too much, which seemed to be happening more frequently lately when he went out for long lunches with his friends. Bob sat and talked to Merriwether for a while, and asked her how things were going at home. They had become confidants ever since she'd told him about her problems with Jeff. She looked stressed when she talked about it. Her previously happy marriage seemed to be going down the tubes.

The agency was quiet for the rest of the afternoon, and Jane stayed at her desk, keeping busy. She left at five-thirty and walked to Martha Wick's office for her six o'clock appointment. Martha was a tall, attractive woman in her early fifties with gray hair. Jane was led into her office. She invited her to sit down and listened to her story with rapt attention. Nothing about it surprised her.

"It's a wonder this didn't happen to him years ago," she said to Jane. "The guy's a menace, and he's gotten away with it for years because no one has had the guts to report him. You're doing the right thing. You've got him on attempted rape, coercion, and several counts of sexual assault and harassment. What are we going to do about it? Do you want to press charges?" Martha asked her. She had a kind, sympathetic face.

"Yes, I do," Jane answered her immediately. "He shouldn't be allowed to get away with it, or he might do something worse." She was shaking again after telling the attorney what he had done in the copy room, and the threats he had made.

"He could go to prison for this," Martha said matter-of-factly. Jane liked her, although she had trouble imagining her with Bob Benson. They seemed very different. She looked like a no-nonsense woman, and she looked older than he did. She didn't make a fuss about her looks. She was neat and professional in a navy blue pantsuit, and she wore no makeup. Bob was a very handsome man.

"How long will the whole process take?" Jane asked her, curious about it.

"Prison will take a while, depending on if he's foolish enough to go to trial. If he pleads guilty and confesses, it will move a lot faster. First the police need to contact the district attorney's office to get a warrant for his arrest from a judge. We need to speak to them first. I'm glad you came to see me today, because technically, you should contact the police the same day as the assault, and since it happened earlier today, you've done the right thing. After he's arrested and bail is posted, the D.A. will take it to the grand jury to set the charges. He'll be indicted and then he'll either plead guilty or go to trial. If the judge lets him post bail, he'll be out during the whole process. It all depends on how he decides to respond: guilty or not guilty. If other women come forward, which can happen with these cases, and he's found guilty or confesses, he'll be gone for a long time." She didn't say that Bob had been worried about something like this happening for years. She had never liked Dan, and was liking him even less over the years, although Bob was loyal to his partner, despite his failings. "You'll need to go to the police and file a report tonight. I can go with you if you like," Martha offered, and Jane nodded. Now that she was actually doing what she'd told Dan she would, she was scared of the ramifications, but she knew it was the right thing to do. She wondered if she'd get fired for bringing charges against him, but she wanted to do it anyway. She thought someone should and he had assaulted her. "There's another matter we need to address," Martha said. "I can't represent you in this matter. I'm happy to advise you or consult on the case, but my husband is your employer, Dan's his partner and will be the defendant. I'm too closely involved, but one of my associates has been handling a number of these sexual assault cases for our clients, as I have. His name is Steve Franklin. I'd like to bring him in to meet you, if that's all right with you."

Jane was disappointed that Martha couldn't take the case, but five minutes later a serious-looking man in a business suit walked into the room, and after talking to him for ten minutes, Jane felt comfortable with him. Martha had stayed in the room too, and would be consulting on the case. She had told Jane that Steve was forty years old, had gone to Yale Law School, and was one of the best lawyers in the firm.

Martha summarized what had happened for Steve's benefit, and Martha's assessment of the charges were attempted rape because he had pulled her underwear down in the copy room, which was a Class C felony, sexual abuse in the first degree for fingering her, a Class D felony, coercion in the second degree, a Class E felony for ordering her to give him a blow job or he'd fire her, and two counts of sexual harassment, which were a misdemeanor, referring to the two earlier incidents in the office kitchen.

Martha asked her if there were any cuts or bruises on her body, and Jane said there weren't.

She left the room to call the police then and returned to tell Jane that they were expecting her at the police station, and offered again to go with her, which Jane gratefully accepted. She didn't want to go to the police alone, and Martha was willing to go with her as a friend and legal consultant.

An hour and a half after Jane had arrived, they left Steve at the office and Martha and Jane took a cab to the police station, where they were ushered into a small office with a stack of overflowing files on the desk. A plainclothes male detective came in a few minutes later, wearing jeans and a Yankees jacket and cap, and a young female Chinese plainclothes officer in jeans and an NYU sweatshirt. Both were pleasant as Martha and Jane introduced themselves, then Martha explained the circumstances. Rachel Yee, the female detective, gently questioned Jane and took notes. The male detective, Rudi Post, brought bottled water for all four of them. He smiled at Jane to put her at ease as Detective Yee continued the questioning.

Taking Jane's statement didn't take long, she was very clear on the order of events.

"So when did this happen?" Detective Yee asked her.

"Around noon today," Jane said in a soft voice. She described what had happened in the copy room in detail, along with the threat to get her fired, and Dan's telling her to give him a blow job in his office at lunchtime if she wanted to keep her job, and the two earlier incidents in the kitchen.

"A real gentleman, isn't he? It's amazing how bold these guys get and think they can get away with it. And many do." Detective Yee listed the charges exactly as Martha had predicted they would. There were two misdemeanor counts of sexual harassment, and felony charges of coercion, sexual assault, and attempted rape. Detective Post told them he'd get the report to the D.A. in the morning, who would go to a judge to have a warrant signed for Dan's arrest. Dan would be arrested in the next few days. "We know where he works," he said, and Martha also supplied Dan's home address, "so he won't be hard to find."

Martha felt sorry for Dan's wife, Rita. She had for years. He had even brushed up against Martha once years before, and she had given him a quelling look and he'd never done it again. She had told Bob about it, but he didn't say anything to Dan, in case Martha had "made a mistake," which she thought was cowardly of him. She thought Bob should have thrown him out of their partnership long before this. Women at the agency had complained about him for years, but Dan seemed to have gotten away with it. But this time he had gone too far.

They were at the police station for an hour. Jane signed her statement at the end of it, and then they stood outside for a few minutes and Jane thanked Martha again. She was grateful for her kindness and support.

Jane took an Uber to the West Village and called Benjie as soon as she got home. She hadn't seen him in three weeks, while she was working on the manuscripts for Hailey. By now, he might be dating someone else. But he answered on the second ring.

"I finished my projects. Can I invite you over for dinner? I'll pay," she said in a serious voice. She felt shaken by the events of the day and wanted company. He laughed when she said it.

"Is that bribery?" He was happy to hear from her, although he'd been mad at her for a few weeks. She was working so hard that she never had time for him anymore. "When did you have in mind?"

"Are you free tonight?" she asked meekly. And then he heard something in her voice.

"Are you okay?"

"Sort of. I'll tell you about it at dinner."

"I'm at the gym. I'll come over in half an hour. We can order in if you want."

He was there in twenty minutes, and they ordered sushi. She looked pale as she told him what had happened with Dan Fletcher, and that she was bringing charges against him, and had just come from the police.

"Good for you. You're doing the right thing. What a sonofabitch. He deserves to go to prison." Benjie looked furious, and sorry for Jane. He still cared about her.

"That's what the lawyer said, that I'm doing the right thing. The police are going to the district attorney tomorrow, with the report.

They'll go to a judge to get a warrant for Dan's arrest. I guess I'll get fired for filing the police report. I love my job, but I still think it's the right thing to do. You can't treat people like that." She felt tired and shaken but still convinced she'd done what was right.

"There are a lot of guys who treat people like that," Benjie said. "I'm really sorry, Jane." They sat on the couch and watched movies on TV after they ate. He didn't feel right trying to take her to bed after what had happened. He could tell she was still unnerved and upset, and it had been weeks since they'd seen each other. After the last movie, she asked him if he wanted to spend the night.

"Are you sure you're up to it? I figured you might want some space."

"I don't want to be alone. We can just cuddle," she said, and he felt sorry for her again and gave her a hug.

"Come on," he said, and pulled her up off the couch. "Let's go to bed." He didn't try to have sex with her when they went to bed, he just held her and she started to cry and couldn't stop. He lay holding her until she fell asleep, and then he did too. He told her again how brave she was when he left for work the next day. He still had some clothes at her apartment, and he wore a clean pair of jeans to work, with an oversized UC Berkeley T-shirt of hers.

When Jane got to work, she saw Dan go into Bob's office later that morning and wondered if he was complaining about her.

"I want that little bitch fired," he said to Bob as soon as the door closed.

"What little bitch?"

"The one that works for Hailey. She's insolent and a troublemaker." He didn't tell Bob she'd slapped him, because he'd have to explain why and he couldn't. "We don't need little sluts like that around here," he said, still angry at how things had turned out the day before. She hadn't shown up in his office to give him a blow job, so he wanted to make good on his threat to have her fired.

"You need to lighten up, Dan," Bob said quietly. "I've said it before. Women don't put up with the kind of fun and games you like anymore. You're going to get into some serious trouble one of these days. I don't want that to happen and neither do you. Did something happen with her?" He could tell Dan wasn't telling him the whole story, and Bob was panicked by what he didn't know.

"First they come on to you with their fake tits and short skirts, and then they bitch when you come on to them. That's what they want, isn't it? You can't treat a whore like a lady. It's a waste of time."

"You need to update your thinking, Dan. Look at what just happened to Rod Talbott."

"I don't go after teenagers. That bitch who works for Hailey must be about thirty. She's no innocent. None of them are."

"They don't want to be manhandled," Bob said bluntly. "You can't just reach out and grab."

"Why not? It's what they're looking for. Look at how they dress."

"It's *not* what they're looking for. That's the whole point."

"Are you going to fire her or not?" Dan asked, looking irritated.

"No, I'm not. We have no grounds and no reason to. You disliking her isn't a reason to fire her. Nor is her rebuffing your advances. Hailey loves her. She says she's smart and a hard worker. Just stay away from her if you don't like her. In fact, just stay away from her, period. We don't need a harassment suit here."

"She's a slut."

"You don't know that and neither do I." It was obvious that the reason for his anger was that she wasn't a slut. He couldn't fire her for that.

Eventually, Dan lumbered out of Bob's office and went back to his own, looking restless and dissatisfied.

Two days later, Dan was just about to leave for lunch when two detectives came to the agency, showed their badges to the receptionist, and asked to see Dan Fletcher. She was about to call Dan, when he walked into the reception area on his way to lunch.

"These gentlemen are here to see you," she said quickly, to warn him. They showed him their badges and asked him if he'd like to go to a private room with them. He was late for lunch and he looked annoyed.

"Why would I want to go into a private room with you?" he asked them, and the senior detective lowered his voice so only Dan could hear him. "So we can arrest you in private. You're under arrest," he said quietly. Dan looked shocked.

"Are you crazy? For what? I own this agency. You can't arrest me. I'm an upstanding citizen." He was shouting, and people around the area were starting to look up to see what was going on.

"Get Benson!" he shouted to the receptionist. She buzzed Bob, who came immediately and approached Dan and the two policemen.

"What's going on?" he asked Dan.

"They want to arrest me. Tell them who I am." He was starting to look nervous.

"What are the charges?" Bob lowered his voice and asked them.

The senior detective spoke in the same tone and told him. Bob looked at his longtime partner in despair. It was a long and frightening list. "You'd better go with them, Dan. This could get ugly."

"Call your goddamn wife and tell her to get me out of this," he bellowed. He had no intention of making this easy for them. Jane had heard him by then and didn't move from her desk. Julia looked at her and knew immediately from the look on her face.

"Did you . . . ?"

Jane nodded, and then held up her head. "Yes, I did."

Julia could see Dan in the reception area from where she was standing.

"I think they're cops and they're going to arrest him," Julia said. Jane nodded again and Hailey came out of her office. Several others did too. Dan was shouting, Bob was trying to calm him down, and the detectives were waiting. They weren't going anywhere. Dan was too old and too fat to make a run for it. It was embarrassing to watch.

"What's up?" Hailey asked her two assistants.

"It's Dan" was all Julia said, and Hailey had an instant bad feeling about it.

"Are those policemen?" Hailey asked.

"I think so," she said, and Jane was silent and watching them too. This was turning out to be a bigger mess than she had thought it would be, but only because Dan wouldn't go quietly.

Francine had come out of her office and was standing still, watching from the distance.

Bob suggested they all go into his office, and Dan was willing, as the two detectives followed them. Bob closed the door, although everyone could see through the glass wall. The detectives read him his Miranda rights and placed him under arrest in Bob's office. They offered not to handcuff him if he would go with them peacefully.

"You'd better go with them, Dan," Bob said firmly. "You don't want to get dragged out of here, do you?"

"For chrissake," Dan said, red in the face by then. "I'll go with you," he told them and turned to Bob. "And have your wife meet me at the police station, or wherever they take me."

"I'll call and see what she can do." He opened the door to his office, and Dan walked across the reception area with the detectives walking closely on either side of him. They took the elevator to the lobby and left the building swiftly. From the windows, they saw Dan get into the back of a police car. Bob called Martha as soon as they left. She took the call immediately and he explained what had happened, and asked her to send a lawyer to Dan, even if she didn't want to take the case. He knew she disliked Dan intensely and had no respect for him.

"I can't," she said simply.

"Why not? You don't have to take the case, for God's sake. Send someone else. He's my partner in the agency."

"I can't take the case, or assign an attorney to it," she said firmly, and Bob understood.

"Oh my God," Bob said, and then was speechless for a moment. "You represent the victim, don't you? How bad is it? The list of charges is awful. I hope it's a false claim." But he knew in his gut it wasn't. Martha had been right. He should have separated himself from Dan years before. He was a disaster waiting to happen, and now it had.

"He should have been stopped a long time ago." There was reproach for Bob in what she said. "He doesn't deserve your loyalty."

Bob called around and sent him a lawyer a few hours later. It was the best he could do. He found a criminal lawyer he knew to take the case, for the preliminary steps at least.

Jane took it one step further. She figured she'd get fired anyway. She drew up a Wanted poster, blew up a photograph of Dan Fletcher's face, and attached it to the poster. She put his name underneath it, and what the charges were. She posted it on Instagram a few minutes later and it went viral immediately. It was over. He was a dead man. He was cooked.

A few hours later, Bob checked with the lawyer he'd sent. He told Bob that since it was Friday, he couldn't get Dan out until the arraignment on Monday, when the judge would set bail, *if* he did. Given the gravity of the charges, he wasn't sure the judge would let him out on bail. He might keep Dan in jail until he pled guilty or was convicted at a trial.

Merriwether came to sit with Bob in his office. He looked profoundly depressed. Dan would get no sympathy from Martha, who had never liked him, nor would Bob, whom she thought should have acted sooner. He hadn't acted at all. Merriwether felt sorry for Bob. In her opinion, he hadn't done anything to deserve this, other than fail to stop Dan earlier, which his wife thought was despicable.

Jane barely said a word all afternoon. At the end of the day, Julia sat down next to her, spoke to her quietly, and said two words. "Me too." Jane looked at her, shocked. "You can put me on a list if you want. He only went after me once. I gave him a hand job in his office, or he said I'd lose my job. I was too scared and ashamed to tell anyone." Jane wondered how many more there were, who might speak up now.

Francine had stayed in her office all afternoon too. She had seen the Instagram of the Wanted poster with Dan's picture on it, along with half the world, and the details of what he was charged with. Everyone would know soon. She didn't feel sorry for him. She didn't feel anything. She didn't give a damn about him. All she felt was relief that he was gone. He was finally getting what he deserved. She hoped he would rot in jail.

Chapter 7

Merriwether stayed late at the office to talk to Bob the day that Dan was arrested. He was deeply upset that things had gotten so out of hand. He was worried about the agency and felt guilty that anyone had suffered. He should have gotten Dan out of the agency before something like this happened. He had never thought Dan was capable of real harm, but he'd been wrong. And he was concerned about what would happen to Dan if he went to prison. He couldn't imagine him surviving prison at his age. He was more of a figurehead and did very little work, but it was going to make them look bad if one of the heads of the agency went to prison. He wondered if the judge would be lenient, given Dan Fletcher's age and stature in the community, but it seemed unlikely. More important men than he were going to prison for similar offenses, justifiably. Bob didn't disagree with the current stricter policies about women being coerced into having sex, trading jobs for sexual favors, or being drugged and raped. But it was such an ignominious end to what had once been a glowing career for a man who had been his friend. Bob wondered if Dan was getting senile, or if too much alcohol had affected his brain.

"The agency will come through it," Merriwether said. She didn't know what to do to cheer him up in the circumstances. It was a serious situation, and he felt terrible for Jane once he knew the story. He didn't want any of his female employees harassed, assaulted, or abused.

"I want people to feel safe here," he said to Merriwether. "That's important to me. I've always wanted the work environment at the agency to be like a family, and a second home. We all spend a lot of time here." He looked miserable.

"I know. Dan is an aberration. Look at all the places where things like that are happening now, in corporations, in the film industry, in politics. Dan has always been a loose cannon as long as I've worked here," she said softly.

"I should have dealt with it years ago. I thought he was harmless. Clearly, I was wrong." And then he looked at Merriwether. "Did he ever do anything inappropriate with you?" He was afraid of the answer now.

"Just a few comments here and there, nothing too shocking. And he never laid a hand on me. I don't think he'd dare, with me as the CFO. He knew it would have gone straight back to you."

"It was stupid and wrong of him to go after Jane. She's young, with an entry-level job. He probably thought he'd get away with it. She's a brave girl. If my wife's firm is representing Jane, they'll ask for the maximum penalty. And they're not wrong. I know her father, and I took full responsibility for her when we hired her. He must be ready to kill me and I don't blame him. I'll call him. It's really an abuse of power on top of everything else. I feel terrible for Jane." He felt sick when he thought about it, and they sat and discussed it for a long time. Merriwether was worried about him, and she didn't leave the office until he did. She got home even later than usual, and Jeff was waiting for her, looking furious when she walked in.

"What the hell was it about now?" he asked her as soon as she came through the door. She was tired and drained and didn't want to have to deal with him too.

"We had a bad incident in the office today. I had to stay late."

"What, did someone commit suicide because their book wasn't at the top of the bestseller list, or some two-bit actress didn't get a part in a horror movie?" He had a way of denigrating everything they did. It didn't used to be like that, but it was now. Everything had changed.

"Dan Fletcher got arrested at the office, for attempted rape," she said simply. "It was very upsetting, and Bob is justifiably worried about the agency."

"Who did he try to rape?" Jeff looked surprised.

"A new assistant. She hired a lawyer, and they went to the police."

"Good for her."

"I agree. Not good for the agency, though. It could give us a bad name, although we're not the only ones with these problems now. It's an epidemic across the country."

"So why did you have to stay late?" he asked her. She could see that he was spoiling for a fight. He'd had little to do all day and she guessed that his writing hadn't gone well.

"I'm a senior officer of the company. I can't just run out the door when something like that happens. He got arrested in the office. That's terrible for morale."

"But a good warning to everyone else."

"That's true," she agreed with him. "How was your day? I'm sorry I'm late."

"No, you're not. You'd sleep there if you could. It's the only thing you care about," he accused her. "And my day sucked, actually. I got a rejection for an article I wrote a few weeks ago. I couldn't get a single goddamn word on the page for my book. I have writer's block." He'd had it for months, but she didn't remind him of that.

"I'm sorry, Jeff. Have you eaten?"

"Obviously. I'm not going to sit here starving, waiting for you." Everything she did was wrong in his opinion, and she was tired of it. It was depressing to come home to at night. She couldn't even remember when things had started to go sour. She hadn't noticed it at first, but now it was a white-hot blaze, which burned her every time she went near him or they talked. She wondered if they'd ever be able to put out the flames and have a decent relationship again. It was beginning to seem more and more unlikely, which depressed her even more. If they couldn't fix it, there was nothing to look forward to except endless years of his accusations and him putting her down. It wasn't how she wanted to live, or an atmosphere she wanted her daughter to grow up in. It wasn't good for any of them. But she wasn't ready to do anything radical about it yet. She wondered if couples counseling would help, but she didn't dare suggest it to him in the mood he was in now, the one he was in every time she saw him.

She took a long hot bath to relax from the stressful day. He was asleep when she got to bed. She couldn't remember the last time they'd made love.

Francine took her son to therapy the night Dan got arrested. Things were going better. The therapy was helping, and with supervision, the bullying had stopped. Tommy was in much better spirits. He spoke to the therapist alone now, and Francine sat in the waiting room, thinking about Dan's arrest that day. It all had an unreal quality to it, and she was sure that with his connections, he'd be back to torture whoever he chose to again soon. And she'd be seeing him twice a week until he was a hundred years old. The rumor was that he'd go to prison, and she hoped it was true. She felt lighter than she had in years, knowing that he was in jail that night. It made her feel braver and more optimistic about life. She was lost in reverie when Tommy came out of the therapist's office and looked at his mother.

"You okay, Mom?" he asked her. The anger that had characterized him for months was gone, or dissipating, and he was grateful to her for helping to stop the bullying and being supportive of him.

"Yeah, I think I am." She smiled at him. They took the bus home to their apartment, where Thalia was looking at pictures of prom dresses. She glanced up at her mother with a smile.

Things were looking up, and Dan Fletcher was in jail for the moment. It made the world seem like a better place, for however long it lasted.

* * *

Phillip picked Hailey up promptly at eight. He was wearing a dark blue suit she had seen him wear on the tour, and he looked handsome in it. He had worn it on the late night talk show he'd been on. There was nothing trendy about him, he was more old school, although he was only forty-eight. Hailey had worn a simple black dress he hadn't seen before. He had told her they were going someplace nice, so she had dressed accordingly. Her dark hair was in a bun and they looked great together.

The boys were happy to see him. Xena had arrived, with Pamela, as she'd promised, and the tiny white Chihuahua was barking frantically. Arianna was still a little suspicious of Phillip. There hadn't been a man in their life since their father died five years before, so having Phillip in their midst was unfamiliar and surprising. Bentley and Will thought it interesting. Phillip talked about baseball with them until they left for dinner.

"They're such cute kids," he said, sounding surprised again. She could tell he wasn't used to children, almost to the point of being afraid of them.

"They're good kids," Hailey confirmed. "I'm completely objective, of course." She smiled at him and he laughed. He was ten years older than she was, and he seemed very "grown up" for his age. He was a serious person, but he did have a sense of humor she enjoyed. He had been an easy person to travel with, which said a lot about him. He was easy to please, not demanding, although they had gone first class all the way because the publisher wanted them to. Phillip was flexible and didn't mind when something changed. With children, something was always changing. It was the nature of parenthood, having all your plans thrown out the window at a moment's notice.

He hadn't told her where they were going for dinner, and she was shocked when they arrived. They had taken a cab from her apartment, and he had made reservations at La Grenouille, the best French restaurant in New York. It had a gorgeous, elegant French interior, and enormous urns filled with exquisite flowers that stood seven or eight feet tall. The food was the best she'd ever tasted, with wines to match. She had been there once with a very fancy client of the agency, but never on a date. As she mulled it over when they walked into the restaurant, she wondered which this was. Had Phillip taken her to dinner to thank her as his agent, or were they on a date? She had a feeling it was the latter but didn't want to ask. She decided to not try to figure it out, and just enjoy the evening.

One of the things she liked best about Phillip, along with his fine mind and generosity and kindness, was that she could be herself with him. She made it a huge point to be businesslike at the office, and never let her personal life interfere. With Phillip, now that he knew about her children and had even met them, she could be herself. She could talk about them, or not, and he could see the other side of her that she usually tried to hide. She could be a whole person with him. At the office, it was all-important not to make a point of being a mother or having other obligations. She had to appear to be focused only on work with no other pulls on her. It was what they expected in the corporate world. She and Francine rarely discussed their children, but she wondered at times if it was stressful for her too. It was as if they had to be superhuman, and almost robotic, with no personal attachments or feelings in order to succeed. She and Phillip talked about it at dinner, and he was intrigued by what she said.

"I didn't even know you had kids for the first few months you represented me, and then I thought maybe you had one," he said as they made their way through the delicious meal. She was very touched that he had brought her to such a lovely restaurant, whether as his agent or his date. "My childhood was so miserable and my parents so unhappy, I could never bear the thought of doing that to someone else if I got it wrong. My mother was a nice woman before she destroyed herself with alcohol. It was the only way she could tolerate my father. I always hoped she would leave him, but she never did. It made me skittish about marriage and human relationships.

"I wasn't a good husband. I was too scared to get attached too deeply, to hurt her or get hurt. I think I was frozen most of the time. I don't blame her for leaving. I'm surprised she stayed as long as she did. She's much happier now. And writing has helped me open up a lot. I've learned a lot through my work, but it's taken a hell of a long time.

"I'm ready for you to read the first draft of the new book, by the way. I love your comments. They're so succinct, to the point, and they bring me back down to earth. I get too lofty at times, and tangled up in the tops of the trees. You ground me." She smiled as they finished the main course. They had ordered chocolate soufflés for dessert, his with sauce anglaise and hers with whipped cream. "Is it too big an imposition, asking you to read the books and give me your opinion?" he asked, looking embarrassed. "Now that I know you've got three people at home, needing your attention, I feel guilty giving you more work to do."

"Don't. That's what agents do. They read their clients' work. I'm honored that you give me an early look and care about what I think."

"I care very, very much, and you share your thoughts so gently." She smiled at that. She tried very hard to not interfere with his writing or ask him to change anything. She just suggested a few clarifications here and there to make the internal light of the work shine more brightly. Some of his books were deep, as he was, and she loved reading them. They gave the reader extraordinary insight into him, and how sensitive and caring he was. If he had been frozen when he was with his wife, as he said, he had grown a lot since. His writing was warm and inviting and very personal. He obviously felt at ease when he wrote, which was true of many writers she had discovered. They were more comfortable hiding in their work, even if very thinly masked. You could always see the writer behind the story and the words, peeking out from their hiding places. Phillip's voice was unmistakable. She loved that about it too. It was like listening to him speak.

"Were you happy in your marriage?" he asked her as they started on their soufflés, which were remarkable. "Or is it rude to ask you that?" He wondered if the rules were different with a widow, and it wasn't appropriate to ask. People seemed to like thinking that their late spouses had been saints, whatever the truth had been when they were alive. She didn't shrink at the question, and answered him as she always did, with her big honest eyes and her heart.

"Sometimes." Her answer surprised him. "We were very different, but we meshed pretty well. I was young when we got married. Jim was a little older. I was more dynamic, he was more laid back. I was angry at him for a long time after he died. He left everything in a mess. He was forty-three, so he didn't expect to die. He wasn't sick, that we knew of. He had an aneurysm, so from one minute to the next, he was gone. He had a good salary, but we had no savings. We spent everything on how we lived and the kids, nice vacations, beautiful apartment. I loved being able to stop working, but all of that meant that we didn't have anything to speak of put aside.

"He had no life insurance, which was crazy with a wife and three kids dependent on him. He could have had a car accident at any age. Neither of us had living parents, so I had no one to help me. I had to give up our apartment immediately, and move to the apartment you've seen. I share a bedroom with Arianna, which is sweet, but I'd love to have my own room again someday." He hadn't realized that when he saw the apartment, and he was impressed. "I had to find a job right away. I hadn't worked in six years, and my salary as an editor wasn't enough for us to live on, so I couldn't go back to publishing.

"My husband knew Bob Benson, so I went to see him, and he offered me a job as an agent with a very reasonable salary, and I've loved working there. It's actually much more fun and interesting than my old job. I was still pretty young then, in publishing, and didn't get to edit any important writers. Bob took a big chance on me, and I've learned a lot. So things have turned out well. I could have a bigger apartment if I moved out of the city, but I wanted to stay in Manhattan. The kids love their school and I'm close to work. I know Francine commutes every day and that takes a chunk of time out of your day. I'd rather spend that time with my kids, and they need my help. I help with homework, and I'm around as soon as I finish work.

"But to answer your original question, were we happy? I think so. Were we ecstatic and madly in love? No, maybe not. But it worked, and I'm sure we'd still be married if he were alive, at least I think we would be. We made the adjustments and compromises we needed to make it work. We wanted to stop at two kids, which we could afford. Will came along as a surprise. That put a strain on us financially, but we managed. Or we would have. As it turned out, I had to make it work. Will was only a baby when Jim died. What would I do without Will now? He's the happiest kid alive, and my joy. Everything's always fine with him. He loves everyone and everything. Arianna and Bentley are both more sensitive, and need more attention and managing. It's been hard for Bentley, not having a dad. I'm a poor substitute for a man in his life. I taught him how to play baseball. I try to be mother and father to them, as best I can."

"I could take them out and play ball with them sometimes. I'd like to do that. Throwing a ball is something I'm good at," he said with a smile. "I played football in college and Little League baseball growing up. Sports and writing were what kept me sane in my family environment as a kid."

"They both play soccer," Hailey said as she finished her soufflé. "I played on a women's softball team in college. I have a pretty good pitching arm," she said with a grin, and he laughed.

"I'll have to check that out. You can show me," he said. He had enjoyed the evening with her. He learned more about her every time they talked. Now that she was home, she was more open than she had been on the trip. She had been focused on making everything perfect for him, and doing a good job, although they'd had some good conversations then too. He really admired her and how gracefully she handled everything she did, including motherhood. "Why don't we go to the park together this weekend? We can throw a ball around, and I'll give you the manuscript then. You don't have to rush to read it. Just do it when you have time."

"Don't worry." She smiled at him. "I have the time." She almost added "for you," but thought it sounded too bold. She was a gentle person, and she didn't want to make assumptions. She had enjoyed the evening too. Going to the park with him and the kids sounded like a nice idea, and appropriately low-key. "I've had a wonderful evening," she said as they finished their wine. They were in no hurry to leave. When they finally did, they walked for a few blocks, with her hand tucked into his arm. It was the first time she had been out with a man, for something resembling a date, if it was a date, in five years. That seemed like a very long time. Suddenly, she wasn't just Mom, or a career person, she was a woman with a man. It was a warm, comfortable feeling with him.

"What were you thinking just then?" he asked her gently. She had been smiling a distant, mysterious, dreamy smile, and he thought she was beautiful.

"I was thinking that I haven't done anything like this in a long time. Most of my clients are female writers, and I've never had dinner with any of the men. Lunch occasionally, but not often."

"I didn't take you out to dinner as my agent," he said quietly, looking at her with a slow smile.

"You didn't?"

"Just to be precise and clear about it, this was a date." He was smiling as he said it.

"It was?" She blushed, but he couldn't see it under the streetlights.

"The first of many, if I'm lucky," he said with a look of determination. "And just for the record, I haven't done this in a long time either. I don't meet a lot of women I want to spend an evening with. In fact, I don't meet many women. I'm at home writing most of the time, and I like to write at night." She knew that about him, and she nodded.

"I actually haven't been on any dates since Jim died. I've been too busy with work and kids."

"Then I'm glad we got off to a good start tonight. This was a memorable first date. We'll both remember it one day, I hope," he said, and a few minutes later, he hailed a cab and took her home. He had the cab wait while he walked her upstairs to her apartment, to make sure she got home safely. He was thoughtful and considerate, and well mannered. He didn't try to kiss her. He knew it would have been too soon. She reached up and kissed his cheek when she thanked him.

"I had a really lovely time." She smiled at him, and then unlocked her front door with her key, and he went down the stairs with a grin and a wave.

"I'll call you about this weekend in the park," he said over his shoulder and then disappeared, and she floated into the apartment, feeling young again.

Allie and Eric went out to dinner that night too. They both wanted Chinese food, and went to Chinatown. They enjoyed everything they did together. They went to the gym together, watched movies, went Rollerblading. They went away for weekends to cozy little inns. They rode on the Staten Island Ferry for the fun of it. They didn't hide, and now and then people recognized him from his previous roles and he'd sign an autograph. They had nothing to be ashamed of, they were both single and their relationship was an honest one. Allie hadn't been in a committed relationship in years, and hadn't wanted to be. She had opted for her career in her twenties, and had no yearning to be married or have kids. Her parents' marriage, however long it had lasted, didn't inspire her to emulate them. She knew that they had both had affairs from time to time, which occasionally erupted in scandal, but they always forgave each other and kept on trucking. She had long since decided she would rather be free to be with whomever she wanted than to cheat on someone she no longer wanted to be with. But it was different with Eric. She liked what they had, and had no desire to move on. She supposed it would end eventually, as all of her relationships did, but she hoped it wouldn't be for a long time. And he was crazy about her, and said so every chance he got.

There was an even more famous actor at the Chinese restaurant, with a well-known female movie star. Allie knew them both and introduced Eric to them. The woman was one of Allie's clients, and they finished dinner at the same time and walked out of the restaurant together. Allie was startled when half a dozen paparazzi leapt at them, to catch the famous couple in a private moment. The male actor was in the midst of a nasty divorce, so it was a juicy photograph for them.

Eric and Allie got caught in the wake of the photographers, when one of them recognized Eric. He and Allie smiled and waved as they got into a cab quickly, but there had been just a moment where they were fully exposed to the paparazzi and made the best of it.

"You'd better get used to that," she said and smiled at him. "They're going to be chasing you around like crazy once the series is on the air."

"I don't like it when they infringe on my private life," he said. "Were you okay with that?" he asked her, always concerned for her, and protective.

"Sure, I'm not hiding a husband and ten kids." She laughed.

"They won't give you shit at the agency for dating a client?" he asked, and she shrugged.

"Fuck 'em, it's none of their business. I'm free, single, and over twenty-one," *quite a lot over twenty-one,* she thought, and laughed.

They went home after that, made love in every possible location and position, and eventually fell asleep in each other's arms on her bed.

They had a busy, fun weekend, as they always did, and on Sunday when they went to buy groceries, Eric spotted one of the tabloids at the checkout counter, with the photograph of them leaving the restaurant on Friday night. It was actually a good picture of them and they looked cute, smiling. Both of them were waving as they ducked into a cab. Allie always told her clients that if they got caught by the paparazzi, at least make it look good and smile. They had. The caption under the photograph was fairly banal, given that it was a tabloid and they loved to make up dirt about celebrities. All it said was "Agent Alabama Moore and hot hunk Eric Clay, soon to be the star of a new series, out for Friday night dinner. A date or dinner with a client?"

"No big deal," she said blithely as she read it over his shoulder. The caption under the famous couple's photo was dicier. They had put a banner across the woman's chest that read "Heartbreaker or home-wrecker?" referring to the man's divorce.

"Christ, their stuff is low," Eric said. They didn't buy the paper and cooked dinner together that night. He was staying at her apartment all the time now, and thinking of giving up his own. They were happy, and Allie was loving being a couple, and proud to be with him. She had never felt this way before.

Chapter 8

O n Sunday afternoon, true to his word, Phillip went to the park with Hailey and her children, and threw a ball around with Bentley and Will, while Hailey and Arianna watched. Then they all played tag, and Bentley won. They bought ice cream from a vendor in the park, and Will had cotton candy too. They were all appropriately dirty, covered in grass stains and ice cream, and Will had cotton candy all over his face when they left.

"I'm out of shape," Phillip said, comfortably tired as he smiled at her. "I had fun."

"So did they." Hailey looked happy too. He was a good sport with the children's antics. Will tripped him while trying to get the ball, and Phillip fell but didn't get hurt. Hailey was surprised by how patient he was with them, for someone who didn't have children, and that he seemed to genuinely enjoy them. "I'm going to have fun tonight, with your book," she said. He had dropped it off at the apartment before they went to the park.

"I don't think I could stay awake to read it," he said, as they walked back to her apartment at the end of the day. "They have a lot more energy than I do, and so do you. I don't know how you manage both sides of your life."

"Sometimes neither do I," she said, and laughed. "I have no choice. If I don't do it, there would be no one to help with homework and it wouldn't get done. No one to organize all their after-school activities or sitters to be with them till I get home and can take over."

"It's a full-time job," he commented with admiration.

"It used to be," she said matter-of-factly. "Now it's only half of what I do."

"And I'm the other half, or part of it," he said, looking guilty. "Thank you for reading the book," he said gratefully. It touched him that she was willing to spend time on it and make thoughtful comments to improve the book.

"Reading your books isn't work. I love doing it."

"That's lucky for me. If it weren't for you and my editor, there wouldn't be a book."

"That's not true. You're the talent, we just help you polish it, like the cleaning crew in a garden. We get rid of a few dead branches and fallen leaves, and then you're all set."

"I've had the same editor for twenty-six years, since I wrote my first book when I was twenty-two. Hannah's gotten older, but she's still working, and she's damn good. She's eighty-six years old. She retired twenty years ago, and now they let me have her edit my books independently. I'd be lost without her. I kick the ideas around with her before I start, although I do that with you too. She always gets me headed in the right direction. I couldn't do it without her."

Hailey knew how much the woman meant to him. She was a famous editor in the publishing world, and she had edited some very important books and authors. She only worked with Phillip now.

"Yes, you could do it without her," Hailey said firmly, thinking of the future. The woman wasn't young, and one day he would have to. She didn't want him to convince himself he couldn't write without her. Most writers felt that way about editors they trusted and were attached to. It was an important relationship, Hailey knew, but he had the talent and she knew he could write a fabulous book sitting alone on a desert island if he had to. As his agent, she didn't want him to forget that. His editor's name was Hannah Frye, and Hailey had never met her. She rarely left her house, according to Phillip, and he kept her busy. He always said she was like a mother to him, or a terrific aunt.

The weekend with Phillip and her children was the perfect antidote to the drama in the office on Friday, with Dan's arrest. She and Phillip had talked about it on Friday night, and again on Sunday. It was a shocking revelation, and once Dan was formally charged, it was going to be even more dramatic for the agency. She knew how upset Bob was about it, both personally and professionally. While they were playing in the park, she knew that Dan was in jail for the weekend. The arraignment was set for Monday, when the judge would decide whether to set bail and set him free pending trial or keep him incarcerated.

"What do you think they'll do?" Phillip asked her.

"I have no idea. I know Bob got him a lawyer, but I don't know how they decide whether to let someone out on bail." Phillip knew some of that from his books but had never known anyone personally who went to jail, or was accused of the kind of crimes that Dan had committed. They both knew that twenty years ago, he might not even have been arrested. Now it was a very different story. Women's rights to be treated respectfully, and not be sexually harassed or molested, were being heavily defended, and their abusers punished severely for their transgressions, both by the law and in their professional lives.

Phillip only stayed for a short time after they got back from the park. He said he had some work to do, and she wanted to get the kids cleaned up, give them an early dinner, do some homework with Arianna that they hadn't finished, and put them all to bed. Then she was going to curl up on the couch and read his manuscript. He could hardly wait to hear her reaction to it. He had discussed it with her, but she hadn't read any of it yet. She would be the first to do so. He hadn't even dropped off a copy to Hannah, his editor, yet.

The evening sped by as she read it, and she was about a third through the book when she finally put it down and went to bed, only because she had to get up in the morning. It was one of those books that she would have read straight through the night if she didn't have work and kids to get to school in the morning. She sent him a text before she went to bed, telling him how much she was loving it.

Predictably, when Hailey got to the agency in the morning, the atmosphere was somber and subdued. She heard from Merriwether that Dan's arraignment was set for ten o'clock that morning. Jane didn't have to be there, only the attorneys and the defendant. But Bob had gone to lend him moral support anyway. Jane was still wondering if she was going to be fired for bringing charges against him. There was a terrible, awkward moment in the courtroom when Martha had turned around, as though sensing Bob in the room, and her eyes met her husband's several rows behind her. Martha was sitting at the prosecutor's table with the assistant district attorney, who was a friend of hers and had been assigned to the case, and Steve Franklin, her associate who was Jane's attorney. They would be filing a civil case too, for damages. She wanted to observe the proceedings, even though she couldn't be Jane's attorney. She also knew the defense attorney, the man whom Bob had managed to hire for Dan. And she knew from Bob over the weekend that Dan's wife, Rita, had said that if he was allowed out on bail, she did not want him back at their home on Long Island. He would have to find somewhere else to stay. Their marriage had been bad for years, and this was the last straw for her. She said that he had slept with half of the women on Long Island, and all of New York. They lived under the same roof but barely spoke to each other. It had been that way for years. Their daughters didn't get along with him either. He was persona non grata in his own home now. It made Martha wonder if he had ever sexually molested any of his daughters' friends. It was possible, given how he behaved.

Bob had let the defense attorney know that he was in the courtroom, in case they needed someone to vouch for Dan in order to get the judge to set bail. Dan's lawyer thanked him and said he didn't think it would be necessary.

Dan's was the first case the judge heard that morning, and the purpose of the arraignment was to record how Dan pled to the charges: guilty or not guilty. It was mostly a formality. And after this, the assistant district attorney would prepare the case to submit to the grand jury, to decide if it would go to trial. And the judge was going to decide on bail. Dan's lawyer stood up next to him when his name was called, and Dan pled not guilty, which didn't surprise Bob. He expected it. Then both attorneys approached the bench to discuss bail. The assistant district attorney wanted Dan to remain in custody until trial. Dan's attorney strenuously objected.

"My client is sixty-four years old, Your Honor. He has a heart condition and is on medication," which was news to Bob, but didn't surprise him. "He's not a flight risk. He has a home, a wife, and a business. He's not going anywhere. He's very involved in the community, and a respected citizen. I would ask that he be released on his own recognizance, but he's willing to post bail." The assistant district attorney looked furious, and gave powerful arguments against it, saying that Dan was a menace to society and particularly to young women. The judge looked unhappy as he considered it, and agreed to set bail at three hundred thousand dollars, which wasn't a problem for Dan. The judge then spoke so that the defendant could hear him clearly.

"You are not to leave the city, Mr. Fletcher, is that clear?"

"Yes, Your Honor," Dan said in a subdued tone. It meant that he couldn't go to their summer and weekend home in the Berkshires in Massachusetts, or their home on Long Island. His wife didn't want him there anyway. So he'd have to stay in the city. He could afford to stay at a hotel, or he could stay at his friend's apartment on Central Park West.

Jane's attorney requested a restraining order to keep him away from her, which the judge explained to him. "You are not to approach, go near, or have any form of exchange or communicate with the victim," the judge told Dan. "If I find out that you have, or have broken any other condition of your being released on bail, I will put you back in jail until trial. Is that clear?"

"Yes, Your Honor." The judge rapped his gavel then, confirming the three-hundred-thousand-dollar bail, and moved on to the next case. Dan had to go back to the jail to wait for the paperwork to be handled. Bob took care of it for him, and posted the bail. He knew that Dan would reimburse him, and it sped up the process since he was there.

Twenty minutes later, Dan was back on the street with Bob, looking like himself again.

"Thanks, Bob. I'll write you a check. I don't have my checkbook with me."

"I'm not worried about it," Bob said calmly, but still looking upset by the situation. Martha hadn't looked at him again before he left the courtroom, and she was conferring with the prosecutor when he did. He was sure that she wasn't happy they had let him out on bail, and Jane wouldn't be either.

"Where are you going to stay?" Bob asked him.

"I have a place I can stay in the city," Dan said confidently. He looked cocky as he said it, and definitely not remorseful, which Bob found very disturbing.

"Have you spoken to Rita?" Bob asked him, concerned about his wife. Dan shrugged and didn't answer the question.

"I'm going to the place where I'll be staying to clean up. The jail was filthy," he said, as though it was an accident that he had been there.

"Take it easy," Bob said, then left him outside the courthouse and took a cab to the agency. Merriwether came to see him in his office as soon as he returned.

"How was it?" she asked, with sympathy for Bob in her eyes.

"Incredibly depressing to watch someone you know go through that process. They let him out on three hundred thousand dollars bail. The judge means business. Rita won't let him come home, which has been a long time coming, and he can't leave the city anyway. I just hope he doesn't drink himself to death while he waits for trial, or get into more trouble. Apparently, he's got a heart condition." Merriwether nodded. It all sounded grim to her too.

Bob then took a folded-up newspaper out of his briefcase and said he had a matter to discuss with Allie, and Merriwether went back to her own office to work.

Martha had already called Jane by then to tell her the results of the arraignment, and that Dan was out on bail but had been strictly forbidden to have any contact with her. She told Jane to call her on her cell if she had any problem with him. Jane promised she would, but didn't expect to. He'd have to be insane to approach her again. He wasn't crazy, just a disgusting old man.

Bob Benson walked into Allie's office with a serious expression and the newspaper in his hand. Allie looked up from her computer.

"How'd it go?" she asked him.

"As expected. He's out on bail. But that's not why I'm here." He unfolded the tabloid and laid it on her desk. It was the one with the photo of her and Eric on the cover. "This isn't going to fly," he said simply.

"What does that mean?" Allie asked him, frowning.

"It means that a partner in this agency is being charged with attempted rape and assorted other charges, one of our biggest clients was charged with the rape of a minor last week, and if the head of the dramatic department is now going to start sleeping with clients, people are going to think this is Sodom and Gomorrah and we have no morals whatsoever."

"First of all, you don't know if I'm sleeping with him or not. The photo shows us fully dressed and getting into a cab, not having sex in the back seat. And what I do in my private life is none of your damn business. Eric and I have been seeing each other for a while. It's the first time the press noticed us. And the only reason they did is because Alan Singer and Elizabeth Fox were having dinner there and the press were after them, not me and Eric."

"Give it a few months. Once his new series starts, he'll be as big as they are. Should I point out to you that, first of all, he's a client of the agency, and, second of all, he's twenty years younger than you are."

"Seventeen," she corrected him, "and no, you should not point that out. It's none of your goddamn business who I date or what I do after hours." Their age difference was even less Bob's business.

"In real time, that might be true. But right now, we need to look respectable," Bob insisted. "You can sleep with whomever you want in normal times, but right now, it looks like shit for the agency and for you." He had raised his voice and so had she. "It's going to hurt your career, Allie. It makes you look like you're not serious about it, that you're just screwing around. And ultimately, it will hurt the agency too. You don't care about this guy. You're just playing. That's what you always do. I know you've had affairs with other clients, and normally, I wouldn't say anything. I never did before, but now I am. You need to give this up before it's all over the tabloids, with you and us looking like shit."

"I'm not going to," she said coldly. This time was different. She really did care about Eric, no matter how much younger he was.

"I can't force you to. But I'm asking you."

"I'm not going to stop seeing him. I happen to care about him a great deal."

"I'll believe that when you're still seeing him in a month," Bob said angrily. "And we both know that's not going to happen. He's a toy for you, and you're playing with fire, with your reputation and ours. No one is going to take you seriously if this gets out right now. I really want you to stop seeing him."

"I'm not going to. I'm not giving him up." She stood up at her desk then, stared at her boss with a victorious expression, and dropped the tabloid in the trash where it belonged. They were just going to have to be more careful. But she was not going to let Bob Benson dictate the fate of her relationship. On principle, if nothing else. Allie was furious when he left, and she hated what he'd said: that no one would take her seriously after this. She was a very serious agent. What fucking business did he have saying all that to her, that she and Eric couldn't date? She was one of the best agents in the business, and got great roles for her clients. She was steaming.

* * *

While Bob was arguing with Allie in her office, Dan had walked in and gone to his own office at the opposite end of the floor and no one had noticed. He took his checkbook out of his desk and wrote Bob a check for what he owed him, and then walked into Jane's office with his checkbook in his hand. By sheer bad luck, she was alone and jumped a foot when she saw him. She stood up and backed away as though she'd seen a ghost.

"Don't act like you're so lily pure and terrified of me," he said. "We both know what you are, now what's your price?"

"For what?"

"To clean up this mess you made and tell them you were lying? What's the price for that? Ten thousand? Twenty?" He didn't want to go too high and whet her appetite. "Twenty-five? I'll write you a check right now, and we can clean this whole thing up."

"No, we can't," she said, feeling stronger. "You can't buy me off. You can't treat people like that. I'm a human being, and you can't grab me whenever you want to, like I'm a piece of meat."

"Isn't that what you are? You're not a virgin. All I did was grab a little ass, and you act like I was trying to kill you. It was just some fun between friends. I could show you a good time, you know, and maybe a few tricks of the trade you don't know yet."

"Get out of my office," she said in a raw voice, "or I'll call the police. The judge said you can't come near me. My lawyer told me so."

"Martha, that bitch, and her flunky. How much?" He walked toward her and she was afraid he'd try to kill her. "How much, bitch?"

"Nothing. I don't want your money." He was two feet away from her, advancing toward her menacingly, when Bob walked past her office on the way to Merriwether's to tell her what had happened with Allie. He walked into Jane's office as soon as he saw Dan.

"Dan, what the hell are you doing here? Get away from her right now, or you're going to wind up back in jail."

Dan gave a start and turned around to face him. "We were just doing a little business," he said, with his checkbook still in his hand.

"No, we weren't," Jane said clearly. It was like a nightmare and she couldn't wake up. It was continuing. "He tried to bribe me to drop the charges, and I'm not going to."

"I understand," Bob said, trying to appear calmer than he felt. "Dan, come to my office. Now, please." Dan looked like a thwarted child. He sat down in one of the chairs and looked up at Bob when he got to his office.

"I figured she'd want the money," Dan said, upset.

"Her father is one of the richest venture capitalists in the country. If he knew what you did to her, he'd put you in jail himself. You'll be lucky if she hasn't told him yet. For chrissake, you heard what the judge said, if you go near her, he'll put you in jail until the trial. Stay away from her, for God's sake!" He was shouting as Dan handed him the check for the bail money, and Bob sat down in the chair across from him, looking defeated and trying to calm down. "Please, Dan, for heaven's sake, take this seriously. You're in enough trouble as it is. You can't come back to the office."

"Why not?" He looked surprised, and Bob groaned. Dan just didn't get that he couldn't do whatever he wanted.

"Because you can't go near her, for one thing. And for another, the agency is on shaky ground. One of our biggest clients has been charged with rape, and now you with this mess. We're going to lose all credibility. Do you want to destroy the agency?"

"Of course not," he said, finally contrite. "We have to get her to drop the charges, though. I didn't realize who her father is. Clifford Addison?"

"Exactly," Bob said. "I went to Princeton with him. And she's not going to drop the charges. You genuinely traumatized her."

"That's bullshit. None of these little sluts are innocent."

"You can't treat women the way you do. And you can't come back to the office until this is over, and you're acquitted or you make some kind of deal with the court or the district attorney's office. I cannot and will not have you here. It will destroy our reputation and any credibility we have left. Give me a break on this, Dan, and be reasonable. It's hard enough as it is." Dan thought about it for a minute and nodded.

"All right, but what am I going to do if I don't come to work?" he said, sounding pathetic.

"I don't know. Play golf, sleep, go to the movies. Don't go out and get drunk. But you can't come here."

"I get it. Give me a few minutes to wrap up some loose ends."

"All right," Bob said, looking stressed, "but don't go anywhere near Jane, or she'll call the cops on you and you'll be back in jail."

"I won't. I promise. And give me a call sometime, will you?"

"Of course. Now do whatever you need to do, and then go. You really shouldn't be here."

"Fine," Dan said, then stood up and walked out of Bob's office. It had been a hellish morning. Dan walked back to his office and took a few things out of his desk and put them in a briefcase he had in his office closet, and then walked down the hall, in the opposite direction of Jane's, until he reached Francine's office. She jumped at her desk when she saw him, and he took two steps in and closed the door behind him. With the door closed, no one could see that he was there.

"What are you doing here?" she asked him, physically frightened of him for the first time.

"I came to see you," he said with a tone of irony and an arrogant smirk on his face. "Don't forget, tonight at seven o'clock." It hadn't even occurred to her that it was one of the two nights she usually saw him. She had thought he was gone forever, or out of her life anyway. "And don't think our deal is over. I can still get you fired. Nothing has changed." It was wishful thinking on his part. Everything had changed. His face suddenly looked vicious as he stared at her. "And if you say anything to anyone about our meetings, I swear, Francine, I'll kill you. Don't even think of doing what that little bitch did. We have history together. You should have some loyalty to me for that. You've kept your job here, and you're the head of the department, thanks to me. And you just got a raise. All thanks to me."

"I'm not coming back," she said coldly. She couldn't do it anymore. "Fire me if you want to. I don't care. And whatever you say about me, no one will believe you now."

"Remember, if you talk, you die," he said evilly. "See you at seven." He needed some release from the stress he was under, and she was the easiest way to get it. She didn't have a rich daddy or a husband to protect her. She had two kids and no husband. She needed him, he told himself as he walked out of her office and went back to Bob's.

"I'm leaving now," he said in a docile tone to Bob. He smiled, and looked like the man Bob knew, worked with, and trusted for so many years. Dan was carrying his briefcase, and Bob felt sorry for him again as he walked Dan to the door of the agency. He had gotten himself in one hell of a mess, and dragged the agency into the mud with him. Bob was worried that Dan's actions would take the agency down. He went back to his office with his head down, thinking about it after Dan left. He hoped Dan would be okay, but he had hard times ahead, and Bob couldn't see a way out for him. What he had done was unquestionably terrible, but Bob didn't want to lose his own life's work because of it. Dan had had no idea how out of line he was. Bob had warned him before. He felt sorry for Jane too. He owed her father an apology, but he wasn't sure he knew yet, or if she was going to tell him. Bob was going to talk to her about it but hadn't had time. There was so much going on.

After Dan left her office, Francine tried to sit quietly and calm down. He had looked so menacing and so convincing when he said he'd kill her. What if he tried? What would happen to her kids? And, if he succeeded? She couldn't let him get away with it. He had no right to terrorize her. She had let him ruin ten years of her life. She couldn't afford to give him another day, another month, another year. She got up from her desk and walked down the hall to Jane's office. Julia was in with Hailey, and Jane was alone. She was still recovering from Dan's brief visit herself.

She looked up when she heard Francine come in.

"Did you see that that bastard was here?" Jane said, looking stressed.

"Sign me up" was all Francine said, with an odd expression. Her eyes were dark pools of pain as she looked at Jane.

"For what?" Jane didn't understand.

"Sign me up. Me too. He got me too," Francine said, and Jane stared at her, shocked.

"You too?" He had gone after the head of the literary division? She wasn't just some little flunky he could push around the way he thought he could Jane. "Do you want to talk to my attorney?" Jane asked her, and Francine nodded. She looked like she was in a daze.

"Yes, I do." Jane called Steve while Francine waited, and she turned to her after she hung up.

"He said he can see you now." Jane wrote down the address on a piece of paper and handed it to her. "Do you want me to come with you?"

"No, I'll be okay," she said, and smiled at Jane. "I'm sorry it happened to you, but at least you stopped him. He just told me he'd kill me if I talk. He looked as though he meant it. We'll be okay, won't we?"

"Yes, we will," Jane said, and got up to hug her. "They'll probably put him back in jail after you talk to Steve. They'll keep him there until the trial. And then he'll go to prison. Martha said there probably won't be a trial. He'll have to plead guilty. There's too much evidence against him. And now with you, he's done." Francine nodded, and walked out of Jane's office. She got her jacket and coat and went to the lawyer.

She told Steve everything. All the years, all the times, twice a week for ten years, using her like a sex slave, threatening to have her fired and to destroy her reputation if she stopped meeting him, all the way to his threats to kill her that morning if she talked. Her story was far more disturbing than Jane's, which included only a few incidents, and he hadn't succeeded in raping Jane, just in terrifying her. Steve took due note of the fact that Francine thought that he had drugged her with something in her drink the first time, which was probably true. He asked her if anyone knew that she went there every week. She said that Allie had alluded to her "dating the boss" a few times, so maybe he had said something to her, putting a spin on it. But she said that the doorman at the building where they met could testify that she had gone there twice every week, and that he knew her by now. Martha wrote down the address of the apartment. She was sure that Bob would know where Dan was staying now, since he couldn't go home. Maybe he was staying there.

Martha took Francine to the police station, as she had Jane, and then Martha called the assistant district attorney and reported it to him, along with Dan's threats to kill Francine and his attempt to bribe Jane that morning, which violated the conditions of his bail. The assistant district attorney assured her that by that night, he'd be back in jail and stay there until disposition of the case, whether a guilty plea or trial. But either way, he wouldn't be out again, maybe ever.

Steve had told Francine that he would be filing a civil suit for her as well, for the trauma and emotional damage she had suffered for ten years, and how it had impacted every area of her life. Dan could well afford any damages the court awarded her. Francine couldn't even think of that yet, she just wanted to know that he was off the streets and that she and her children were safe.

* * *

Steve called Francine at seven o'clock. They had picked Dan up at the apartment on Central Park West. This time, they had taken him out in handcuffs. He had cried when they took him back to jail, but Steve didn't tell her that.

"You can sleep peacefully tonight, Francine," Steve told her in a kind voice. "You don't ever have to worry about him again. He's gone, and he won't be coming back."

Martha called Bob and told him that Dan was back in custody. He was still at the office, conferring with Merriwether again about how to handle the press once the story hit the papers, because it would.

"Did Jane call and tell them he tried to bribe her?" Bob asked his wife in a saddened voice when he heard the news.

"I can't discuss that with you, but we had new evidence today, from another victim. Two, in fact." Julia had called Steve too, about Dan assaulting her in the past.

"Oh my God, who? Anyone I know?" He hoped it wouldn't be.

"Francine, in your office. And Julia, Hailey's executive assistant." There were tears in his eyes when she told him. He had felt sorry for Dan before, but not anymore. He had done damage to so many people, and to the agency that Bob had worked so hard to build.

"The agency will never survive this," he said grimly.

"Yes, it will. You have a great staff, and you all do a terrific job for your clients. And you have had an immaculate reputation until now. In the long run, that will outweigh all this miserable stuff with Dan. You just have to batten down the hatches and ride out the storm," she encouraged him. "It may be a rough time, but I know you'll

weather it. I'll see you at home," she said, and hung up. He was crying when he ended the call, for all of them. Jane, Francine, Julia, and
even for himself. He had no tears left for Dan.

Allie was still angry when she got home from work that night. She
told Eric about it when he came back from the gym.

"Do they have an official policy about not dating clients?" he asked
her.

"Of course not. Everybody does that at some point. It happens.
Francine doesn't. I think she's been depressed for ten years since her
divorce, so she didn't date anyone. And Hailey has no time because
of her kids. But I know some of the other agents do date clients. Merriwether is married and she's crazy about her husband, so that leaves
me. I think he's just sensitive right now, because of the mess with
Dan." They talked about that then. She didn't know Dan was back in
jail. Or that Francine and Julia had made statements. The news of
that was too recent.

"Do you think we should cool it for a while? Or go underground
and not be seen in public together? I don't want you to lose your job
because of me," Eric told her seriously.

"No, I don't think any of those things. To hell with them. This is
our business, and no one else's. They can't tell me who I can and
can't date."

"You're sure?" He worried about her.

"Totally," she said with confidence. The one thing that worried her
was Bob telling her that this would diminish her credibility in the
business. She didn't see how that could happen, but her priority had

always been her career, and she didn't want to sacrifice that for romance now. But she loved Eric, and wasn't willing to give him up and stop dating him. He was the first man she had cared about that way in years, maybe ever. She didn't want to lose him now. Not even for her career. She hoped Bob was wrong about that.

They forgot about it after a while and made love as passionately as ever. There was no way she was going to give him up.

Chapter 9

Bob had lain awake all night, thinking about Dan, now that he knew he was back in jail and would stay there. His bond would be returned to him, but Dan had ruined what was left of his life. It was unlikely he'd be free again, unless his attorney could make a deal with the district attorney and he pled guilty. Maybe they would shorten his sentence if he did. The only other possibility was if the women who had accused him dropped the charges, but he couldn't see that happening either.

After a sleepless night, he decided to talk to his wife about it before they both left for the city, to go to work. He took the train and she drove every day. She didn't want to be tied to train schedules and she claimed that she enjoyed the drive. It gave her time to think. She only took the train when the weather was really awful, making it too dangerous to drive.

Martha saw how rough Bob looked when she came down to breakfast. Their youngest son had already left for school. He had early football practice, so they were alone in the kitchen. Bob looked at her miserably, and decided to broach the subject. All she could do was refuse.

"I was thinking last night that there is only one way out of this for Dan," he said with a morbid expression, and she looked shocked.

"I hope not. That would be a terrible thing to do to his wife and daughters, no matter how angry they are at him." She assumed that Bob meant suicide.

"That's not what I had in mind," he corrected her.

"Oh. I do think Rita will divorce him for it, though. Their marriage has been dead for years. I think this will be the coup de grâce. I can't say I blame her. He must have a screw loose or he's getting senile to have gone around threatening women if they wouldn't have sex with him. I can't see the satisfaction in that."

"Martha, you've got to get them to drop the charges," he said, looking desperate. "It's the only way out for him, and it will save the agency too."

"Are you insane? He doesn't deserve a way out. He deserves to go to prison for what he did."

"I know. In a real sense, that's true. But he didn't actually rape Jane. He's sixty-four years old, he's sick, and maybe he is getting senile."

"He has impacted the lives of three of your employees, and maybe others we don't know about yet. How can you suggest they drop the charges?" she said coldly.

Bob was shocked into silence by what she said, but he wanted to find some way to save the agency. He was so distraught he wasn't thinking clearly. "He *has* to go to prison, Bob. Maybe if he confesses, they'll give him less time, but I doubt it. It's much too serious to let him off the hook. He's incredibly foolish if he tries to go to trial. No decent attorney will let him take this to trial. A jury would kill him." Bob nodded. He knew Martha was right. He wanted to rewind the film and cut this part out. He still couldn't believe it was happening. "It shows you how little we know people sometimes. I always thought he was an asshole about women, I never thought he was as sick and vicious as this. Any lawyer defending those women is going to recommend the maximum sentence for his crimes," she said matter-of-factly.

"Why do you always have to be so harsh about everything, and so black-and-white. Where's your compassion?"

"My compassion is with the women he assaulted, physically and emotionally. Even Jane will be marked by this. None of them will emerge from this unscathed."

"Prison will kill him."

"He should have thought of that before he committed the crimes. It's time to honor the women whose lives have been impacted by men like him. Dan is a terrible guy, whatever the reason for it. You have to accept that."

"Prison won't change that. I just hate to see him die there. I think that's what will happen to him. If none of the other prisoners kill him, which is a possibility in a case like this, his health will get him. He called me crying last night."

"That's appropriate. I listen to women cry every day. A guy like Dan Fletcher doesn't deserve to be free. Personally, I think that given the chance, he'd do it again."

"I hope they put him in a decent prison."

"That's up to the judge," she said without emotion in her voice, and it irked her that Bob was so desperate to help him. She thought it was carrying friendship too far, in a case like this. He was also trying to save his own hide and the agency, which she could understand even if she didn't agree. "I'm not sorry for him," she said again as she put their breakfast dishes in the sink. "What about us?" she said to him suddenly. "Is there any point continuing this marriage? We have nothing in common anymore. There's nothing we agree on. Our kids are pretty much grown up. Wesley is leaving for college in the fall." He had been accepted at Princeton, like his father before him, and his grandfather. "Sometimes I wonder why we're still married."

"We love each other, we're family," he said weakly. He couldn't disagree with what she said, but he couldn't deal with a divorce on top of everything else. Martha had a cold, dispassionate way of looking at things. She didn't used to be that way. She had been a warm, loving woman, and even passionate when they got married. Somehow life had beaten it out of both of them. They lived together like brother and sister. He hid at the agency and had for years. He never came home until everyone was asleep. He had been an absentee father for most of his boys' lives, staying in town to have dinner with important authors and big movie stars. In a way, he had had a glamorous life, and she had never been a part of it. She was too busy with her law practice to participate in his life and he had never wanted her to. He wanted to keep his family and his business separate, and in the end, he wound up married to his business and no longer to her.

"Sometimes I think we'd both be happier if we were divorced," Martha said clearly. "You might find someone who suits you better and makes you feel young again."

"Is that what you want?" he asked her.

"I'm happy with my work, my friends, our boys, and a peaceful life. We live in this house like strangers. What'll we do when Wesley leaves? We won't have anything to talk about, if we even see each other." He had the feeling that she was pushing him away, and he had already done that to her in his own way. The feelings between them had died a long time ago. They had both been careless with their marriage, and hadn't protected or nurtured it. Now it lay at their feet like a dog or a plant that had died, or any living thing they had ignored and hadn't bothered to feed or water. He had no idea how to fix it, and she didn't seem to care. She was no longer the woman he had married. She hadn't been for years. He had changed too. He had more to say to Merriwether every day, and he enjoyed it. She was alive and fun, and as unhappy in her marriage as he was in his. She was still hoping there was something she could do to revive it, and their little girl was still very young, but his marriage to Martha seemed to be beyond salvation. It was like trying to breathe life into a corpse that had been dead for years, and she was much more willing to admit it than he was.

"How did we wind up here?" he asked.

"We both worked too hard. We went in separate directions. We forgot about each other and focused on our work. We didn't talk to each other about anything that mattered. We came home late at night, separately. We did everything that people shouldn't do, and we thought we'd get away with it, and we'd fix the damage later. There comes a point where there's nothing left to fix. I think we're about there," she said. She had always been honest with him, sometimes too much so. He didn't dare ask her if she still loved him because he knew the answer, she didn't. He could see it in her eyes every time he looked at her, and he was no longer sure that he loved her. It was hard to measure.

He walked her outside to her car, and then watched her drive away. It was a lonely feeling, standing there, watching her. He was sure that she must be just as lonely in their marriage as he was. She had been lonely with him for years. She had allowed it to linger, they both had, and neither of them had had the courage to end it.

He was still thinking about it as he rode the train to New York. He wondered if Martha was too, or if she had put that aside, gone to work, and was now engrossed in what she was doing for the day.

He didn't see the answer right in front of his face. When he walked through the agency to his office and Merriwether walked into his office a few minutes later, his face lit up like Christmas, and so did hers. He hadn't felt that way about Martha in years, if ever.

Within days of the first photograph the paparazzi took of them, Eric and Allie became the hot item and the most fun to pursue. They were both good-looking people. He was a star growing in size and brightness, and she was a big-deal agent. They looked great, they were having fun, and the press had fun chasing them down and trying to get a story out of it. There was no story. They just loved each other, and were living day to day. But the pressure of having to deal with the paparazzi constantly was wearing on both of them, and Bob Benson's words that it would kill her career were still ringing in Allie's ears. That was the one thing that frightened her the most, and Bob knew it. It was like a bomb he had dropped down her smokestack to explode everything at a later date.

A week after Dan went back to jail, Francine walked into Bob's office, and dropped another bomb on him he didn't expect. She had made a decision and acted quickly. With Dan in jail and totally discredited in the industry, no one would believe a word he said, and he could do her no harm. He could no longer cost her her job or reputation. His threats were empty. The vile serpent he was had been defanged and her own prison walls, built by him, came tumbling down. She was free. She told Bob she had realized that it would never be the same for her again at the agency. The specter of Dan would be there for her forever. She had lived through ten years of torture almost since her first day on the job. And now everyone knew it. Even if they sympathized with her, she didn't want to live with the curiosity and the humiliation, the gossip and the pity. She had called a headhunter when Dan went back to jail and was shocked at how quickly they had lined up interviews for her. Her credentials, history, and client roster were flawless. She had thought of going back into publishing as a senior editor, but couldn't afford to with college on the horizon for Thalia. She needed a job that paid at least as much as the one she had. They found her a better one at a rival agency that was thrilled to have her. It was exactly what she had always said she didn't want, but it was perfect for her now. It was in the literary department of one of the big impersonal, factory-like agencies that she had always avoided because she didn't want to get lost in the crowd. But that was exactly what she wanted now: to get lost and become anonymous, where no one would remember that she was one of Dan Fletcher's victims, and possibly the most damaged one.

The salary was higher than any she'd ever made, and would make life easier for her and her kids. The new agency's list of clients was excellent, and she had a suspicion that two or three of her important writers would go with her, much to Bob's chagrin.

They wanted her to start in two weeks and she had agreed. It was too painful for her to stay now. Everyone felt sorry for her, she could see it on their faces and in their eyes.

She gave Bob two weeks' notice, and he nearly fell out of his chair when she did. She was the head of the literary department and he relied on her. She ran it efficiently with military precision, paid close attention to every one of her clients, and kept a watchful eye on the younger agents, who represented less important writers. He didn't see how he could manage without her. His only option was to put Hailey in Francine's job, but he wasn't sure that she was ready for it. Francine had more experience. Hailey managed beautifully as second-in-command, but being head of the department was a much bigger job. He begged Francine not to leave, but she had made up her mind. She didn't feel that she could do a good job anymore where she was, with a dark cloud hanging over all ten years of her employment. It was too heavy a burden to carry. And she was excited about her new job. She was going to look for a new apartment in Manhattan. In desperation, Bob offered Francine a sizable increase if she would stay. It was less than the other agency was offering her, and what she really wanted was a fresh start in a new place. She declined Bob's offer and apologized for the abrupt change. She felt she couldn't stay.

Bob was panicked when he talked to Merriwether about it. More than ever, she had become his chief adviser and his most trusted employee and friend. Together, they had also decided to take Dan's name off the agency. They were going to call it Benson Associates, and hoped that people would forget quickly that Dan had ever been a part of it. Bob was trying to bring a fresh look and feeling to the agency, while maintaining stability, which was hard to do with Francine leaving on such short notice.

Merriwether came up with an idea to boost morale. She said they needed some kind of happy event to bring them together and raise spirits, which would be an even bigger challenge once everyone knew that Francine was leaving.

Bob decided to make Jane a full-fledged agent, under Hailey's supervision. It was early to do so, but she was doing well, and had a good eye for new authors. She had already suggested three to them, and Hailey and Francine both agreed with her choices. Bob and Merriwether both felt she would grow into the job. And he made Hailey head of the department. It was a big responsibility for her, and a big decision to accept it, knowing the time it would take from her life at home and her kids. Bob offered her a big raise she couldn't afford to refuse. It would make a big difference for her kids.

Merriwether suggested having Bob host a staff barbecue at his house in Greenwich. They all needed something fun to look forward to. Francine's announcement that she was leaving cast a pall on all of them, and the staff was touched by the invitation to a party at Bob's home. He put Merriwether in charge of the party and told Martha what he planned to do. She was going to be out of town for a golf tournament in Jamaica, so the timing seemed perfect. She had no desire to be there. Hailey invited Phillip to go with her, and he thought it was brave of Bob to host the event. Through Hailey, he had heard all the details of the upheaval at the agency. Jane invited Benjie. He wasn't happy about her promotion, because he knew it meant he would see even less of her, but she was on a career path now, and nothing was going to stop her.

The party was scheduled for the week after Francine left. Francine's departure was silent and discreet. It was very emotional for her the day she left but it was a relief too, the nightmare was truly over. Bob, Merriwether, Hailey, and Allie came to say goodbye, walked out with her, and hugged her. She took nothing with her. She threw everything away.

Bob had invited Francine to the barbecue, and she decided not to go. Her time in their midst was over, and she wanted to put it behind her.

Allie had invited Eric to come too, but he was nervous about it because he knew Bob was upset that he and Allie were still dating. Eric didn't want a confrontation with him. And by sheer bad luck, the paparazzi were still hot on their trail, and they were in the tabloids every day that week. No matter what they did, they couldn't get away from the photographers who were following them to the gym, the dry cleaner, and the grocery store. They couldn't go out for a meal. Bob was particularly annoyed when the tabloids called her "Eric Clay's high-flying, gadabout agent girlfriend."

"You expect our clients to take you seriously, or the casting directors you're sending our clients to?" Bob said angrily, pointing at one of the papers. "You're single-handedly destroying your career, Allie, for a twenty-six-year-old kid you won't be dating six months from now. This is insanity. He must be fabulous in bed for you to risk everything you've built here."

"I'm not risking anything. I'm dating a man I love. We're not out doing drugs and going crazy. We go to the gym and stay home at night. They'll get bored with us." But they hadn't so far. It created tension in the relationship and Bob was harping on her constantly that she was throwing her career out the window. She and Eric had a terrible fight about it one night. He said the same thing, and that he didn't want to be responsible for destroying her career. Eventually she'd hate him for it. They'd both been drinking, and he'd had a stressful week in rehearsal for his series. He wasn't getting along with his leading lady, and he took it out on Allie. In a burst of flame, Allie said fine, why didn't they break up, if he was so worried about her career. Not risking her career had finally won the argument. Afterwards, she wasn't sure if it was what he had wanted, or what she did. They both ended up in tears, and he went back to his apartment that night. He hadn't slept there in months and couldn't even find sheets to put on the bed, and he didn't come back to Allie's in the morning. He was devastated, and so was she.

She sent him a text in the morning, and didn't go to the gym because she was too hung over and didn't want to see him.

"Are we broken up?" she asked him by text. He took an hour to respond, being equally hung over and feeling sick about the fight the night before, but he had said he thought it was better for her. She had spent twenty years building her career as an agent, and he didn't want to be the one to destroy that for her. He knew how much it meant to her. He figured Bob Benson was right. He was crying when he answered her.

"Looks like it to me. Do you want me to find a new agent?"

"Whatever," she answered, and spent the rest of the day in tears, heartbroken over their breakup.

The barbecue in Greenwich was the next day. She wasn't going to go, she was too upset about Eric, but Hailey called her and said she had to. Allie told her that she and Eric had broken up, and she was in no shape to go anywhere. Hailey said that as head of the department, Allie had to show up and put a good face on it, for Bob's sake. So she booked a car and driver, and took a Xanax before she went. She was in a daze by the time she got there, and started drinking as soon as she arrived. Everyone at the agency had shown up and there was an atmosphere of celebration after weeks of mourning. Merriwether was right. It was what they all needed. Jeff had come with her, and looked like he was sulking. He was convinced that her job was destroying their marriage, when in fact he had done most of the damage himself.

Merriwether looked beautiful in a white lace dress, and everyone had made an effort to show up and look festive.

Jane and Benjie had come with Phillip and Hailey, and they had a good time on the drive. It was the first fun Jane had had since her encounter with Dan Fletcher, and all the fallout ever since. She had had thousands of responses to her Wanted poster with Dan's photograph on it on Instagram. Dan was in jail, determined to go to trial. She wasn't looking forward to it. In the era of social media, the entire world knew every detail of what had happened. She had told her parents about it, and they were upset, but her father was glad that she had gone to the police and pressed charges and that Dan would wind up in prison. He had called Bob and discussed it with him, and Bob had been deeply apologetic.

There were waiters circulating at the party with trays of champagne and margaritas. Allie had one of each, and then stuck with the margaritas. She had worn a shocking pink silk dress that was so low cut you could see most of her breasts, and it had a slit up each side. It was the sexiest thing she owned, which she thought would cheer her up after the breakup. But it didn't. Nothing did, and she found herself talking to Benjie as they both lay on deck chairs at the pool. She didn't feel steady enough on her feet to mingle, and she wasn't in the mood. She was wearing six-inch heels, and Benjie said he'd had a lot to drink too, and the margaritas had hit him.

"Yeah, me too," she confessed. "I broke up with my boyfriend two days ago and I feel like shit," she admitted.

"That's too bad. He must be crazy if he let you go," he said, admiring her cleavage and the slits in her dress.

"Thank you," she said, wondering if she should go home. She wasn't having fun, and no one would notice if she left. She spotted a hammock in a back corner behind the pool under a tree, took off her shoes, stood up unsteadily, and told him she was going to lie down for a minute.

"I'll come with you," he volunteered, and then held the hammock for her so she could get in it without falling out. The party was in full swing, with most of the people around the other side of the house where there was Mexican music and dancing. Then Benjie rolled into the hammock with her, and they both nearly fell out as it moved and swayed. She giggled as the hammock rocked. They held on to each other to steady themselves, and he found his hand on her breast without meaning to. She looked at him and didn't stop him, and he slipped his other hand easily into the slit in her dress, and his fingers into her thong. She moaned softly and closed her eyes, but then had to open them again so she didn't get sick. He kissed her, and she arched her body toward him, trying to pretend to herself that it was Eric and not this awkward, drunken boy who belonged to someone else. She didn't care who he belonged to at that moment, he was inside her by then. They both came quickly and it was over within minutes. He wondered where Jane was. He hadn't seen her in a long time. But Allie was too exciting to leave, so they continued lying in the hammock for a while, her dress had slipped below her nipples, and she didn't care. After a while, she noticed Hailey walking toward them. She was looking for someone or something, and Allie waved. The hammock started rocking again, and Benjie hung on to her as Hailey reached them.

"I was looking for you," Hailey said, starting to smile, and then she saw that Allie's dress had slipped, her bare breasts exposed, with Benjie's hand resting on her thigh, and she could guess what had happened. "Are you okay?" Hailey asked her in a low voice, and she shook her head.

"No, I'm not. We're broken up," she said drunkenly as Benjie tried to get out of the hammock, finally managed it, and stood up. He looked at Hailey, coming to his senses a little, and straightened out his clothes.

"I'd better find Jane," he said, and stumbled off.

Allie started to cry. "I'm such a mess. I really love him."

"Benjie?" Hailey looked horrified.

"No, Eric," she said forcefully, and then looked chagrined. "I think I just had sex with Benjie," she whispered, and Hailey looked at her intently.

181

"Allie, listen to me. Don't tell anyone that. Ever. You're out of your mind tonight. Forget that you said it or did it, or whatever happened. You don't want him, and he's Jane's."

"I know." She nodded, lying there. "He's Jane's. She can have him. I don't want him. I want Eric."

"Then go back to him, and don't let Bob bully you into breaking up with him. If you love him, get him back. He loves you too. Don't tell anyone what happened tonight. Not Eric or Jane or anyone. Now let's get you cleaned up so you can go home." She helped Allie get to her feet and pull up her dress. Hailey got the slits of the dress back in the right place and covered Allie's thong again. They found her shoes, and Hailey smoothed down her hair, like a child. Allie thanked her and wrapped her arms around her neck and leaned against her.

"Everything's been so fucked up since Dan left, hasn't it? And Francine left. I never really liked her, but I'm going to miss her. And now you have her job and I love you," Allie mumbled to Hailey.

"I love you too. If I put you in your car, do you think you can get home okay?"

"Yeah, but I might throw up on the drive," she said as Hailey put an arm around her waist and walked her to the parking lot. She had her shoes in her hand.

"Leave the windows open in the car," Hailey told her, and asked one of the valets to find Allie's car and driver, and he pulled up a minute later. He could see the condition she was in and helped her into the car. Hailey put her seat belt on and made sure that he had Allie's address. They pulled away a minute later and Hailey hoped that no one ever found out what had happened that night. She went to find Phillip and saw Benjie sitting in a chair, looking glazed, while Jane danced with a group of young agents.

"Where were you?" Phillip asked her.

"Dealing with a minor problem. Everything's fine now." It wasn't, but at least Allie had left.

"Allie?" he asked her, and she nodded. "She was in bad shape when we arrived. I gather that she and her boyfriend broke up. You look beautiful tonight, by the way." He loved her dress, which was ladylike but just sexy enough.

"So do you." She smiled at him. He had worn white slacks and a white shirt, and a navy blazer. He led her out onto the dance floor. They made a handsome couple, and she noticed that Merriwether was dancing with Bob Benson, and Jeff was hanging out at the bar. They had provided jitneys and cars and drivers for everyone, so they could drink as much as they wanted, and no one had to drive home drunk. She was happy to note that Phillip wasn't drunk, nor was she. She still had to go home to her children, and she had wanted to be helpful to Bob and Merriwether. She was grateful that she had found Allie and Benjie before someone else did, particularly Jane, who didn't seem to care that he was blind drunk. She hadn't even noticed that he'd been gone for a while. She was having fun with her colleagues and loved being a full agent now.

Phillip kissed Hailey for the first time on the dance floor that night, under a full moon. It was the perfect moment, and she forgot everything else while he did—Benjie and Allie and Jane and all the others. She stood smiling at him afterwards, and he kissed her again.

* * *

The party was winding down by the time they left. Benjie was passed out in the front seat of the car and slept all the way back to New York, and Phillip and Hailey and Jane sat in the back seat, talking about how much fun it had been. Merriwether and Bob had done a beautiful job putting it together, and the party had been just what everybody had needed. Bob had spared no expense to cheer up his staff.

The only mishap of the evening had been Allie and Benjie's little escapade in the hammock, and Hailey hoped Jane would never find out.

They dropped Jane and Benjie off first when they got back to the city, and the doorman helped Jane get Benjie inside. Then Phillip took Hailey home, and smiled at her as they walked up the stairs to her apartment together.

"I think we started a new chapter tonight," he said to her, then stopped her on the stairs and kissed her again. "I just wanted you to know that I meant it, and that wasn't an accident on the dance floor. I didn't get carried away by the party, or the margaritas." He smiled at her as they walked the rest of the way to her apartment, and he kissed her again. She had finished his book and had given him notes on it that he was very pleased with, and he was waiting to hear from his editor. She was taking longer than usual. Hailey unlocked the door and he watched her go in with a longing look. They had opened a door that night, and inevitably there would be more to follow, at a later date when her children weren't around. It was something to look forward to.

He looked back up at her window before he got back in the car, and she was standing there, watching him. She waved, he smiled and waved, got back in the car, and he was still smiling when he got home.

Chapter 10

Hailey had just dropped Will off for a playdate on Saturday. She had taken Bentley and Arianna with her. She stopped to buy groceries on the way back, and they each helped her by carrying a bag upstairs. She was about to unpack them, when Phillip called her and he sounded strange.

"Are you okay?" she asked him, and his answer surprised her. He had a tremor in his voice. He sounded deeply shaken.

"No, I'm not. Hannah's daughter just called me from New Orleans. Her mother has been visiting her there for two weeks. Hannah was in the hospital and never told me. She's had leukemia for a year, and didn't want anyone to know. She was feeling worse so she went to be with her daughter, who's a nurse. Hannah passed away last night. She's been working more slowly lately, but I had no idea she was sick." He sounded as if he was in shock. She'd been his editor for his entire career, and he always said she was like a mother to him. It was an immeasurable loss to him. "She was eighty-six years old, but she

was so vital and energetic. I could just never imagine her dying."
Hailey could hear that he was crying, and she felt terrible for him. It
was a double loss for him. He had lost his creative mentor and his
dearest friend. And Hailey knew that editors were all-important to
writers, especially great ones like Hannah. She had been the last of a
dying breed. You never heard about great editors anymore. Now
they were mostly young people with entry-level jobs, who knew little
about the editing process and were more interested in the advance
they paid an author than the quality of the work.

"Oh, Phillip, I'm so sorry. Do you want to come over?"

"I don't know. I think I need to be alone for a little while to absorb
this. Hannah wasn't religious, and she left instructions that she didn't
want a service. There won't even be a funeral. Her daughter is going
to scatter her ashes. She's going to take them to Venice when she has
time. It was Hannah's favorite place." He sounded devastated.

Hailey called to check on him an hour later, and he didn't answer
the phone. He called her back that afternoon, after Hailey had
dropped Arianna off at a friend's. Bentley was catching up on homework in his room, and Hailey had time to talk. She tried to console
Phillip, but she knew how hard this was for him. He felt like the bottom had fallen out of his world.

"I don't even know if I can write without her. She helped me organize my ideas for every book. We talked them through for months
before I'd start. The only other person I've ever shown my early drafts
to is you."

"It's going to take time," she tried to reassure him. "But eventually
you'll find someone you can work with. Maybe not in exactly the
same way, but Phillip, the talent here is you. It's within you. She

didn't write the books, you did." She wanted to remind Phillip of that.

"It won't be the same without her," he said.

"No, it won't, but you'll remember everything she said to you and taught you, and working without her may open up a new dimension to your work." Hailey knew how important the relationship with a long-term, creative editor was for any writer. She had total confidence that his work wouldn't suffer, but she couldn't convince him of it yet.

"I just can't believe she's gone." His reaction reminded her of how she felt when her husband died, leaving her with two young children and a baby. He was only forty-three and it seemed completely unreal to her, but Hannah was exactly twice his age. Phillip had been in denial about the fact that she would die someday. That may have been why Hannah didn't tell him she was sick. Or maybe she didn't want to face it either.

"Bentley's doing homework in his room, and the others are at friends'. Do you want to come over for a cup of tea or a glass of wine, or just sit and talk for a while?"

"Yes, I do," he said, sounding lost.

He came half an hour later, and he looked stressed and pale. Bentley came out of his room to get something to eat, said hi to Phillip as though seeing him there was a regular occurrence, grabbed some cookies and an apple from the kitchen, and went back to his room. Hailey liked the fact that her children were getting used to Phillip, and liked him. It would have been hard to deal with if they didn't. But he had been very nice to them.

Phillip talked about Hannah for a while longer and reminisced about some of the books they'd worked on. Hailey invited him to stay for dinner, but he said he needed some time alone to think, and mourn her. He kissed Hailey when they got to the front door, and he smiled.

"You're the bright ray of sunshine in my life," he said. "You're going to be busy now with Francine leaving, and your big promotion."

"I'll always have time for you, Phillip," she said. "I'm honored that you let me read your work." He nodded, and after kissing her again, he hurried down the stairs. She'd brought some work home that weekend. She was trying to get up to speed on Francine's files. That was going to be a big change in her life too, being head of the literary department now.

She had a text from Allie that afternoon. "Sorry I was such a mess last night." It reminded her of finding Allie with Benjie in the hammock. She just hoped again that Jane never found out. It had been a disturbing scene and a foolish thing to do. If Jane had come looking for them, she would have seen it too. He wasn't the love of Jane's life, but he was the man she had been dating fairly steadily since she had come to New York, and she thought he was faithful to her. Jane was a very direct, honest, clean-cut person. She didn't have Allie's more casual views about sex, and she had had enough upheaval over Dan Fletcher. The last thing she needed was trouble with Benjie now. And Allie was clearly distraught over the breakup with Eric.

Hailey's quiet, slow-burning romance with Phillip was very different from the turmoil and passion in her coworkers' lives, and she was grateful that Phillip was a steady, responsible person too. It helped that he was older. At twenty-six and twenty-nine, neither Eric nor

Benjie was fully mature yet, although Hailey thought Allie should have known better at her age than to have drunken casual sex at an office party. She was playing with fire and someone was likely to get burned. She was leading the life of someone half her age, with very liberal views about sex and relationships.

Hailey was reading one of the manuscripts she'd brought home on Sunday night when Phillip called her. They had exchanged short text messages all day. It was ten o'clock and the children were asleep when she answered. He sounded tense, though less disoriented than he had the day before.

"Can I come over?" he asked her.

"Now?"

"Are you in bed?"

"No, I'm reading on the couch. Are you okay?" She had asked him that dozens of times since the day before when he learned of Hannah's death.

"I think so," he said quietly. "You'll be busy tomorrow." Her workdays were nonstop now with Francine gone. "I'd like to talk to you tonight."

"Okay. Don't ring the buzzer. Text me when you get here and I'll buzz you in. The kids are asleep."

He was there ten minutes later and she buzzed him in. He came up the stairs quickly, and she was waiting for him with the door open. He kissed her lightly and followed her into the apartment. She offered him a glass of red wine, and he accepted and she poured one for herself too. Then they sat down on the couch and spoke in whispers, so they didn't wake the children.

"I've been thinking about it all day," he said after a sip of wine. He looked wide-awake and very tense and earnest. She gently touched his cheek and he smiled. She always had a way of making him feel better and reassuring him.

"It's going to be okay, Phillip." He had had a shock, but she knew he had all the expertise and talent he needed to go on without his longtime editor. He just didn't know it yet. She felt maternal toward all the clients she represented, and particularly Phillip, although their relationship had deepened and changed since they'd been on the tour together and gotten to know each other as more than just writer and agent.

"Maybe this will sound crazy to you, but hear me out," he said nervously. "I want to offer you a job." She looked startled. It wasn't what she had expected him to say.

"What kind of job? I'm happy to read your draft manuscripts. That *is* my job. You don't have to pay me to do that. You pay the agency ten percent of what you earn from your books for my attention and support, and for anything you need me to do with your publisher."

"I know that. I want more than that from you, Hailey. It's unusual, but I know of several writers who've done what I want to suggest to you. I'd like you to become my editor and my agent, and work just for me. I know of at least one famous writer who did that with his editor, when his agent died. And from everything I've heard, it worked really well. The man who became his agent, whom he hired away from his publisher at the time, started his own agency, which is a big success. I'm not suggesting you do that. But I'd like you to work just for me, as my agent and my editor. I think we'd make an amazing team. You were an editor before, and you've had five years' experience as an agent. Hailey, you're perfect for it. You can work from home if you want to, or set up an office elsewhere, however you want to do it. You can decide your own hours, and you'd be at home for your kids. You wouldn't have to deal with all the corporate bullshit, all the agents you're responsible for now, and the writers you don't like working with. It would be what we do now, only just the two of us, and you can hire an assistant if you feel you need one."

"I can manage it myself," she said quietly, trying to absorb what he had said. It was totally unexpected. "Poor Bob will go crazy if he loses me too, with Francine gone." The agency would be on its knees with one partner gone and the two main literary agents leaving, if she left too. Jane was still very new as an agent, and young, although she was a bright girl. But she couldn't handle the department alone. Bob needed a strong, experienced agent to run the department. He'd have to hire one from outside the agency. Allie wasn't in great shape these days on the dramatic side, after her breakup with Eric, although she'd get over it. "I don't know what to say," she responded to Phillip. She wondered if it would complicate things too much now that they had started dating. What if things went wrong? It could be very awkward for both of them. Or incredibly wonderful if their relationship went well and continued to grow. It might turn into a partnership on all fronts, but it was too soon to tell. He could sense what she was thinking.

"We just have to figure things out slowly on the personal side. It seems very positive to me, and we can go at whatever pace you want." She had a lot to deal with, with her children too. His personal life was simpler than hers. She was dedicated to her children. "On the professional side, I know this would be perfect for me. You're already my agent, and your editing is flawless and as good as Hannah's was. You have a younger perspective, which is good for me, and you've been an editor before. Hannah and I had history, but whatever I do, I'll need a new editor now, and I don't want to start with someone brand new. You've been doing it unofficially for a while. I want this to be a lucrative arrangement for you, not just the right one for me." He quoted a number for the salary he was offering her that made her eyes open wide. It was far more than the agency was paying her, even after her recent promotion to head of the department.

"Are you serious? That's insane!"

"I did the computation and went through my records. It's what I paid Fletcher and Benson last year for their percentage. I'd be willing to pay you the same. Why should Bob make all the money? And you could get out of this tiny apartment, and even get one big enough to have an office for you right at home." He wanted to make her life better, and his own too. The number he had quoted would not only restore the way she'd lived before, when Jim was alive, it would be a major step up for her. She would have a cushion for her children, and be able to provide things for them she couldn't now, lessons and vacations and good schools as they got older. It would give her security that she'd never had before, and certainly not for the last five years once she was widowed.

"I'd feel guilty earning that much from you," she said gently.

"Don't. You deserve it. Will you think about it?" he asked her, and she nodded.

"I will. I would love to work for you, and just for you. It's a big decision. And I'd have to give Bob decent notice." She thought that Francine had been too radical, only giving Bob two weeks, but once the mess with Dan became public, it was too hard for her to be there, which even Bob understood. Hailey's circumstances were different, and had nothing to do with Dan. It was all about Phillip's needs now, and he was offering her an extraordinary opportunity. Bob had saved her by giving her a job five years before, and a decent salary, although she could just barely squeeze by on it with three children. Phillip was offering her a huge one, which put her in a whole different league. "I promise I'll think about it. I just don't want to make a hasty decision, or one that either of us will regret. If you don't like the way I work and you fire me, I'd be in a terrible situation."

"We can have a contract, and I could guarantee you a year's severance if it doesn't work out, which would give you a chance to find something else. And you'll make a hell of a lot more money than you do now, starting from the base I want to pay you, and I'd be willing to pay you a ten percent fee for anything you improve over what I make now." He was being incredibly generous as well as fair. "And what don't I know about the way you work? I learned even more about you while we were on tour together." She had learned a lot about him too, and liked him even better now. To complicate matters further, she was falling in love with him, and had high hopes for their relationship working. She hadn't seen anything about him she didn't like yet. And he was nice to her kids. The boys loved him, though Arianna was still somewhat on the fence. But certainly as a boss, he would be amazing. It would be hard to turn down an offer like the one he'd made.

"Give me a few days, so I can try to be coolheaded about it, and make the right decision." It would be less time than what she did now at the agency, which would be great for her kids.

"That's fine. I'll try not to pressure you, although I desperately want you to do it. It seems perfect to me."

"It does to me too." She smiled broadly at him. "Almost too perfect. I would love the job, and a salary that would change everything for me and my children." He looked happy that she hadn't rejected it out of hand. He had been thinking about it all day and had no idea how she'd react. So far, it seemed very favorable.

He had another glass of wine as they sat on the couch and talked about it, and then he kissed her again. He was more passionate than he had been with her until then, and for a minute he wished she lived alone, or at least had her own bedroom. He whispered to her.

"How do you feel about sleeping with your boss, although it would really be more of a partnership." For a minute, he looked worried. What if she put an end to their budding relationship if she went to work for him? He didn't want that to happen either.

"I've never done that before," she whispered back. "But we have a prior relationship, so I think I could make an exception." He grinned when she said it, and kissed her again. Then he asked her a question that he had meant to ask her the day before, after the party.

"Did something happen between Allie and Benjie at the party the other night?" He was curious about it.

"Not that I know of," she said with a knot in her stomach. It was the first lie she'd ever told him. "Why? Did you see something?" She hoped not, for Jane's sake, and even Allie's, however liberal her morals were. Although Allie had seemed to be faithful to Eric, and deeply in love. But she'd been very drunk at the party. And very foolish.

"No, I just got an odd feeling about them. They both disappeared for quite a while, and she looked kind of disheveled when she turned up again. But she was very drunk. Maybe that was all. And Benjie could hardly stand up by the time he showed up and was back with Jane. She seemed perfectly happy, so I don't think she had the same odd feeling I did."

"I think the drinking just got out of hand. And they weren't the only ones." A lot of people had gone overboard with the margaritas, and the release of the tension of recent weeks.

"Her dress looked kind of cockeyed," he commented, "but too much alcohol does that. I think all the upset about Dan and Francine leaving built up a lot of anxiety for everyone, and then they all went crazy at the party." He explained it easily and Hailey nodded, praying again that no one else had seen what she did, and that Jane wouldn't get her heart broken. Allie's already was, which was a new experience for her. She had always had short-term, superficial affairs that meant nothing to her, with younger men, in the five years Hailey had known her. It had been different with Eric, and Hailey was sorry that Bob had put pressure on her to end it. They genuinely seemed to love each other. But with his new series, Eric was going to become a very big star, so it might have ended anyway. The entertainment field was not famous for fostering stable relationships. There was a big age difference between them, which could prove hard to navigate long-term, even though she did look and act years younger than she was. They looked right together and had seemed happy.

Phillip kissed Hailey hungrily again at the door, and she promised to think very seriously about his offer. It was not only flattering, it was miraculous, and would be hard to resist. He had given her much to think about. After he left, she lay in the narrow twin bed in the room she shared with Arianna and thought about how much she could do with the salary he had proposed. She didn't want to make the decision just based on money but there was so much she liked about it, and if the romance continued to go well between them, it could be a remarkable arrangement for them both. But it was too soon to tell how that would work out. She had to make the decision based on the business side of it, and she tried not to think of how Bob Benson would react. She knew he'd find someone good to replace her if he had to. She couldn't let that deter her or be part of her decision. She had to think of herself and her kids.

Allie looked particularly gloomy in the office on Monday. She had spent the whole weekend hung over, and feeling guilty and sick. She couldn't believe how stupid she had been, having sex at an office party with a guy she hardly knew, and didn't care about or even like. If Eric ever heard about it, he'd think she was a slut, and she thought that herself. She was so drunk that she had no idea if anyone had seen them. She vaguely remembered Hailey helping her straighten her dress, and getting her to her car. She had no recollection whatsoever of her doorman and driver carrying her to her apartment, which she assumed must have been what happened, but didn't want to ask.

She'd had three calls from a big film producer in L.A., but didn't feel up to returning his call until Tuesday. When she called, she missed him. She didn't even care why he was calling. She wondered if Eric was really going to change agents. Bob would be even more pissed about that than her dating him.

Eric would be going into preproduction soon on his new series. She had been so excited about that for him. She missed him terribly. The life she'd led before, of casual affairs that meant nothing to her, held no appeal now. They were just bodies. She had never really fallen in love before, and this time she had fallen hard. Now it was over.

She hated Bob for implying that their relationship would jeopardize her career. Her career had meant everything to her, just as her parents' did to them. And what had they ended up with? A bad marriage held together with tape and baling wire, which they kept together out of laziness and convenience between their random affairs. She was beginning to feel she'd wind up like them, except not even married. She had run away from L.A. for all those reasons, but re-created the same scenario in New York.

She ran into Hailey in the kitchen, getting more black coffee, and lowered her voice to a whisper.

"Sorry I was such a mess at the party. I was upset about Eric, and I stupidly took a Xanax before I went. The margaritas hit me like a bomb. Thanks for getting me to my car and getting me out of there." Then after a pause, she asked her another question. "Did Jane say anything?" Hailey shook her head.

"I don't think she noticed. She'd had a few drinks too, and she was dancing with the younger agents from your side." The dramatic agents tended to be younger than the literary ones, with the exception of Jane. "Let's hope Benjie keeps his mouth shut and doesn't confess." Allie nodded agreement.

"He's an idiot if he does." But people did stupid things at times, just as she had.

"Have you heard from Eric?" Hailey asked her.

"No, and I won't. The breakup is all over the tabloids. I don't know who told them, but someone did. Maybe he did. He'll have every twenty-year-old actress in New York and L.A. after him soon, once the new series is on the air."

"They're not you, Allie," Hailey said kindly. She was sorry for her.

"Yeah, lucky for him," Allie said, and went back to her office with a tall glass of iced coffee, and Hailey went back to hers. She had a lot to think about, and she had made lists of the pros and cons of Phillip's offer. The list of cons was short, and the pros list was long.

The office was settling down after all the upheavals over Dan. Francine had been right. Without her in the office there was less to talk about, and Jane wasn't mentioning it at all. She had talked to Steve and Martha, and they had to wait now for the grand jury decision and the next court appearance while the attorneys on both sides studied the case and the assistant D.A. presented the evidence to the grand jury. Bob had been to see Dan in jail and told Merriwether he was a sorry sight, and had already aged ten years in the short time he'd been there. His wife was filing for divorce, and his daughters wouldn't see him.

Hailey made her decision about Phillip's offer on Tuesday night and called to tell him. She was sure and thrilled, and she was ready to move ahead. He invited her to dinner for the following night, so they could celebrate, and she told him she was going to tell Bob in the morning. She didn't want to wait. She wanted to give him all the time he needed to replace her. He was only going to have the younger, less experienced agents on the literary side now, for a while. He needed to find someone with solid experience for her job, with Francine gone and Hailey planning to leave. She wasn't looking forward to telling him, but she was also excited and eager to move forward with Phillip. She wanted to find an apartment and move as soon as she could, so she could set up an office at home. She hadn't told her children that they'd be moving yet. It was still all very new. She wanted to find a place they'd love before she told them. It was all good news, but change was hard for kids, and they'd already had some big ones.

When Hailey told Bob, he looked as though he'd been shot. He stared at her for a minute without speaking, as though he didn't understand or must have heard wrong.

"You're *leaving*?" he asked her in a shaking voice. "To work for Phillip White? Christ. I never thought one of our authors would start poaching agents." He looked angry at first.

"His longtime editor died last weekend," she explained, "and I've read the manuscripts for his recent books and made comments on them. We work well together." She looked at Bob. "And it's a financial opportunity I just can't pass up. I have three kids to support, and I can barely make it living in the city now, and commuting would be just too hard, trying to get home at a decent hour to have dinner with them and help with homework. I share a bedroom with my eleven-year-old daughter now, and have for the last five years. It's been hard ever since my husband died."

"As head of the department, we can make some more improvement on your salary and your annual bonus," he said hopefully, but when she told him what Phillip had offered her, he looked crestfallen. "There's no way we can come even remotely close to that," he said bleakly. She had gotten a raise when she became head of the department, but it barely made a difference.

"I know. I didn't make the decision lightly, Bob. And I don't want to leave you in the lurch. I'd like to leave in a month," she said, and he looked panicked.

"With both you and Francine gone, we really have no one to run the literary side. Jane's a bright girl, but she's nowhere near your league yet or Francine's. Making her a full agent was a stretch, although she seems to have a real knack for picking talented young writers from the internet."

"I know. Jane's found three really good ones recently. She's a good agent but she needs time and maturity."

"We're going to need someone experienced and solid." Without saying it, he felt that Dan had put the agency at risk. With one of the two owners in jail and likely to go to prison, both their agents and their clients were feeling insecure and nervous. Francine was a direct casualty of that, and maybe Hailey too. "You know, it's not smart to put all your eggs in one basket," he said to her. "If things don't go well with Phillip, you'll be out of a job, and you may not find the right one again, and certainly nothing to match what he's paying you." He tried to frighten her into staying.

"Then we'll just have to make it work," she said brightly, unwilling to let him manipulate her into staying. He had nothing to offer her compared to what Phillip did. She could work from home and set her own schedule so she could be with her kids. She loved Phillip's work and understood it intimately, and he was going to pay her a fortune, enough for her to have a decent life again, and not live in a West Side walk-up apartment too small for their needs, where she had to scrimp and save and count every penny. Phillip White was going to take away a lot of the stress that had been her lot in life for the last five years. He had suddenly become the light at the end of the tunnel, regardless of their relationship. Even without it, this was a fantastic deal.

"I want to wish you luck, Hailey, but I wish you'd stay," he said.

"I can't, Bob. I love it here, and I think the agency will survive the shock of Dan's criminal activities and poor judgment, but I think this is an amazing opportunity I just can't turn down and that will never come again." He couldn't deny it, and he couldn't compete with Phillip's offer. He knew when he was beaten. He shook her hand when she left his office and wished her well. He said he would start looking for a replacement immediately and keep her posted. He just hoped he could find good candidates in the next month.

He walked down the hall to Merriwether's office as soon as Hailey left, and he looked sick when he sat down in a chair across from her desk. "More bad news," he said glumly.

"Another victim of Dan's came forward?" Merriwether asked, and he shook his head. He could see that she had spreadsheets all around her and was working on projects for the coming year.

"No, thank God. Hailey is leaving. She just gave me four weeks' notice."

"Why?" She looked shocked. "And it has nothing to do with Dan?"

"No. Phillip White's longtime editor died. She was a brilliant editor, but the poor thing was ancient. He and Hailey seem to have a strong rapport over his books. He just offered her four times what we pay her, to become his agent and his editor. So we're losing a client and our new head of the literary division. We no longer rep his books, *and* we lose her." He looked desperate. Merriwether was thoughtful for a minute, as though she were trying to remember something.

"There's a guy I went to Harvard with who works for ICM. I haven't seen him in a while, but he handles their literary division in New York. Maybe we could steal him from them. That would be more in our ballpark financially than trying to compete with a crazy offer from Phillip White. Successful writers will pay anything to keep the editors they trust, so we can't match that," she said. "The guy at ICM is smart and a strong agent from what I've heard. I think you'd like him. Why don't we take him to lunch and see what he thinks? Some of the guys in the big agencies like the idea of moving to smaller ones so they can give their clients more personal attention, and he might bring a couple of his clients with him." Bob liked what she was suggesting, and it gave him some hope. Merriwether always seemed to have a solution to their problems. "His name is David Bristol. I'll give him a call," she said as Allie showed up in the doorway of Merriwether's office.

"I've been looking everywhere for you. I thought I'd find you here." She looked at Bob. She was still angry at him for objecting to her relationship with Eric, which was none of his business and had been their undoing. She had Bob to thank for it. "I just talked to Quentin

Park in L.A. He's a huge Hollywood producer," she explained, and Bob looked annoyed.

"I know who he is. What does he want? Actors for a show?"

"He's making a big movie, with an all-star cast. He's in New York looking for financing, and he wants our help. He's offering us a big cut of the profits, both at the front and back ends, if we find it for him. After that, we can talk about casting and a package fee, although he already has his big stars. He wants to meet with you." She looked at Merriwether then. "And you should be there, I assume, since it's mostly about finding financing right now. I can deal with the casting later. It would be a huge deal for us if we can land it." Bob looked visibly cheered. "When can you see him?"

"Anytime he wants," Bob said quickly.

"He wants you to come to L.A. too, after the meeting here."

"No problem. I can do that. And by the way," he said, looking gloomy again, "Hailey just gave me notice. She's leaving in four weeks."

"Shit. How did that happen?" She looked sad. They had almost gotten to be friends, although they weren't close. But Hailey had definitely bailed her out and covered her ass at the party.

"Phillip White offered her a fortune to be his agent *and* editor."

"That must have happened while they were on tour together. She's a good agent and editor, and she's very organized. It sounds like an amazing offer." Allie wasn't jealous, she was happy for Hailey. She liked her own job as it was. She liked the movie side of the agency, and didn't like working with writers. The dramatic side was more fun. "What are we going to do without her?"

"Merriwether has some ideas." She nodded at Allie.

"I'll call Park back and tell you when he wants to meet. I'll let you know."

On her way back to her office, Allie stopped at Hailey's, walked in, and Hailey looked up from her desk.

"I hear you're leaving," Allie said. "Bob just told me. It sounds like a terrific opportunity for you." She smiled at her.

"It is. But I'm sad to leave too." The two women had worked together for five years and had never become friends, but they had mutual respect, and Allie was happy for her. She knew Hailey couldn't have an easy life as a widow with three kids, living from paycheck to paycheck at the agency. "We'll keep in touch," Hailey said, and got up to hug her. "I'll stay in the city, and it's going to be nice just focusing on his work and no one else's. We work well together."

"He seems like a nice man," Allie said, although she had no business dealings with him. So far, there had never been a movie of his work, but he hoped that would happen one day. Maybe Hailey would change that.

Allie went back to her office and called Quentin Park to make an appointment for the four of them to meet. Merriwether called David Bristol at ICM, and made a lunch date with him, and Hailey texted Phillip that all had gone well. They were off and running in the busy life of the agency. There was never a dull moment, but she couldn't wait to get started with Phillip now. The future was looking very bright.

Chapter 11

The meeting with Quentin Park went extremely well. Bob agreed to assist with finding the financing, and negotiated an even higher front- and back-end participation for the agency. The next step was for him and Merriwether to go to L.A. for further meetings with various potential investors. After the meeting in New York, Bob looked at Merriwether.

"Can you come to L.A. with me?" he asked her, knowing that her home situation hadn't been easy recently.

"Of course, that's my job," she said smoothly. "I'm the CFO."

"To be honest, I need you with me. It'll go a lot better if you're there, and I want your opinion on the people we meet with." She nodded, excited by the thought of going with him and putting together a package for a major feature film. She loved working on the dramatic side, although she enjoyed the literary side too. And thinking about Quentin Park's new project distracted Bob from his worries about the agency: Hailey's departure, filling Francine's shoes, Dan's eventual trial and whatever bad press that would bring, which would be massive and cast a bad light on the agency.

He and Martha hadn't been getting along recently, even more so than usual. She was very vocal that his failure to sever the partnership with Dan Fletcher years ago had caused all the problems he had now. She blamed Bob and no one else for that, and told him he had been in dreamland to have stayed in denial about Dan. Dan was a misogynist and a sexual deviant, and the fact that he was clearly going to prison did nothing to lift Bob's spirits. Quentin Park's movie did, and the fact that they were going to make a huge amount of money from it was good for the agency.

Merriwether had had a very satisfactory lunch with David Bristol from ICM. He was intrigued by their offer and said he would consider coming to work for them. Things were looking up.

Everything was going well for Merriwether except at home. When she told Jeff she had to go to L.A. with Bob about a big movie deal, he went through the roof.

"What the hell is that about? Are you sleeping with him?"

"Of course not. I'm the CFO and there's a lot of money involved. I need to be there to help make financial decisions and structure the deal. That's what I do."

"And screw the boss on the side?" he accused her. She lowered her voice and her tone went cold.

"I've never cheated on you, Jeff," she said.

"I don't believe you," he said in an aggressive tone. "I think everybody fucks like rabbits in those creative agencies. I saw Allie Moore bang that girl Jane's boyfriend at the party when no one was looking.

You probably do the same when I'm not around." Merriwether was shocked to hear it about Allie, and had no idea whether it was true or not. And she hated what he'd said to her and the assumptions he made.

"I don't know what you saw, or what's true, but they're all single adults and they can do whatever they want. I'm married to you and I behave accordingly and always have." Her feelings were hurt by his accusations.

"Tell that to someone who believes you. I've seen you with Bob. You two look more married than we do. You're always laughing and smiling and flirting with him. All we do is fight."

"Yeah, I wonder why. Because you're always bitching at me and accusing me of something. I'm not home enough, I work too hard, I come home too late, now you accuse me of sleeping with the boss. I'm tired of it, Jeff. I'm a good wife, and you never have a kind word to say to me. I support our family, I give you a good life, and all you give me is grief. I used to think we had a great marriage. Now I can't remember the last time I spent a happy day with you, or even an hour." It was true.

"You think you own me because you pay the bills," he said viciously.

"Actually, I don't, but an occasional thank-you or kind word might be nice. I work my ass off for us, while you whine about your writing and writer's block. If you're having such a tough time with it, then get a job. I'm tired of working insane hours in a stressful job so you can be nasty to me and lie around on your ass." It was the bluntest she had ever been with him. He stormed out of the house and didn't come back that night. She didn't know where he went, and didn't try to find out. He stayed away for three days without contacting her, and she didn't see him before she left for L.A. She left Annabelle with the nanny, she hired her to stay at the house while Merriwether was away. But she had no idea where her husband was. She was quiet on the flight to L.A., thinking about it. Bob noticed and asked if she was all right.

"The usual." She smiled at him. "Ivan the Terrible and I had a falling-out a few days ago, and I haven't seen him since. I'm thinking of calling a lawyer when I go back. It's not going to change."

"Once things get that bad, it usually doesn't improve. It just keeps getting worse. Martha and I seem to be reaching that point too. She blames me for not getting rid of Dan years ago, and says that every- thing that happened is my fault, because I didn't. She may be right. I kept thinking he'd straighten up too. I had no idea how bad he was, or that he was doing things like he did to Francine. I do feel guilty about that."

"You didn't do it, he did," Merriwether reminded him.

"True, but even the small inappropriate things he did were too much. Maybe Martha's right. She said I failed every one of my female employees, out of friendship to Dan, and I'm as morally responsible as he is. She says she has no respect for me anymore.

"It's a little hard to get up every day and know that's how your wife feels about you. I think she's felt that way about me for a long time, and this mess with Dan has just made it worse. She's very tough, very black-and-white in all her points of view. You're good or you're bad, right or wrong. Somehow I slipped off the pedestal with her a long time ago, and never managed to get back up. It's out in the open now because I didn't fire Dan years ago. I never thought something like this could happen. I thought he just talked big. I never believed he could sink so low with women. And Martha will blame me forever for what happened to someone like Francine. There are no reprieves with her, no suspended or commuted sentences. If she doesn't give you an acquittal, you get death row with her. That's where I am now."

"That sounds miserable," Merriwether said. She was more forgiving than that, and willing to make allowances for people she loved. She had made many for Jeff.

"It doesn't sound like a picnic with Jeff either," he said softly. "Do you really think you'll call a lawyer when you go back?"

"Probably. Now or soon. I can't do this forever, hold down a serious job and be a good parent for Annabelle, with no joy between Jeff and me, and no happy moments. Instead of putting gas in my tank because he loves me, Jeff drains me and takes away the energy I have." That was how Bob felt about Martha now. He had told himself he could live without love for the rest of his days, but he was finding it hard to do, much harder than he thought it would be.

When they landed they were going to the Beverly Hills Hotel, where Bob had booked a two-bedroom bungalow, with a big living room between the two bedrooms. It was perfectly respectable, with a patio and a private pool. The hotel had a vintage 1950s feel to it, and movie stars had stayed there for years. It had old Hollywood glamour, restaurants, and the Polo Lounge, where stars and people in the film industry hung out. Merriwether thought it sounded like fun, and she'd never stayed there before.

* * *

The plane had just landed when she got a text from David Bristol at ICM. He had a good job there, and he had been torn about the decision. His text said that he was accepting their offer to head up their literary division. Merriwether handed her phone to Bob without comment while they waited for their bags. She was smiling, and Bob was too.

"All right! Now we're cooking." The problems were starting to get solved. She noticed that she didn't have a text from Jeff when she turned her phone on after the flight. She wondered if it had been one fight too many and if he'd move out while she was away. Anything was possible. He was so resentful of her job and suspicious of her that he couldn't even be civil to her now. She tried not to think about it while they were in L.A. She had work to do. They had a free evening that night and their meetings started the next day, at Park's office.

After Bob and Merriwether left their meeting in New York, Allie had had drinks with Quentin Park. They had worked together before on his movies, mostly on casting, with actors she represented, and they had always gotten along well. There had been an incident years before where they got a little too drunk together during the filming of a movie, and had wound up in bed one night. It had been a fun moment and a one-time occurrence, which had never been repeated. It was more of a slip than a decision, but they had ended on friendly terms, and the option was always there, if either of them wanted to open that door again. They didn't. Quentin had been married and divorced since. She was married to her career, and preferred lightweight affairs to relationships. She accepted with pleasure his invitation to have a drink with him after Bob and Merriwether left. They went to the bar at the Sherry-Netherland, which was walking distance from the office.

"So what's new in your life?" he asked her after they sat down and he ordered a martini and she ordered champagne.

"Nothing much. Busy, actors, movies, casting, the usual," she answered casually. He was a very attractive man, her own age, in great shape.

"I read about you and Eric Clay for a while," he said with a raised eyebrow, and she smiled. "What was that about? He's a nice kid. He's got a big show coming up. Did you get him that?"

"I did."

"Big break for him. Big romance for you?" As he recalled, she shied away from anything long-term. It was all about her career with her, and Eric was young.

"No, just a fling," she said with a shrug. "No big deal," she lied.

"Sounds like you had some nasty goings-on with Dan Fletcher. That sounded like a real mess," he commented. "I saw it on Instagram." So did half the world.

"It was. He's in jail, and he'll probably go to prison," she said. But they had breezed right past the subject of Eric, and she had dismissed him as a fling. It made her heart ache even having said it, just like having sex with Benjie had. It demeaned everything she felt for Eric. But she could hardly say to Quentin that Eric was the love of her life and he dumped her, and she let him, to "protect my career." So she said nothing. One drink led to three for each of them. He was staying nearby at the Plaza. He invited her to have dinner with him and wanted to drop off his briefcase in the suite. She went upstairs with him. She could justify having drinks or dinner with him as a professional contact she wanted to maintain, but as soon as they got to his suite, he dropped the briefcase and kissed her. He didn't force her or coerce her. She had a choice all along. She had forgotten how sexy he was, and he had her panting for more, and feeling more than willing to skip dinner and go straight to bed. She followed him to the bedroom of the suite. They both took their clothes off and got into bed. He was fully aroused and so was she, and he excused himself for a minute to go to the bathroom. She lay in bed waiting for him, and suddenly she had tears in her eyes, thinking of Eric. She realized that this was a turning point for her. She could try to get over him by sleeping with as many men as she could. Benjie, Quentin, and others like them, young, old, eligible or not, drunk, sober, assholes or good guys. But it wouldn't change anything. It wouldn't bring him back. It would just make her a drunken slut who thought sex was the final solution as the substitute for love. It wasn't. She knew that all too clearly now.

She didn't know what he did in the bathroom—maybe he was taking Viagra, or looking for a condom, or snorting coke. But by the time he got back, she was dressed, with a woebegone expression.

"Did I miss my chance?" he asked her with a smile. He had lots of opportunities for sex that he took full advantage of. He didn't need one more. He was a good sport when she nodded. He didn't get mad, as some men would have. He really was a good guy.

"I lied to you," she said with tears still in her eyes. "I'm in love with Eric. We broke up, and I've been acting crazy ever since. It's time to stop. I need to go," she said as he stood naked in the room. He wasn't embarrassed with her. He was at ease with who he was.

"I hope you get him back. He must be a big deal for you to do something like this."

"He is. To me."

"Well, good luck then. Call me if you change your mind. I'm always open to a little fun, and we're old friends. Too bad you're not coming to L.A. with Merriwether and Bob. I might have worn down your resolve to be faithful to the ex-boyfriend. That's not like you, Allie."

"No, it's not. Scary, isn't it?" she said with a grin, and escaped gracefully while she still wanted to. Quentin was a good-looking guy, and a hot bachelor in Hollywood. But she was in love with a twenty-six-year-old who suddenly meant more to her than her job did, or anyone else.

She took the elevator down to the lobby and a cab to Tribeca, then sat alone in her darkened apartment for the rest of the night. She wanted to call Eric, but she didn't dare. What could she say to him? *I'm sorry? You mean more to me than my fucking career and that scares me to death?* That she didn't care what Bob Benson thought of their relationship or even if he fired her? Eric was on his way to stardom now, and she had missed her chance. She was just glad that she hadn't slept with Quentin. Sleeping with random men she didn't care about didn't fill the void anymore. She was in love with Eric. It was as simple as that. And it was too late to do anything about it.

* * *

The week after Bob's party for the agency in Greenwich, Jane was swamped. Hailey had given notice. Bob was panicked. Jane had a stack of new manuscripts to read, and some producer from Hollywood was meeting with Bob, Merriwether, and Allie. Benjie had texted Jane several times and she just didn't have time to see him. She tried to explain it to him by text, and he made it clear he was pissed. She finally texted him on Thursday night, and asked if he wanted to come over on Friday. She hadn't seen him all week, and the weekend before he'd been hung over. She had rarely seen anyone so drunk at a party. But she was happy to spend Friday night with him. She realized that with Hailey leaving, her workload would be even heavier in the future.

Merriwether had told her they were trying to lure an agent away from ICM but he hadn't decided yet. She promised they'd find someone really good to fill Hailey's shoes. But change was in the air with Francine gone and Hailey leaving. She and Julia talked about it over lunch. Julia was worried about her job and hoped the new agent, whoever it was, would like her. For now, with the new promotion, Jane's job was secure.

She was smiling when she opened the door for Benjie on Friday night. She was in a good mood and had stopped on the way home to buy flowers and the Thai food they both liked. She was wearing jeans and a soft white cashmere sweater with a low V-neck. Benjie looked cautious as he walked into the apartment. He'd been nervous about seeing her all week. He had no idea if anyone other than Hailey had seen what he and Allie did at the party, or if they had told Jane in the meantime. He wondered if that was why she had avoided him all week.

"Are you pissed at me?" he asked as soon as she closed the door. He couldn't stand the suspense any longer.

"No, of course not. I told you all week, I was insanely busy. I had lots of manuscripts to read. That's not an option now. It's my job, with the new promotion I got. Hailey quit. Some producer is in town who's a big deal, and he kept Allie and everyone else busy. They're trying to find someone to head up the literary division, and Bob and Merriwether are leaving for L.A., something about the movie they're packaging. It's been nuts." She poured them both wine and he drank half the glass immediately. He looked nervous.

"Why did Hailey quit?" He was worried about that too.

"She's going to work for Phillip White. I told you, it was crazy all week."

"I had a busy week too," he said vaguely, but his job was never as hectic as hers at the agency, where there was always a lot going on.

"That was a fun party last week," she said over dinner, and he stared at her suspiciously. "Okay, you got pretty drunk, but it was fun, wasn't it?"

"What do you mean by that?" he asked her, and she stared at him.

"What do *you* mean by that?" she said. He was acting weird. "I just meant it was fun, even if you got blind drunk and passed out. I had a lot to drink too. Margaritas always go down too easily."

"Did Hailey say something to you?"

"No. Why? Why would she? What about?"

"Or Allie?" He looked like he was about to choke on his dinner and stopped eating, and so did she.

"Do they know something I don't?" she asked, totally baffled by the confusing conversation, and Benjie hung his head, stared at his plate, and then looked at her.

"I can't lie to you, Jane. I did something stupid. I got so fucking drunk, I didn't know what I was doing. I was out of my mind. I had sex with Allie in the hammock at the pool. She was even drunker than I was. I don't know how it happened. I think she was on drugs or something. She said something about Xanax. Anyway, I fucked her. That's all it was, a fuck. It didn't mean anything. I wasn't thinking straight. And neither was she." Jane was staring at him with her mouth open.

"And you had sex with Hailey too?" She looked like she was going to faint. She could believe it of Allie, but not Hailey.

"No, she saw us, that's all."

"Who else saw you?" Jane said with red cheeks and narrowed eyes.

"I don't know. I was too drunk to care if anyone was watching. It was hard to see, where the hammock was, and everyone else was pretty drunk too. Maybe no one saw us. But I didn't want to lie to you. It was a stupid thing to do and I'm sorry." He looked remorseful and Jane was livid.

"You had sex with someone from my agency, at a company party that I took you to, right out in front of everyone, where anyone could see you? I don't care how drunk you were. That's a shit thing to do. And Allie too. What are you, some kind of animal? If I take you to the office Christmas party, are you going to fuck one of my coworkers then too?"

"No. I told you I'm sorry. It was dumb."

"It was not 'dumb,' it was disgusting. You have no respect for me, or yourself." She stood up then and stared at him. "Get out of my apartment, and don't ever call me again. You're a jerk."

"Jane, come on . . . I admitted it, I apologized. I didn't want to lie to you."

"You're pathetic, and stupid on top of it."

"I felt guilty all week."

"Good, you should. Now get out, I mean it." To illustrate the point, she walked across her living room and opened the front door wide. He realized that she actually did mean it, slunk across the room, looking like a guilty teenager, and tried to talk to her in the doorway. "There's nothing you can say that I want to hear," she said. "I'll put your clothes in the garbage, that's where they belong anyway." She shoved him out the door and slammed it behind him. She felt stupid and used and furious. She didn't love him, but they had an easy, fun relationship. And he had made a fool of her. She was too angry to cry. She threw away the rest of their dinner, put his ragtag cutoff jeans and torn T-shirts in a garbage bag, and dumped them in the garbage can. Then she sent Allie a text. She didn't want to wait until Monday and create a scene in the office.

"You're a bitch and a slut," she wrote to her. "Benjie just told me about last Friday night at the party. You're welcome to him. He's all yours. He's a shit and so are you. I hope someone tells Eric." Allie shuddered when she read it and hoped no one would tell Eric. She had narrowly escaped sleeping with Quentin Park that night and was glad she hadn't. She found Jane's text when she woke up to go to the bathroom at two in the morning, and responded then.

"You're 100% right. I was out of my mind, which is no excuse. I'm truly and profoundly sorry. It was a lesson to me. No more slut scenes. I'm sorry, Jane. Truly." There was nothing else she could say. They had to work in the same office. Jane didn't answer her when she read it. She was still awake. Benjie had tried to call her six times that night, and texted her five times, apologizing. It made her realize how little they cared about each other, and that it was time to end it. She was disappointed in all of them: Benjie, who was an asshole, Allie, who was a bitch and a slut, and why didn't Hailey tell her? She thought they were friends. She felt as though all the women she knew only cared about their careers and had no morals or loyalties. It didn't matter anymore. It was over. Benjie was history.

Chapter 12

O n the first night of their trip, Bob and Merriwether had dinner at the Polo Lounge in their hotel, a famed meeting place for movie stars and anyone of any importance in show business. Many of them Merriwether didn't know, but Bob did and pointed them out to her. Studio heads, major directors, producers, and a head of a network. He knew all the important people at the top. She recognized famous actors and actresses. It was fun having dinner there, and it was a balmy evening in the garden. The weather was beautiful.

They talked about the meeting the next day, who they would be meeting with and what they hoped to accomplish. They had other meetings set up with three different possible investors, and Merriwether had done extensive research on all of them. She was fully prepared, and as always, Bob was impressed. She was incredibly bright and a pleasure to work with, and the consummate professional.

"Any news from home?" he asked her after dinner as they ambled back to their bungalow, which was more of a cottage and extremely luxurious. The suite had a living room, a dining area, three bathrooms, two huge bedrooms, and its own patio and garden. It also had a private pool for their own use, as well as the main pool of the hotel, where you could have lunch and eat and drink all day with flocks of attendants to serve you. The suite had every possible kind of drink, snack, and amenity: terrycloth robes, slippers, even a pink dog bed. The hotel was sublimely comfortable and very glamorous.

"No, no news," she answered his question. She had thought about it constantly when they weren't talking business. Her husband had walked out during an argument, and she had no idea where he was. If he hadn't gone home, he didn't even know she had left town. The babysitter had told her he still wasn't back, when she called to say good night to Annabelle before their dinner. She really had no choice. It was time to deal with it when she got back. He had gotten too venomous. It wasn't healthy for her or their daughter to live that way. She had to put a stop to it. She wasn't looking forward to it. Divorces were ugly. He had managed to kill everything she'd ever felt for him. She just wanted it to be over, and the fighting to stop. There would have to be a settlement, since he was financially dependent on her. She didn't begrudge it, but it would be something else to fight about—spousal support, and the house, which belonged to her. She tried not to think about it. She would deal with it when she went back.

When they walked back into the bungalow, she saw that there was a huge bouquet of white roses in a vase on the desk and a card next to it. She opened the card, wondering if Jeff had sent them and was apologizing. They were from Bob, and the card read "Thank you for coming to L.A. with me. You're the best. Bob." She was touched, and she smiled at him.

"Thank you. You always make me feel special."

"You are special, Merriwether, and you should be treated that way." She sighed. She hadn't felt special in a long time, and when she went to her own room, she had an idea. She had brought a bathing suit with her, and slicing through the warm water and forgetting her problems was immensely appealing. She knocked on Bob's door a few minutes later, in her bathing suit and one of the hotel's terrycloth robes, and he smiled when he saw her.

"Do you mind if I use the pool?" she asked him.

"Of course not. Enjoy it. I was thinking the same thing, but I'm too lazy," he admitted. She let herself out the back door of the bungalow, the pool was lit, and it was dark around it. She slipped into the water in her trim black bathing suit that showed her perfect body, and she had her long dark hair held high with a clip. She swam laps for a while, until she started to relax, and then did the backstroke across the pool. She was a strong, graceful swimmer. Then she saw Bob in the doorway, watching her.

"Mind if I come out?" He didn't want to intrude on her.

"Not at all." She laughed. "It's your pool too. Do you want to come in?"

"Maybe I will," he said, and disappeared. He had brought a suit too, and was back in a few minutes, dove in, and swam toward her. "Not a bad life out here, is it?" he said. "I always like visiting L.A., but I can't imagine living here. I love New York."

"Me too." She smiled, and then they both swam for a while, and came to sit on the steps, next to each other.

"It's amazing how complicated life can seem at times, and it really isn't, or it doesn't have to be," he said. "All that terrible shit that Dan did, and look where he is now. His wife and kids hate him, he's going to prison. And in a less extreme version, Martha and I had everything for a happy life: good kids, a nice home, great careers. We used to get along and enjoy each other, and then we ruined it and let all the important stuff slip away from us."

"I keep thinking that about me and Jeff too. It only took us seven years to blow everything. The perfect marriage has gone to hell in a handbasket. He keeps telling me that my career did it, but it didn't. Careers don't wreck marriages, people do. I think the big mistake was letting him not work, and my being the only provider. He wound up hating me for it. The truth is I don't think he has what it takes to be a writer like Phillip White and our other clients, and he doesn't have the balls to admit it, so he blames me for it, and is too lazy to get a job."

"That makes sense," Bob said. He was watching her closely. He didn't want to ruin what they had. He also didn't want to compound the problems in her life by doing something stupid that she didn't want and would hate him for. The one thing he had learned was that couples who loved each other had to be partners. They had to be equal in some area of their life, they needed strong hearts to make a marriage work, and they had to want it. Martha was cold as ice, and he was warm. Merriwether was a hard worker and Jeff was lazy. People didn't have to have the same amount of money or brainpower, but their hearts had to be equally matched, and their willingness to love each other, and desire to be together. It was all about their hearts and their commitment to each other. As they sat there together on the steps of the pool, Merriwether leaned her head on his shoulder. It was a small gesture, and a big statement, and what he needed to know from her. He put an arm around her.

"I'm older than you are," he said softly. He was fifty-three and she was thirty-seven. They were sixteen years apart. "Does that bother you?" he asked her.

"I'm shorter than you are," she answered him, "do you care?" He laughed. She always found a way to lighten the moment, to laugh or make him feel good.

"You're very special to me, Merriwether." He didn't know what else to say, and it was true. She was more than that to him, much more, but he didn't want to scare her.

"You are to me too," she said in a whisper, matching him point by point, and then he kissed her, which made it all easier. They kissed on the steps for a long time, hungry for each other, gently discovering each other's bodies. He slowly peeled off her plain black bathing suit, and revealed the marvels of her body, and she slipped off his trunks, and they glided through the water together, naked, with the water warm and the air cooler above them. It was exhilarating and felt like a dance between them. She stood with her back against the side of the pool, with Bob pressed against her, and he kissed her breasts and her neck.

"I've wanted you since the first day I met you. You were so happy with Jeff then. I would never have wanted to interfere, or upset you and confuse you. I didn't want to hurt you. I didn't just want you physically, I wanted to be part of you, to share hearts and souls, and this," he said as he kissed her and throbbed against her under the water. She guided him into her, and they hung there for a moment, tantalizing each other, and then she kissed him and whispered.

"Let's go to bed." It was their time now. Martha was over, and so was Jeff. Their stories had taken years to play out, and now Merriwether and Bob were ready for each other. She was happy it hadn't happened sooner. It would have been wrong then, and shoddy, for both of them. They didn't have to hide now. Merriwether knew without a doubt that the heart and soul of her marriage to Jeff was dead. And Bob knew it about his own. They were free now. They ran into the bungalow in their bathrobes and went to Bob's room because it was closer. He dried her gently with the robe, and she pressed against him, and then they slipped onto the bed, and made love with the hunger of all the years they'd known each other, the relationship they had built, the things they had learned about each other. They had brought it all with them, and now it was theirs.

Merriwether had never given herself so freely to any man. She didn't know it, but she had been waiting for Bob, building a nest for him, opening her heart and her mind to him, and he poured all the years of love he had saved for her into her that night. They couldn't imagine a life apart from each other now. They had waited so long for this, and they fit together now like two puzzle pieces that had been carefully carved by loving hands over time and were made for each other.

They made love until first light, starving for each other, and then slept for two hours until they had to get up for their meeting. He showered and she went to bathe and dress and they met in the living room. He had ordered breakfast for them, and he beamed when he saw her. It felt like a honeymoon, even though they had business to do, but it was business they shared. They complemented each other. It felt as though their future had been sealed the night before, their vows had been made. It had taken years to get here, but they had arrived.

He spoke to her softly over breakfast. He didn't want her to worry about it. "I'm going to straighten things out when we go back." He didn't want any sneaking around or stolen moments or lies. He didn't want to taint what they had or disrespect her.

"So will I," she promised, "if I can even find him."

"He'll show up. Don't make him angry. I don't want you at risk," he said. He knew that Jeff was jealous of him and had accused her of sleeping with him, which wasn't true then but was now, which made things different. "There's no life left in my marriage to Martha. She doesn't care. She's wanted out for a while, and I thought we should stay for the boys. She didn't think it was necessary. I may be a poorer man when you get me. We were young when we got married and we didn't have a prenup, so she'll want half of the business, but it may be something of a wash with hers, we're pretty equal on that score. I'll give her the house in Greenwich. She loves it, I don't. I'll get a place in the city so I can be close to you." He had already been think-ing of all the details he had to address now.

"I'll have to see what Jeff wants. Probably a lot. I will be poorer too," she said, and they both smiled.

"What we have right now, this minute, are all the riches we need." She could see that he meant it and she leaned over and kissed him. She was wearing a chic beige dress and jacket, and he was wearing a charcoal gray suit. They looked like a very elegant pair when they left the hotel for their meeting. He stopped her before they left the room and kissed her. She didn't have a doubt in her mind about how much they loved each other or how right this was for both of them. She would have married him on the spot the night before, and in all the ways that mattered, they already were.

"Let's go make a deal," he said, excited about the meeting they were going to.

"We already did, last night," she said, smiling.

"That too," he said, and kissed her as they walked hand in hand out of the hotel to the car and driver waiting for them in the driveway.

The trip to L.A. accomplished what they wanted it to. They found the right investor and came to an agreement. Quentin Park was thrilled, and so were they. They spent their nights at the hotel, and the days doing business, and they stayed an extra day to savor what they had established between them while they were there. They both had challenges to face when they went back, and were ready to face them. They promised to come back here to celebrate where their love had been consummated.

Bob spoke to Martha the night he got back. The conversation was as bloodless as all their dealings with each other. She said their lawyers and accountants could sort out the details. He told her he was moving out, and she could have the house. She looked relieved. He hated the commute and she loved it, and the boys would be happy to have their childhood house to come home to, and Bob wanted them to have that.

She asked if there was someone else and he said there was. She looked wistful for a minute, remembering what they had lost so long ago. He told her it was Merriwether, and she said it was the right choice for him. They both had tears in their eyes when he left the next morning. He was going to come back for his things when he found an apartment. He wanted to find one near Merriwether. Even if he stayed with her, he thought he should have his own place. It was too soon to move in, whenever Jeff moved out. He wanted the dust to settle before he moved into her home.

Merriwether waited until the next day to tell Jeff. He was at the house when she got back. She didn't want one of their long, drawn-out fights the night she came home. He acted as though nothing had happened when she got there, as though he hadn't disappeared for several days after their last fight.

"Where were you?" she asked calmly.

"None of your business," he said with a smug look, and she nodded and didn't comment. She wasn't going to fall into the trap of one of the fights he loved to create with her. In the morning before she left for the office, she told him she was going to call an attorney, and he needed to move out.

"You can't make me leave," he said, jutting his chin out, standing with his legs wide apart.

"I couldn't make you stay either, when I left for L.A. I won't play games with you. I own the house. You have to leave."

"Then you have to buy me an apartment, and pay me alimony," he said, and she wondered if that was what he'd been waiting for. "You *owe* me," he said angrily, but he didn't seem sad to lose her, or surprised. She wondered if he had someone else. But she didn't want to know, or to tell him about Bob. Jeff had tried to make love to her the night before, and she had said no, and he had slammed out of the bedroom and slept in the study, but he didn't leave the house. She wondered if he'd seen a lawyer to advise him. She had that feeling.

"The lawyers will have to figure it out." Unlike Bob, she did have a prenup. She had been thirty when she married Jeff, and her father had insisted. Jeff had nothing, and she already had a good salary and some money she'd inherited. They had to sort it all out now. By legal standards, seven years was not a long marriage.

Jeff left the house before she left for work, and she was excited to see Bob when she got to the office. This was going to be an exciting time, despite any bumps they encountered. Their life together was just beginning, and they had so much to look forward to.

"Did it go okay?" he whispered to her as they walked into a meeting with Allie and several of their agents about the film they'd been to L.A. about.

"It was fine," she whispered with a smile. "You?"

"Perfect. A little sad. But I think she's happy, and I gave her the house. There will be lots more," he said ruefully, and she smiled and they sat down in Allie's office.

"You two must have made one hell of a great deal," she commented, looking at them as they sat down. "You're absolutely glowing." After she said it, she realized what had happened. She and

Merriwether exchanged a smile and Merriwether laughed. Allie was no fool. She knew love when she saw it, even if she had lost it herself. She was happy for them. They deserved it.

Phillip and Hailey had had a lucky weekend before Merriwether and Bob went to L.A. All three of her children had sleepovers with friends from Friday night to Sunday. It was rare when all three left at once, and they decided to seize the opportunity. They thought about going to an inn in Connecticut or somewhere else in New England, but then he asked her if she wanted to stay with him, and they both liked the idea. She didn't have a bed big enough for the two of them in her apartment. Will and Bentley had bunk beds, and she and Arianna had twins, so her place was out.

They planned it like a robbery or a prison escape, and she showed up at his apartment at seven-thirty on Friday night with a small overnight bag with everything she needed for the weekend. He had filled his apartment with roses for her and had bought wine and groceries. She had her cellphone so her children could reach her. His apartment was a small but elegant bachelor pad with deep hunter greens and dark blue velvet couches, a very masculine pearl-gray bedroom, and his office was full of antique red leather chairs he'd bought in London. It was warm and inviting, but he only had one bedroom, and it was the perfect place for him to write. Everything was set up for his comfort during the long spells of isolation and solitude when he wrote. He had a fabulous sound system and a view of Central Park.

He had bought lobster for dinner. They ate it cold, with white wine, and while they were eating, he shared an idea with her. "I had a crazy thought today, before you look for a new apartment for you and the children. Apartments don't come up very often in this building. It's kind of a legend. There's a family selling theirs two floors down. I looked at it today. It's a duplex and very well set up. It needs some paint and a new kitchen. It's big enough for you and the children, with an office for you, and it's even big enough for me, if that's how we end up. I could keep this apartment to write. They're selling it at a very good price, and I'd like to buy it as an investment. If things don't work out, I can always sell it. But I feel like I should grab it while I can. How does that sound to you? We can look at it tomorrow. It has the same view of the park I do." She felt as though she was dreaming.

"You would do that, Phillip?" she asked in an awed voice. He didn't have any idea yet how things would work out with them. They were about to spend their first night together. She had been struggling for so long that she couldn't imagine anyone doing that for her.

"It's a good investment," he said, so he didn't scare her, but he was sure of what he wanted now, and he was certain it would work. Keeping his bachelor apartment to write in was a comfort for him, and it was familiar. It would give him the space and privacy he needed to work. It was as though the other apartment had just been waiting for them and had fallen into their hands at the right time. The owners had four children, all grown up now, who lived on the West Coast and in Europe with families of their own. "Let's see how you like it tomorrow. You might hate it. It looked good to me, but I'm a man. I don't know what you need for the kids."

She laughed.

"Is it as nice as the one I have now?" she asked with a serious expression, and they both laughed.

"Well, not quite, and Arianna would have to sleep on her own, and she might not like it if I become your roommate and she doesn't."

He put music on his sound system after dinner, and they relaxed and talked for a long time. He had put her suitcase in his bedroom. It had been a long time since a woman had stayed there with him, in his totally masculine apartment. It looked like an English gentleman's club to her, and she loved the smell of the leather in his study, mixed with the cologne he wore. She felt shy being there with him at first, and they sat in his living room talking and kissing for a long time. His dark blue velvet couches reminded her of a sky at midnight, and she loved looking at the park from his windows. She followed him into his bedroom and there was a wall of leather-bound books that made the room cozy, and some handsome paintings. "Welcome to my world," he said gently, and kissed her. They found their way to his big, comfortable bed with the down comforter, European square pillows, and crisp white sheets, and her shyness fell away as he held her. She suddenly felt she had come home to the place she was meant to be, with the man that she loved.

He was a gentle, skilled lover, and she felt as though she was discovering a world she had forgotten and never really known. She and Jim had never perfectly fit together and they had made do, but being with Phillip was the perfect fit of interests and hearts and bodies, and she lay next to him afterwards, smiling. She looked like a happy child in his bed, and he laughed looking at her.

"What are you looking so pleased about?" he asked. It had gone exactly as he had hoped. It was perfect. They were lucky. They had started making plans before they knew the details, and the details were turning out to be just right, better than either of them had dreamed.

"You make me so happy," she said, giggling, "and you're so good to me."

"That's the idea," he said. "Although I've turned a page here."

"Have you? How?" she asked. He had a strong, masculine, lithe body, and he loved hers.

"Well, I've never slept with my agent or my editor, and certainly not at the same time," he said, she laughed at him, and he kissed her and made love to her again.

They looked at the apartment together the next day. He was right, it was perfect. It had five bedrooms: three for the children, a big master suite for them, and the fifth one as an office for her. Good kitchen, once it had new equipment, big enough for family dinners, nice bathrooms, high ceilings in the living room and dining room. It was bright and sunny. He said he had some spare furniture in storage she could use, since she had very little for their tiny apartment.

"What do we think?" he asked after they went back upstairs to his place and sprawled on the couch to talk about it. She was still stunned at what he was offering to do, and planning, so quickly.

"We think I'm the luckiest woman in the world and I must be dreaming."

"And I'm the luckiest man." They went for a walk in the park after that, then came home. She felt comfortable in his apartment now, with all his beautiful things. She was surprised by how quickly she felt at ease with him, as though they'd always been together. He was shy too, but not with her. He welcomed her into his life and his bed and his arms, as he had wanted to do for so long and hadn't dared. Now he could.

By the time they picked up the children on Sunday afternoon, and went back to her apartment for a boisterous but relaxed spaghetti dinner in her kitchen, she had a new life and a new world and a new man, and soon they would have a home together. Phillip played video games with the boys and chess with Arianna, and she almost beat him. He smiled over their heads at Hailey, remembering the weekend, and she already missed waking up with him in the morning. The future couldn't come soon enough for both of them, but they could reach out and touch it. It belonged to them now, and was already real.

Chapter 13

Phillip got a thirty-day closing on the apartment from the family that owned it, at the price he wanted, and he was very pleased. It still felt like a dream to Hailey. They picked out kitchen equipment and paint colors together, and she told the children they were moving. It was going to take a month or two to paint and do the kitchen, and by then Hailey hoped the children would be ready to accept Phillip living with them. She was heading in that direction, and they would stay in their old apartment in the meantime, and he was working on a new book.

Francine, Julia, and Jane were meeting with Steve Franklin regularly to prepare their testimony for the trial. Dan's attorney deposed all three of them and their testimony was so damning that Martha was stunned Dan hadn't pleaded guilty yet. Steve was proceeding with the civil suit against him.

By the time Hailey left the agency, a month after she had given notice, Bob had found an apartment two blocks from Merriwether's house. Jeff had rented a very expensive apartment downtown that Merriwether had to pay for as part of her spousal support. They were still negotiating the details of that, but he wanted the moon. And so far he hadn't had Annabelle stay with him at his new apartment at all. He said he wasn't set up for it yet, although he had charged Merriwether for a truckful of very expensive furniture. He was making the most of the separation, and his attorney wanted the maximum he could get from her. Merriwether's attorney assured her he wouldn't get everything he wanted. He had a wish list a mile long, including half the value of her house, which he wasn't entitled to.

Bob's new apartment was a floor-through in a brownstone, which was small but elegant and cozy. He was happy there and spent most of his time at her house, except for the nights so they didn't shock Annabelle. Jeff came to see his daughter, but he never took her to his place, and Merriwether suspected that he wanted visitation at her house so he could watch her and check out what was going on. He didn't know about Bob, and they didn't want him to until the financial settlement was final.

By the time Hailey left the agency, David Bristol, the new head of the literary division, was settling in nicely. He was thirty-nine years old, very bright, and he made a point of trying to get to know everyone he was responsible for. He was good-looking in a rugged, intellectual way, and Allie had eyed him a few times, but he spent a lot of time with Hailey, trying to learn all the important details. Hailey thought he had an eye for Jane, who hadn't seen Benjie again and didn't want to.

Allie had a jolt when she saw Eric in the tabloids with a young actress from his series, which had recently been released. She was an extremely pretty up-and-coming actress, who had been in several feature films, and they had gone to a big splashy event together. They made a beautiful couple, and Allie's heart ached when she saw the tabloids in the grocery store. He looked as handsome as ever. Allie hadn't had a date since he'd left, and didn't want one. Her only transgression had been Benjie, which she was still embarrassed about, and Jane was still cool with her. She hadn't forgotten.

A few days after Hailey left the agency, David came in to ask Jane a question about one of their new authors. He had been reading her manuscript and was surprised by how good it was.

"Do you have any biographical material on her?" he asked Jane about the author, and she printed it out on her computer and handed it to him with a smile. "How did you find her?"

"Just digging around on the internet. Every now and then I find a gem."

"You certainly do. That book is going to sell a million copies and make her—and us—a fortune." His own taste was somewhat loftier, but he was very knowledgeable about commercial fiction. "You wouldn't want to go to the ballet tomorrow night, would you?" he asked her innocently. He'd been waiting for the right moment to do so. "I happen to have two tickets someone gave me." He wanted to get to know her better, but he was attracted to her too, which was delicate now because of Dan. They were all a little skittish at the moment.

"Tomorrow?" She looked startled. "Sure, why not? I love the ballet." That's what Hailey had told him when he asked her advice before she left. She was amused. He'd been circling Jane since he got there and was waiting for the right opening, but he seemed like a nice guy, and he really liked the agency. He had no interest whatsoever in the theatrical side, only the literary.

Bob and Merriwether's big film deal was coming together well. They were going back out to L.A. again soon for some final meetings.

They were approaching the date of Dan's trial, and Bob felt sick about it. Martha had convinced Bob that Dan was committing legal suicide if he went to trial, given the testimony of his three victims, but no one had been able to convince Dan of that. Bob had gone to see him in jail a couple of times, and tried to urge him to plead guilty. Dan stubbornly refused to admit his guilt.

The trial was only three weeks away when Martha got an unofficial call in her office from the assistant district attorney.

"We think he's going to plead," he told Martha. She wondered if Bob had finally convinced him. Or maybe he was finally listening to his lawyer. Martha wanted to draw up papers at the same time, to settle the civil suit she was bringing against him, for damages for all three of his victims.

Bob was depressed after he saw Dan in jail. Dan wanted to sell his half of the agency to Bob, and Bob wanted to buy him out, but he was also settling accounts with Martha. Dan's wife, Rita, was divorcing him, and trying to get every penny out of him she could. Dan was going to prison a poor man.

Martha surprised Bob in the end by being more reasonable about the divorce than he'd expected. They weren't touching each other's businesses, which were equally lucrative. He was giving her the house in Greenwich, and she wanted roughly half of his investments. She wasn't leaving the marriage empty-handed, but at least she hadn't touched the agency. And Bob made an agreement with Dan to pay him for his share of the partnership over time, although Rita was going to get half that money from Dan in their divorce. "What's the point of working our asses off for thirty years, in order to give it all to the bitches we married?" Dan said to Bob when he saw him. His attitude toward women hadn't improved. But at least when he left jail and went to prison, he'd have more space to move around in, more comfortable quarters than he did in a jail cell with a roommate. He was getting no special treatment whatsoever in jail.

Five days before the trial, he finally pled guilty to all the charges. The district attorney's office wouldn't make a deal with him to reduce the charges. The judge was going to sentence him. Steve was in heated negotiation with his attorney over the civil suit for Jane, Julia, and Francine's benefit. The civil suit allowed them to negotiate a financial settlement. Steve wanted to get them the best deal he could. Dan had to disclose his full financial statement, and Steve was basing his demands on that. Steve wanted his clients to at least have financial compensation for their pain.

There was a formal court appearance to change his plea, and Steve asked all three women if they wanted to attend. Francine was hesitant and didn't really want to, but she decided to go in the end. Jane was adamant that she wanted to be there, and Julia decided to go with her, although the offenses against her were the least onerous. Francine's was the worst case of all. But none of that testimony would be heard when he pled guilty.

They would all go back one last time for the sentencing, and then it would be over and he would be gone forever. Francine could hardly wait for that to happen.

All three of Dan's victims went to the formal plea change. Hailey and Phillip went with them for support. Merriwether and Bob went too. Jane's parents offered to fly in for it, but Jane said it wasn't necessary and would be brief, so they didn't come. She had grown up during her time in New York, and they were acknowledging it and treating her like an adult. Allie decided to go at the last minute, and David asked Jane if she'd like him to go with her. It was a piece of the agency's history that predated him, but he'd had a nice evening with Jane at the ballet and dinner afterwards, and he was happy to offer his support, since there would be no graphic testimony to embarrass the three victims.

All of them were shocked at how old and broken Dan looked when he shuffled into the courtroom in a jumpsuit, leg irons, and handcuffs. He could hardly walk in the leg irons, and he looked at where they were sitting with hatred in his eyes. It tore Bob's heart out to see him. He was a ruined man.

The three women were talking softly before the judge entered the courtroom, and Francine had been saying how much she loved her new job, and her kids were doing well. They had moved to an apartment in Chelsea a few weeks before, and were happy with their new home and fresh start. And so was she.

They talked about the changes in the office, and Jane introduced Francine to David, since he now had her old job. There was a sense of the agency continuing, despite all the terrible things that had happened and the people who had left. There was a continuity to it nonetheless.

"Merriwether and Bob?" Francine asked with a look of surprise, and Jane nodded with a smile.

"And Hailey and Phillip?" Francine smiled. Allie was alone without a partner in the courtroom, and Francine didn't want to ask about Eric. She had heard that that was dead and buried. Allie looked as young as ever, but Francine noticed that she didn't look happy. Her eyes were sad.

The judge arrived finally and mounted the bench. They all stood, and then were told they could sit down again.

The judge addressed the defense lawyer and said that he understood that the defendant wanted to change his plea, and the attorney said that was correct. As Francine listened, she could suddenly remember all those terrible nights when she arrived at the borrowed apartment on Central Park West and did whatever Dan wanted her to, and then she left, like a hooker who had done her job, and went home to her children feeling filthy. She used to scrub herself in the tub or the shower for half an hour on those nights and emerge red from the friction of whatever brush she used. She could never feel clean after she'd been there, and then she'd have to go back again to keep from losing her reputation and her job.

Dan stood and pled guilty when the judge asked him how he pled to the charges. The judge pointed out that, in addition, Dan had been guilty of abuse of power, which made it all seem worse, and would increase his sentence. Then he told Dan and the attorneys that sentencing would be in thirty days, and from there he would go directly to prison.

Steve conferred briefly with Dan's attorney as he was led away. Dan glared viciously at his victims and looked as though he would have liked to kill them, but fortunately that wasn't possible. He was trussed up in chains. He could have been out on bail for all this time if he'd behaved, but he hadn't. He had come back to try to bribe Jane and threaten to kill Francine if she talked, so he went back to jail. As Bob said, he was his own worst enemy.

There was a brief exchange of papers between Steve and Dan's attorney, and then they all disbanded and went their separate ways.

With a guilty plea, Steve could conclude a settlement of the civil case, and it strengthened their position immeasurably. There was no debate now as to whether he was innocent or guilty. With the charges leveled by all three women, he was going to prison for a long time. None of Dan's family was at the hearing, neither his wife nor his daughters.

On their way back to the office, Merriwether was thinking about how drastically their lives had changed in the time since Dan's crimes had come to light. Francine and Hailey no longer worked at the agency, both had new jobs, Francine was delighted with hers, and Hailey had been given an extraordinary opportunity, with a man to go with it. She was working for one of their biggest and most successful clients now. Merriwether herself was involved with the boss, and they were both getting divorced. Jane was a full agent, and had stood for principle to the fullest degree in exposing Dan for what he was. She had been fearless about it. Allie had the same job, but had lost the man she loved. So some of them had been winners, and some losers, but most of them had benefited in some way from their jobs and their circumstances. The torture Francine had lived through had been stopped thanks to Jane's courage, and her own willingness to speak up finally because Jane and Julia had.

Two weeks after Dan entered his guilty plea, Steve Franklin called all three victims, and invited them to come to his office for the results of the settlement of the civil suit. He and Dan's attorneys had reached an agreement, which was going to be confirmed by the court, and Dan had agreed to it. If they hadn't reached a settlement agreement, the civil suit would have gone to trial, and the damages might have been even greater for him. He had decided not to fight it. Steve had used all the measures available to him to get them the best settlements he could. He asked each of the women if they were amenable to meeting with him together, or if they preferred to be alone with him in each case, and all three had said that they were perfectly satisfied to be together when he told them the results of the settlement negotiation, and resulting agreement. They found a day that suited the three of them and made an appointment to meet at his office. They looked relaxed when they got there. They had no idea what to expect. Whatever the amount was, they felt sure that Steve had done his best. It was a matter of principle, as much as anything. How could you put a price on fear and humiliation, trauma and degradation, and the nightmares they would have forever when they thought of him, and of what Francine's children had suffered as a result of their mother's depression for an entire decade.

Once they had all arrived, Steve spoke to them. He had three sets of papers on his desk, and the former coworkers chatted for a few minutes, waiting to hear the results. None of them had inordinately high expectations, and Steve explained that they truly deserved what Dan had been forced to give up for their benefit.

They were shocked when Steve said that the settlement for Julia for the hand job she'd had to give Dan was a hundred thousand dollars.

"Oh my God," she said, covering her mouth with her hand. The amount seemed enormous to her. She couldn't imagine having that much money all at one time. Steve smiled at her response as Julia thanked him profusely.

And for Jane, for the attempted rape she suffered and the trauma, and two incidents of sexual harassment before that, the defendant had agreed to three hundred thousand dollars. Jane was shocked too. She had had no idea what the award would be. She smiled at the other two women. Even though the money didn't make up for the fear and humiliation, it was a real acknowledgment of what they had suffered at his hands, and it would be nice for each of them to have. Jane was less in need than the others, but it was tremendous validation that she was grateful for.

Steve turned to Francine then. "We struggled with an amount that seemed reasonable for you, Francine. But even I couldn't assess what ten years of torture twice a week would be like, and how does anyone pay restitution for that? Add to that the constant threat of losing your job if you didn't comply, and a death threat when he was out on bail. The defendant's attorney came up with an amount I'm satisfied with, and I hope you will be too. They've agreed to a settlement of three million dollars for you."

Jane and Julia gasped, and Francine's eyes filled with tears. She was speechless. Never in her life could she imagine having that kind of money, and what it could do for her children. It was life-changing after ten years of soul-crushing sexual and emotional abuse. She would never forget what she'd been through, but it would make such a huge difference in her life and her children's. They could go to good colleges, live in a nice home, and be secure. A prom dress would no longer be out of reach, or lessons, good food on the table, and vacations together. Three million dollars was like giving Francine and her family a world that would never have been open to her otherwise. The other two women hugged her, and she hugged them and Steve, crying uncontrollably.

"I don't know . . . I can't . . ." She couldn't put her feelings into words, but they all agreed that it was fair. She had suffered by far the most. She hugged Jane again, because if Jane hadn't spoken up, she never would have either. They all signed the papers, agreeing to the settlements, and Francine was shaking when she stood up. She still looked dazed when she left. She had to go back to work, but she couldn't think straight she was so stunned. The judge was going to validate the agreements and confirm them that afternoon, and Steve said that they would have the checks in two days. He hadn't handled the civil suit on a contingency basis, they had agreed to pay his hourly rates, but he told them before they left his office that he had conferred with Martha and her partners and there had been unanimous agreement that the case would be handled pro bono. The women would have no fees to pay and would get the full settlement amount. It was Martha's contribution to alleviate what they had suffered at Dan Fletcher's hands.

They hugged Francine again before she got in a cab to go back to work. Her mind was racing in a thousand directions at once, and Jane and Julia were still talking a mile a minute when they got back to the agency. Bob and Merriwether came in quickly to find out what had happened. They were impressed by the amounts, and Bob was proud of Martha for doing it pro bono. She was a woman of principle. As much as it drove him crazy at times, this time it made him proud. They had just settled on the final amounts for their divorce settlement, and it wasn't inexpensive, but it was fair enough and an amount he could live with. She hadn't crippled the agency to prove a point, which he was grateful for.

Merriwether was having more of a battle with Jeff through her attorneys. Despite their prenup, which he was contesting, he was still demanding the moon and they might have to go to trial over it, but he wouldn't win the amount he wanted for a seven-year marriage, from a woman who had supported him fully for all seven years. Bob could wait for however long it took for her to be free. They were together as much as possible now, and once the finances were settled, he was going to move in with her and her daughter. In the meantime, he was close by. He was with the woman he had loved from afar for years, he could wait a few months longer. They were going to get married quietly at city hall when the divorce was final. They had much to be grateful for.

Francine told her children that night, because they would be the most affected by the settlement. She had told them an abbreviated version of the circumstances when Dan's crimes came to light. It explained a lot to them about why their mother had seemed so emotionally unavailable for so long. They were both proud of her for standing up for herself in the end. And it was a lesson for them both. Now Thalia could go to a really good college, and Tommy would too one day. They already had a new apartment they loved, thanks to her new job. Thalia had been accepted by several good colleges, and now she could accept the one she preferred. And Tommy was excited about high school in the fall. They hugged and cried, and Francine seemed happy and at peace. She had taught her children a valuable life lesson, to fight for what was right, and stand for principle, and not let someone take away your freedom and your self-respect, no matter what the consequences. Francine knew she would owe Jane a debt forever for her courage.

After Merriwether and Bob left Jane's office, David was hovering outside. He hadn't wanted to intrude. She told him to come in.

"How did it go?" he asked her, concerned. She told him all about the settlement agreement, and he thought she was a very courageous woman. He admired her for what she'd done, and for sticking with it, in the face of embarrassment, threats, and fear. "Well done," he said. "Can I invite you to dinner tonight to celebrate?" She smiled and nodded.

"I'd like that," she said. He was courting her slowly, and not making any fast moves, which seemed appropriate to both of them. He didn't want to rush her or frighten her, but he thought she was a very cool woman. He was ten years older than she was, which seemed comfortable for both of them. They enjoyed working together and were both serious about their careers, but Jane had realized that she wanted a personal life too, not just work at the expense of everything else.

Ripples went through the office all afternoon, which reached Allie's ears. She hadn't wanted to go to Jane's office to find out. She was still uncomfortable with her, and Jane hadn't warmed up to her again. She wasn't angry anymore. She thought Benjie was a jerk and didn't miss him, but she still didn't like what Allie had done, whatever the excuse. It was a mean thing to do.

Allie was checking her emails late that afternoon, and was surprised to see one from the producers of Eric's show. It was on the air now, and the ratings were through the roof, as she had predicted they would be. The email was a standard notice of some papers he had to sign to complete his files, and a few had been missed. It was standard housekeeping stuff from their accountants. She didn't know who to send them to because he had never notified her of who his new agent was, and she had no idea or record of it. He hadn't communicated with the agency since he broke up with her. The producers of the show were threatening to withhold his payments until he signed the documents in the attachment, so it was important that he get them and take care of it. She debated whether she should just email them to him, but he might not notice them or think they were important. As his agent, she would have printed out the documents and had him sign them, but since she assumed she wasn't his agent anymore, she wasn't sure, and she'd had no notification of a new agent. He just disappeared.

She decided to text him instead, and if he didn't respond, she'd call him. She didn't want to talk to him. She knew it would upset her too much. He had moved on, and his new girlfriend was gorgeous. That was hardly surprising, he was too. She'd been lucky to have him for as long as she did. Their relationship had all worked seamlessly for a while, and then it didn't, thanks to Bob Benson. And he was with Merriwether now, one of his employees, which was no more proper than her being with Eric, in fact probably less so. She was still angry at Bob for his interference. Pathetically, she realized, she hadn't gotten over Eric. She kept waiting for the missing him to diminish, but it hadn't.

She sent Eric a simple text that she had received documents from his producers that he had to sign, and asked what agency she should send them to. She didn't expect an answer from him for a while. He was usually slow to respond to texts and emails, and didn't like dealing with them. She had always handled everything for him of that nature. She did it for most of her clients. Most actors didn't like dealing with the housekeeping.

He called her on her cell in less than five minutes.

"Why did you send me that text?" he asked her. He didn't sound friendly, and his voice was cold.

"Because you need to sign their paperwork or they won't pay you. One of them is a tax document. Who do you want me to send them to? Who's your agent?" She tried to sound neutral, but her heart was pounding just hearing his voice.

"What do you mean? Aren't you my agent?"

"I don't know. Am I? You didn't switch? I thought you had. You said you were going to."

"No. I was busy. What would you normally do? You used to send stuff over to me with a guy when I had to sign it," he said, sounding petulant, which was worse. Unfriendly she could deal with. Petulant made her want to protect him.

"I can do that. I'll send a courier over. Where are you?"

"On set at the studio. We shoot in New York," he said, as though she didn't know the show.

"I'll have someone bring them over. And I'll get them back to the producer after you sign."

He sounded as though he wanted to say something else then, but he didn't. All he said was "Thanks," and hung up. She sighed after the brief exchange.

She printed up the documents in the email, and was about to call for a courier, when all of a sudden she thought of Jane and how brave she had been, and the results of her bravery. What was the worst he could do? Spit in her eye? Have her thrown off the set? Yell at her? That wasn't his style, he was more likely to just be cold to her, sign them, hand them back to her, and walk away. And if he did, she'd survive it. It couldn't be any worse than a lot of other things that had happened in her life, or the last months without him. They had been the worst months of her life. At least this way she could see him. She put the papers in a manila envelope, grabbed her purse, and headed for the elevator. She told the assistant in the hallway she'd be back in an hour, and didn't say where she was going. She realized that she looked a mess, but she didn't care. She was wearing jeans, a purple sweatshirt, and running shoes, and her hair looked like bats had flown through it. She just wanted to see him. It was a twenty-minute ride across town, and a few blocks down on Tenth Avenue. The studio was housed in a full block of warehouses.

She was nervous in the cab, and she was clutching the envelope in her hand. It was her ticket to see him, the excuse she needed. And if he wouldn't talk to her, so be it, at least she would have tried, and not wish forever that she had.

She knew her way around the studios they were using, although she hadn't been there in a while. She asked a guard what set they were on, and took a freight elevator to get there. She was standing between a resin dinosaur and an elephant from some kids' show, and got out on her floor, walked down several hallways, and stopped at the set in case they were shooting and the cameras were rolling. But they were on a break so she asked for his dressing room. The person she asked pointed her in the right direction, and she stood outside the door with his name on it for a minute, holding her breath. She was about to knock when he pulled open the door, and he was standing there, staring at her from inches away. They both stayed frozen for a minute.

"What are you doing here?" He didn't look happy to see her. He looked annoyed, and pained.

"I brought you the papers to sign."

"The agency can't afford couriers anymore?" he said and took the envelope from her. "Do you want to come in? They're relighting the set and I've got a twenty-minute break." He stepped back so she could walk into his narrow dressing room, and she did. There was a small pink settee, some mismatched chairs, a setup for hair and makeup, and a rack of what he had to wear on the show. There was

250

nothing glamorous about it. There were some bottles of water, a big bottle of Coke, and some Power Bars on the table.

"Why did you bring me the papers yourself, Allie?" he asked her in a gentle voice. It was the opening she'd been waiting for, for months, and she felt paralyzed for a moment, not sure what to say.

"Because Bob Benson is an asshole, and he had no business telling me who I can date or what's good for the agency. Fuck the agency. His partner is going to prison for heinous crimes. And I don't give a damn about my career anymore. That's all I ever cared about for the last twenty years. What was good for my career. And you know what? I discovered that I don't care. I finally found someone I love more than myself and my precious career. Bob's dating the CFO, for chrissake. That's a lot more improper than what we did. I love you. I know you have a new girlfriend, but I just wanted you to know. Now sign the goddamn papers, so I can get out of here before I cry and make an even bigger fool of myself than I just did."

"What new girlfriend?" He stared at her.

"The one I saw you in the tabloids with. She's gorgeous and about twelve years old."

"She's on the show. They had me go to an event with her for publicity, and she's a raving bitch. I love you too. I've been miserable since we broke up. I can hardly make it through the show every day. I didn't want to fuck up your career. And just for the record, I don't care how old you are, or if you're Grandma Moses. I love *you, YOU.* Now shut up for a minute, will you?" She started to say something, but he kissed her, and whatever had happened, whatever had gone wrong, whatever he had meant to do, didn't matter now. And her age didn't matter to either of them. She loved him, more than her job or her career or all her other clients. He wasn't a client, he was the only man she had ever loved. And he loved her too.

"I'd rather quit my job than lose you." He beamed when she said it. "And I don't care if they put us on the cover of the tabloids every day, *or* what Bob Benson thinks about it."

"Good. Me too. Now that we've gotten that clear, what are we going to do about it?"

"I don't know. What do you want to do?"

"I want to never let you out of my sight again. Let's have dinner when I finish here, get a great picture of us on the covers of the tabloids, and go home and make love till the sun comes up. And we'll figure out the rest after that." He pulled her into his arms then, held her so tight she couldn't breathe, and kissed her harder than ever. It felt familiar and wonderful, and was what she had missed every hour of every day while he was gone. They were both smiling when he stopped. "Where's the stuff you want me to sign?" She pointed to where he'd thrown the envelope on the table. He grabbed it, opened it, found a pen, signed all of it, and handed it back to her. He was beaming. "I love you, Allie."

"Yeah, me too. You're the only man I've ever loved," she said, and it was true. "I never realized how much, until you were gone."

"Let's not fuck it up again. We'll get married if you want. This is it for me," he said seriously.

"I'm a hundred years older than you are," she said, grinning. "You shouldn't marry me."

"Why not? We'll ask Bob to be best man. Marry me, don't marry me, just don't leave me, Allie. I want you with me forever. My life was shit without you, a wasteland. I thought of you every day."

252

"Me too. I won't let you leave me again. If we fight we'll have to fix it, because I'm not going through this again."

"Good. I'm glad you showed up with the papers. That was brave of you."

"I know. I figured it was my one shot at seeing you. The worst you could do was have me thrown out." He pulled her tightly in his arms again and held her. "You feel so good. I have to be back on the set in five minutes." He took a long swig of the Coke, and then walked her out on the set with his arm around her, smiling broadly. He introduced her to the technicians and actors who were hanging around. "This is my agent *and* my girlfriend," he said proudly. "Never mind dinner," he whispered to her as the hair and makeup people headed toward him. "I want to go to bed with you."

"Me too," she whispered back. "I'll pick up something to eat."

"See you around seven. I'm in the last shot." He gave her one more quick kiss and she scampered across the wires on the set. She ran down the hallway, and was smiling when she got in the elevator, went outside, and hailed a cab. She called Hailey on the way back to the office.

"I just saw him," she said triumphantly.

"Who?" Hailey sounded busy. They were finishing up the painting and the kitchen in the new apartment.

"Eric."

"Oh my God. What happened?"

"I got brave and went to see him, with some papers he had to sign. We're back together."

"That was fast."

"Very. He's been miserable too. And I don't know why, but he's the

253

one. After all these years of guys I never cared about. He turns out to be it."

"You didn't tell him about Benjie, did you?"

"Of course not. He was an idiot. I don't know why he told Jane. She still barely speaks to me. The new head of literary likes her. He's a good guy. I just wanted you to know what happened. I'm on my way back to the office now. Eric's coming home tonight. How's the apartment coming, by the way?"

"Almost finished. It's gorgeous."

"We came out winners," Allie said to her. "You with Phillip, and me with Eric. And Francine got three million dollars. She deserves every penny of it. And Dan got what he deserves. All these years I thought that all that mattered was my career. It's not enough, Hailey. In the end, it really doesn't matter."

"I know. The same thing happened to me," Hailey said.

"And poor Jane is heading down that path. She's just starting," Allie said.

"She's young. She'll figure it out." Hailey had faith in her, she was a bright, courageous girl.

"None of it matters," Allie said. "I don't even care how much younger he is, and neither does he. It's not about age, or money, or careers. Maybe in the end, it's just about courage, and having the guts to go after what you want." The cab pulled up outside the agency then, and they hung up. It was also about having the good luck to find the right person, Allie realized, by some miracle finding the right one. She and Hailey had, and so had Merriwether and Bob. They were all the lucky ones.

Chapter 14

D an Fletcher's sentencing happened right on schedule, thirty days after he had pleaded guilty. Bob and Merriwether went, and so did Julia and Jane. Francine decided to go at the last minute. She hadn't been sure before that. David Bristol went to lend Jane support, and sat with her respectfully. Hailey couldn't go because it was their moving day, into the new apartment. Allie went, although she hadn't been one of Dan's victims, and Eric went with her. He took half a day off shooting to go.

Dan was led into the courtroom in chains and leg shackles again. His hands were cuffed and attached to the chain around his waist. He hadn't shaved in a few days, his hair was matted and dirty. And there were dark circles under his eyes. He told his attorney he hadn't had a decent night's sleep since he'd been in jail, and he looked it.

The judge talked for a few minutes about the seriousness of his crimes, aggravated by the abuse of power, threatening to take their livelihood away from women with children to support. The judge called it a reign of terror, and Bob winced.

The judge sentenced Dan to state prison. All of his crimes were felonies, three of them with indeterminate sentences, the misdemeanors were dismissed when he pleaded guilty, and the judge sentenced all of Dan's crimes consecutively. He sentenced him to one count of rape for Francine for three to fifteen years, attempted rape for Jane for another three to fifteen, two counts of sexual abuse for seven years each, and three counts of coercion for one to four years each. And the judge enhanced each sentence by two years, for abuse of power, which added another fourteen years to his sentence. The minimum amount of time he would serve was thirty-seven years, and at most seventy years. It was unlikely that he'd be paroled in his lifetime. He was going to spend the rest of his life in prison.

There were tears sliding down Francine's cheeks when the judge read off the sentences. He fully understood the devastating effect it had had. Dan looked as though he didn't. Bob Benson sat there wondering how Dan could have gone so far off track, how he could hate or disrespect anyone so much that he could do the things he did.

It was grim watching him being led away. It was the end of the story. He was being taken by bus that night to state prison, to live in a cell for the rest of his days, no fewer than thirty-seven years. He had destroyed his own family while having a devastating impact on everyone else's. And God only knew how many other women had been his victims and never came forward. He would die in prison.

They walked out of the courtroom together after Dan had been taken back to jail. He didn't turn to look at anyone before they took him. He looked straight ahead, already separate from the human race.

There was a broken piece in him that nothing would ever fix. Bob doubted he would ever see him again. Dan had nearly taken them all down with him.

They stood in the sunlight outside the courthouse, huddled together, not speaking at first, because it was hard to know what to say. Allie put an arm around Francine's shoulders. They all kissed Jane and Julia and Francine. Jane had been the bravest of all. They had all learned from her to stand up for their principles, to speak up, to refuse to be silenced or cowed or bullied or threatened into silence. Her lone voice had carried the day, Julia and Francine had followed, and Francine had finally won her freedom.

They all went to lunch together afterwards. The restaurant was friendly and loud. They were all part of it. They had earned the right to go after what they wanted, to stand for what they believed in. Some of them had paid a high price, the others had supported them. When they left after lunch, they hugged each other and it meant something. They had been through the wars together.

They went back to work, to life, to the business of living, to their jobs and careers and the people they loved. When they kissed each other and their children that night, they were part of the victory and the blessing. They had earned the right to their happiness because they were brave.

About the Author

DANIELLE STEEL has been hailed as one of the world's best-selling authors, with almost a billion copies of her novels sold. Her many international bestsellers include *Invisible, Flying Angels, The Butler, Complications, Nine Lives, Finding Ashley, The Affair,* and other highly acclaimed novels. She is also the author of *His Bright Light,* the story of her son Nick Traina's life and death; *A Gift of Hope,* a memoir of her work with the homeless; *Expect a Miracle,* a book of her favorite quotations for inspiration and comfort; *Pure Joy,* about the dogs she and her family have loved; and the children's books *Pretty Minnie in Paris* and *Pretty Minnie in Hollywood.*

daniellesteel.com
Facebook.com/DanielleSteelOfficial
Twitter: @daniellesteel
Instagram: @officialdaniellesteel

About the Type

This book was set in Charter, a typeface designed in 1987 by Matthew Carter (b. 1937) for Bitstream, Inc., a digital type-foundry that he cofounded in 1981. One of the most influential typographers of our time, Carter designed this versatile font to feature a compact width, squared serifs, and open letterforms. These features give the typeface a fresh, highly legible, and unencumbered appearance.